LOVE'S COURAGE
Copyright ©2018 by Elizabeth Meyette
PUBLISHED BY: Boris Publishing

BORIS PUBLISHING
ISBN 10: 0-9960965-4-6
ISBN 13: 978-0-9960965-4-6
eISBN 10: 0-9960965-3-9
eISBN 13: 978-0-9960965-3-9

Interior Image: Meyette Photography
Cover Design by Steven Novak
Interior Format

LOVE'S COURAGE

THE BRENTWOOD SAGA
BOOK 3

Linda,
Wishing you peace, love,
and joy Betty

Elizabeth Meyette

Elizabeth Meyette

*Being deeply loved by someone gives you strength,
while loving someone deeply gives you courage.*

~ Lao Tzu

To all who love deeply

BOOKS BY ELIZABETH MEYETTE

THE BRENTWOOD SERIES

Love's Destiny

Love's Spirit

Love's Courage

The Brentwood Saga

THE FINGER LAKES MYSTERIES

The Cavanaugh House

Buried Secrets

CHAPTER ONE

❡

July 1777, Yorktown, Virginia

*W*HEN HAD LYING BECOME SO *easy?*
"Did you hear me, Jenny?"

"Yes, Uncle Jonathon." Jenny Sutton pulled her white linen scarf snug, crossing her arms over her stomach against the visceral guilt that pulsed there. She stared into the slate-blue waters of the York River, avoiding his gaze. Captain Jonathon Brentwood's integrity was known far and wide. He was respected by Patriots and hated—perhaps feared—by the British.

An honest man.

"You're certain of your mother's wishes? That she wants you to join her? New York City is thick with British troops since they occupied Manhattan last December. I can't understand Constance demanding your return." He braced his forearms on the brass railing of his ship, the *Destiny.*

"Yes." That was all she could say. She could not repeat the lie. She didn't want Jonathon to sense her dishonesty. She wanted him to continue to think of her as courageous ... and honorable. Her hand moved to her bodice where Mother's letter lay heavy against her skin, heavy with the lie Jenny had told him. Mother's letter detailed Father's wounds but assured her that he was receiving excellent care and would recover soon. Mother had insisted she *not* sail to New York, saying the city was too dangerous with the British occupation.

When she had first read the message, Jenny had sensed a graver injury to Father than the letter revealed. Whatever it took, she had to help Father. Even if it meant lying to Jonathon. Even if it meant never seeing Andrew again. How was she to make this choice—her father or the man she loved? Well, she had decided, thus Andrew was lost to her forever. Her gaze flicked to Water Street, running along the shoreline, then up to the ridge above.

Jonathon's gaze followed hers. "We can wait no longer to set sail. I'm sorry that Andrew didn't arrive in time to see you off."

She nodded, knowing that Andrew would not arrive in time, but unable to resist searching for him. Finally, she turned to Jonathon. He was the epitome of a ship's captain, with broad shoulders and tanned skin. A gust of wind blew down from the ridge, blowing about his dark brown hair, gathered in a queue with a leather strap at the nape of his neck. His eyes, the rich color of coffee served at Charlton's, reflected his concern.

"How badly was Edward injured?"

"Mother said that he was involved in a skirmish with a Tory. Father was nearly killed—he's bedridden and the wound isn't healing. Mother is anxious about his recovery and needs me there. She must be devastated."

"So, of course, she wanted you to join her ..."

"Of course."

Her knuckles turned white as she clutched the brass railing tighter. The metal scorched her hands, like the lies that burned her heart. Lies that were necessary if she were to accomplish this journey.

Lies that were growing too heavy to carry.

Lifting her chin, he forced her to face him. His brows drew together as his eyes bored into hers, his mouth pulled taut in a thin line. "You must understand the danger inherent in this voyage. The sea will always challenge those who sail her waters, and she is temperamental, changing from fair to foul in the blink of an eye. For your safety, you are bound to my orders, just like the crew. Also, there's a good chance we'll encounter British ships." He glanced down the river toward its mouth, then back at her. "I cannot guarantee we won't be captured … or sunk. My responsibility for your life weighs heavy. I wish you would reconsider this voyage."

The temptation was great. Simply walk down the plank to the wharf and wait for Andrew. Run into his arms and never leave him. Return to the safety and comfort of Brentwood Manor. But the image of Father, lying wounded, perhaps dying, loomed in her mind. "Mother and Father need me." She looked toward the shore as she spoke. Perhaps lying had become easier, but looking into a person's eyes as you deceived them never would.

Following her gaze, he softened.

"It's not easy leaving the one you love," he said.

"No." Jenny shook her head.

"Fighting for the cause of liberty is never easy. It requires sacrifice. Your father understands that, and so did you and Andrew when you risked your lives to rescue me from the British. If not for you, I surely would have been hanged. As I recall, you were quite audacious in facing down a British contingent to rescue me."

"Yes, but Andrew was beside me. We rescued you together—as a team. Somehow I don't feel as brave without him by my side." What was it about Andrew that made her feel she could accomplish anything? In her eighteen years, she had never met a man who so seemed to be a part of her, whom she had somehow known before they'd met, and recognized instantly.

The burden of also deceiving Andrew weighed her down like a ship's anchor.

"How have you endured these past years, Uncle Jonathon?

How have you left Emily behind, and now your daughters? Not knowing if you will ever return? Not knowing if they are safe or if you will be killed?" Her voice rose as she spoke. "How do you bear it?"

"When I was held captive by the British, I thought I would never see Emily and my children again." He pulled her to him and kissed her forehead. "Every day was a struggle to survive. Every day they thought of new ways to torture me, trying to discover information about our fight for freedom." He pulled back to look at her. "But you and Andrew faced possible capture to save my life."

She placed her hand on his forearm. "A possibility well worth facing if it meant bringing you home to Emily. Andrew couldn't bear to see his sister's sorrow, nor could he bear the thought of you imprisoned and tortured by the British."

"When I first sailed for the Committees of Correspondence and the Patriot cause, it was because of what Parliament's laws are doing to the colonies." He watched the seagulls swooping to the water's surface. One rose triumphantly, a fish thrashing in its beak. The other birds chased and scolded as the first flew off with its prize. "Mine was an economic fight then. Brentwood Manor, the *Destiny*, my profits were at stake." He faced her. "Now I am fighting for freedom for the ones I love. For Emily and the children. Before, my antagonism stemmed from my wealth, my account books—now I feel it here." He patted his hand against his chest. "Love gives me the courage to fight this war. And you, too, will find your courage in love. Remember, 'love casts out fear.'"

She looked toward the shore. At this moment, for her, life cast out love.

"But I entreat you one last time to reconsider this voyage. I only agree to it because of your mother's frantic plea for your presence. If she understood the potential danger, not only in the voyage, but in Manhattan, she would never ask you to return."

His words were a knife through her heart. Did he suspect her subterfuge? She stood taller and shook her head.

He scowled. "I see. Now I must ready the ship to set sail." He bowed slightly.

As he strode away, the breeze picked up again, blowing strands of hair across her eyes, a veil of curling, black lace. She brushed them away and tucked them back in her cap. One persisted, caressing her cheek softly like a kiss. Andrew's kiss. Soft upon her cheek, nuzzling against her neck. Oh, God, how could she leave him?

Behind her, the crew hurried about setting the sails and weighing anchor. Men called to each other as they worked, and the ship slipped out of port. She stared out at the wash, waves rolling out from the ship to the shore in an eternal motion. Entranced, she surrendered to the gliding ship's cadence.

She glanced at the shore again as the ship passed the end of the wharf on its journey up the York River to Chesapeake Bay and out into the Atlantic Ocean. A flash of color along the ridge caught her eye. Her heart thumped as a rider careened along the road that ran down the Great Valley leading from the ridge to the port. Even from this distance, she recognized Andrew. How could he possibly have made that journey so quickly?

The letter she had sent him should not have arrived in time for him to see her off. She had never intended it to. His presence would make her departure impossible, and she could not bear that. So, she had delayed sending her letter.

That had been first of her lies.

Snatching his hat off his head, he waved it and whistled, piercing the heavy air as he reached the base of the hill and thundered along the riverbank. He pulled the horse up causing it to plant its hooves, its rigid front legs angled straight out. As he slid from the saddle, he again whistled shrilly, waving his cocked hat.

"Jenny!" The sleeves of his white linen shirt billowed as he signaled to the ship.

How could it be? He must have ridden at break-neck speed.

"Jenny! Jonathon, turn back!" Andrew ran along the wharf until he reached its end.

Would his brother-in-law hear Andrew's plea? But neither Jonathon nor anyone in his crew looked up. They would not hear him over the sails slapping the wind, arcing and spreading high above the deck, or over the bosun's piping Jonathon's orders. The crew were all occupied with raising the sails and navigating the departure from Yorktown.

She did nothing to call their attention to Andrew.

She could see errant strands of his light brown hair blowing about his head. The disheveled look of his shirt, untucked, flapping in the breeze was quite a contrast to how he had looked the last time they'd been together at a formal dinner at Brentwood Manor. Then, he'd worn a cream-colored long coat and russet breeches, his cravat billowing at his neck. His tawny hair had been tied back in a neat queue, as usual. He'd swept off his wool cocked hat in a regal bow, his blue eyes smoky with passion as they shared a secret smile. He'd pulled her to the empty parlor and wrapped her in his arms.

As the ship continued its slow passage along the York River, she leaned against the rail, Andrew's form ever more distant. She stretched out her arm toward the shore as if, somehow, she could reach him. But it was no use. She dropped her arm to her side. This was what she had hoped for.

This was what she had dreaded.

"Andrew." His name escaped her throat in a moan. How she had wanted to hold him and kiss him goodbye. She would never hold him again.

"Jenny. I love you, Jenny."

Although he bellowed the words, they floated over the water to her in a shimmering, faint declaration. Tears ran down her cheeks, and she hugged herself to stop the sobs that shuddered against her ribs.

"I love you, too, my dearest Andrew," she whispered against the catch in her throat.

❦

"Shite!"

Blurting out "Sorry," and "Pardon me," Andrew Wentworth pushed and shoved at the porters, sailors, and merchants who blocked his way as he sprinted along the wharf. Two riggers stretched lines across the pier, forcing him to leap over the ropes and race ahead. Blood pumped in his ears, muffling the curses that followed him. His heart pounded with the rhythm of his hurtling feet. He skidded to a stop, sliding to the edge of the pier.

"Damn!"

The *Destiny* had already set sail.

"Jenny! Jonathon, turn back!"

He whistled and bellowed to the captain of the *Destiny*, waving his arms to get his brother-in-law's attention, but Jonathon must not have heard him. Jenny did, for she waved from the ship's rail. And did he hear her call his name?

He had been so close to embracing her, to pleading that she remain at Brentwood Plantation.

He had not run fast enough. Jenny was gone ... perhaps forever. He fell to his knees, ignoring the pain of the jagged splinters digging into his skin. With his heart still hammering from the exertion of his swift horseback ride and sprint, he doubled over. Burying his face in his hands, he moaned. *Why didn't I ride faster? Why didn't I read Jenny's note sooner? I would have arrived in time to take her into my arms and convince her to stay.*

He looked up, watching the *Destiny* sail away.

He closed his eyes. Her face floated in his mind: Jenny laughing, revealing the single dimple in her right cheek that tempted him so sorely, her gray eyes, soft as a summer's dawn, alight with mischief. How he loved twining his fingers in her hair, as wayward ebony tendrils caressed her heart-shaped face. The determination in her face when, together, they faced certain death in rescuing Jonathon from the British. So brave. So beautiful.

He stared out at the ship as she sailed out of his life.

As he watched, the *Destiny* slipped down the York River toward Chesapeake Bay on her voyage to New York City. His shoulders drooped. He'd heard so many reports of increasing unrest there. Last September, a fire had destroyed a third of the Island of New York shortly after the British had arrived. Loyalists blamed Patriots, but nothing had been proven. Reports from New York had been grim, the British presence there ominous.

And now Jenny would be surrounded by that violence.

Damn. The opportunity to attend George Wythe's lecture and hear him describe the pride with which he had signed the Declaration of Independence was a highlight of Andrew's experience at the College of William and Mary. In his excitement, he'd tucked Jenny's letter in his pocket. Why had he not read her letter first? Instead, he had wanted to enjoy it later, as he always did, sitting at the coffee house near the college, drinking in her every word. He might have made the ride from Williamsburg to Yorktown in time if he'd skipped the class. Through his blurred vision, the ship grew smaller as it slipped down the river. He stood.

"I love you, Jenny." *I love you.*

Above him, the screeches of seagulls echoed his desolation. Sweat streamed from his brow and merged with the tears sliding down his face, catching in salty rivulets at the corners of his lips. He wiped his sleeve across his face, dampening the white linen. He threw his cocked hat on the wooden pier.

"Damn, damn, *damn!*"

A strong hand gripped his shoulder.

"Come, Andrew. I will buy you dinner and a tankard of

ale."

He turned, startled by the brogue of Randolph O'Connor.

He reached out as if to comfort Andrew, but Andrew pulled away. His blood was lava flowing through his veins, his mind unable to make sense of what was around him. A primal rage surged through him impelling him to strike out, to satisfy his anger.

Andrew punched the Irishman in the gut.

The burly man staggered back, more surprised than injured.

"What the devil are ya' doing?" He stumbled toward Andrew again.

Andrew yielded to the fury that whirled within him like a hurricane. He wanted to hit something, throw something, break something. He swung again and landed an upper cut on Randy's jaw.

Randy stood his ground, fists clenched at his sides. "Andrew …"

Andrew jabbed a fist at the Irishman again. Randy caught it midair, swung it forward, pivoting Andrew around, and locked his arm behind his back. Randy pulled up on it.

"Ow," Andrew cried.

"You need to settle. Just settle."

Randy held Andrew's arm against his back, sending a sharp throbbing to his shoulder. Andrew almost welcomed it, merging the pain with the misery running through him. He finally relaxed and Randy let go.

"Sorry, Randy." Shaking his head, he bent forward, leaning on his knees, breathing deeply to regain his senses. He stuck out his hand, which disappeared into Randy's as they shook. He admired Randy whom he'd met upon his arrival in Virginia two years ago. Even back then, he had joined Randy and Jonathon in their battle to fight the British and further the Patriot cause. Now, the sympathy in Randy's hazel eyes only deepened Andrew's sorrow—and fury.

Randy retrieved Andrew's hat, handing it to him. Andrew crushed one of its three corners as he clutched it.

"I could have arrived in time. I failed to read her note when it arrived—I thought it was her weekly letter. I could have been here in time." He bunched his wool felt hat into a crumpled mass.

Randy took the hat and shook it out, trying to reshape its three corners. "Lad, mind your hat. With the damned Parliament's stranglehold on shipping, you might not find another to buy." He clapped it on Andrew's head. "Aye. Perhaps you could have done all those things, but the fact is, Jenny is gone. That is the truth of it." He turned toward the shore. "Come. Let me buy you an ale and some food. I may have an idea that will help us both."

Andrew turned to face him. "What do you mean, 'help us both'?"

Randy smiled and slapped him on the shoulder, almost knocking him off the edge of the pier. Andrew scrambled to regain his balance.

"You'll see, lad. You'll see.

☙

Andrew and Randy sat in a far corner of the tavern where eavesdropping was less likely. Voices emboldened with too much ale rang around them as Andrew tapped his foot, his fingers drumming the table. Thoughts bounced in his mind like hail on a roof. How to get to New York City? To Jenny? He had never ridden that distance, and he knew nothing about the roads or where the British camps were. He shifted in his seat, his legs tingling with the need to act, not waste time in some tavern. A serving maid deposited another two tankards in front of them, then hurried off to the beckoning cries of other patrons. An air of camaraderie and shared purpose swirled around them as men discussed the overbearing reach of Parliament and the intrusion of British troops.

Leaning forward, Randy took a generous swig of his ale, scanned the room, then spoke in tones just loud enough to be heard above the din. "You want to join Jenny in New York, and I have messages to deliver to the colonies to the north. Together we can accomplish both."

The din faded as Andrew focused on Randy's words. "I'm listening."

"You will be working for the Sons of Liberty, providing information along the route to New York City. Stephen Alcott's farm—do you remember it? Jonathon hid from the British there."

"I know the farm."

"I'll meet you back here tomorrow, then you'll ride to Alcott's farm. He will provide you with directions to your next stop."

"But I want to leave tonight."

"I know, lad. But if you leave tonight, you will raise suspicion at the college. Tomorrow I will know the safest route to Alcott's farm. The British roam the countryside, Andrew. What if you encounter a regiment? Worse yet, what if someone recognizes you? You were there when Jonathon killed Captain Walters. And you've been to New York with Jonathon. This will be a hazardous mission. You need to be prepared."

Andrew sank into his chair and scrubbed his face with his hands. "You're right, Randy." Sighing, he cupped his hands around his tankard. "I'm worried about Jenny. I feel in my heart that she is in danger, too."

Randy stared at him as if weighing his next words.

"Your heart is correct, lad. Jenny is in grave danger."

CHAPTER TWO

ℂ

JONATHON PACED THE DECK, STOPPING every so often to lift the telescope and study the western horizon. Jenny could see nothing there, but he was intent, scouring the seam of the sea and sky. Crewmen glanced surreptitiously in that direction as they bustled about their duties. The air was thick with anticipation. Jonathon propped the telescope against a barrel and pulled out a parchment, unfolded it and read it, combing from top to bottom twice. He replaced the letter in his pocket, then stared though the telescope again.

Finally, he turned to her. The concern on his face did little to quell the nerves that jumped along her skin. Though he smiled at her, his eyes remained steely.

Was it fear for her or anger?

He glanced to the west again. "This voyage is perilous. General Howe has troops aboard an armada of more than two hundred British ships now sailing along the coast of the colonies. We may very well engage them. I am keeping as far out to sea as possible while still making it feasible to complete our mission. Our stop in New York was to be quick, but ..."

Jenny understood. She was delaying them already. A confrontation with a British ship—or two hundred—put his mission at risk.

"I'm sorry, Uncle Jonathon. I didn't realize ..."

But had she realized, her plan would have been the same.

She brushed her arms up and down as urgency raced through her skin like a thousand ants. Father could lie dying right now—she had to reach him as soon as possible. Her twin sister's face floated to her mind. Kathryn's curly black hair and gray eyes had mirrored Jenny's. Their gleeful shouts echoed in her mind as she remembered their games and competitions—Kathryn winning every race. Kathryn running into the road, Jenny not fast enough to save her from the oncoming carriage. Kathryn's pale face, gray eyes staring at nothing. Jenny blinked away stinging tears, shaking herself back to the present. "Yes. If I do not run to him, he will die."

"You carry a tremendous burden, Jenny."

Puzzled, she frowned at him. How could saving Father be a burden?

He took her hand. "You saved Andrew's life from a British bullet and my Emily from certain death when Deidre was so deranged she sought to kill her." He frowned for a moment. "My Lord—you even endangered your own life to save *me* from the British. But, you carry a weight of responsibility that is too heavy for the strongest person." His voice softened on the misty air. "You cannot save the world."

She rose to her tallest stature. "But I can save Father. If there is any chance, I cannot ignore it."

He leaned on the brass rail, staring toward the west. Pushing off it, he grimaced. "I will get you to your father as quickly as I am able. I promise. But I as I cautioned you, it will be dangerous. British warships sit off Long Island and the island of Manhattan, requiring us to land elsewhere and travel over land as well. That, too, will be a difficult journey."

"I understand. I hate to place you in such jeopardy; New York is a dangerous place for you as well."

"Yes, if I'm seen, I'll be arrested again … and this time I would surely swing from the gallows. I cannot accompany you on the entire journey."

"Whatever you can do, wherever you can drop me … but I must return to my parents. All I need is a good horse. I can make it on my own."

He grunted. "You have enough courage for ten men. I will certainly not leave you to make the last of the trip on your own. Mr. Gates and some of my men will accompany you until they can turn you over to trusted people outside of Manhattan. Those friends will see you safely to your parents."

As if on cue, a tall man with a neatly trimmed beard and gray hair that curled around his collar joined them, retrieving Jonathon's telescope. He wore a black wool cap, his face tanned and weathered save for the creases around his smiling blue eyes where, crinkled from laughter or squinting, white lines fanned out.

"Good day, Captain. Miss Sutton." He bowed slightly.

"Ah, Gates, we were just speaking of you. I'm explaining to Jenny that you and a few of our crew will escort her to the countryside near Manhattan. There you will entrust her to our colleagues in the area."

He nodded to her. "I'll be honored to do so, Captain."

"You'll be in safer hands than if I were to accompany you." Jonathon grinned at her, then at his second-in-command.

"Thank you, sir." Gates again bowed. "Any sign of …"— he glanced at Jenny— "company?" He offered the telescope.

Jonathon again searched the horizon. "Nothing. If our luck holds out, we will not encounter any British vessels."

Mr. Gates glanced at Jenny again.

"I've told her, Gates." He raised a brow at his niece. "She is fully aware of the many risks inherent in this trip."

"I'll leave you to discuss the plans." Tapping his finger to the brim of his woolen fisherman's cap, he sauntered off.

Jonathon placed his hands on Jenny's shoulders.

"Truly, you will be safe with Mr. Gates."

"I know I will." She inhaled the salty air and squared her shoulders.

He scanned the horizon. "I hope your arrival in New York will be our only challenge."

&

Andrew drummed his fingers on the smooth wood of the table as he sat in the back of the tavern waiting for Randy. Scanning the room, he looked for Randy's red hair among the patrons. A man his size would not be missed. Not seeing his friend, he sighed and slapped the table—he wanted to be on his way. The sooner he could reunite with Jenny, the better.

Leaning back, he balanced his chair against the wall and closed his eyes. He envisioned her face glowing in candle-light, remembered the scent of lilac when he pulled her near. When she smiled, that single dimple, just to the right of her angel-bow lips, invited a kiss, turning his innards to jelly. His arms longed to hold her. He remembered her silken skin, smooth beneath his fingers, and her eager response when they kissed. How he missed her already. His jaw clenched; he might never see her again. News was rampant of the dangers of New York, and if her father had been injured by the British, what did that mean for Jenny? Would they now go after her?

"Based on the lovesick look on your face, I assume you're thinking of Jenny."

Randy's voice startled Andrew back to reality. He brought his chair upright with a bang.

"My God, man, you scared me half to death."

Randy grinned at him. "I thought I'd best pull you out of your reverie before you embarrassed yourself." He waggled his brows.

Andrew sat up and pulled his long coat around his hips. His face grew hot with embarrassment at Randy's insinu-ation.

"Aye, you are a hot-blooded youth. Do not fear, Andrew. I will see you reunited with your beloved Jenny."

Andrew puffed out a long breath. As Jonathon's lifelong friend, Randy was a frequent visitor at Brentwood Manor, Jonathon's boyhood home. Andrew trusted him as he trusted his brother-in-law. If Randy said he would see Jenny again, then he would.

"We'd best get busy so you can be on your way." Randy pulled a piece of parchment out of the pocket of his long coat. He placed his cocked hat on the edge of the table to conceal from any curious observers what he was about to show Andrew. He scanned the room, then pulled in his chair.

Peering at the parchment, Andrew studied a roughly drawn map of the coast of Virginia and the colonies to the north. Several places were labeled or marked with an X. Ships were crudely drawn along the coastline from New York to the Chesapeake Bay.

"This will be your route." Randy ran his finger along the dotted line joining the locations.

"There are too many stops here. I want to get to Jenny as fast as I can."

"Lad, you can help the Sons of Liberty with our fight— we have a war going on."

"But Jenny …"

Randy's fist slammed the table, jarring their drinks and making Andrew jump. The pub went quiet as patrons stared in their direction. Randy glared at them and they returned to their conversations. He bent toward Andrew, his face a thundercloud. "This is bigger than you and Jenny, for God's sake. People are dying, losing everything, being arrested and hanged. Wake up, boy. The world doesn't revolve around you."

Andrew's nostrils flared and he balled his fists. "Jenny could die. Her father could be dead already. I have to get to her."

"And I will help you do that. If you ride off half-cocked, you'll run into British troops for sure. You sitting in their jail won't help her. Now listen to me." He glanced around, staring down those who still chanced a look at them. His voice was low. "Now listen to me," he repeated.

Andrew strained to hear him over the din of the pub. "Your fastest route is the King's Highway, which runs from Charleston all the way up to Boston, but you must be careful. British troops will be plentiful along that road. But sailing is hazardous, too. A British fleet is sailing toward Maryland with General Howe in command. He has more than two hundred ships with thousands of soldiers aboard. General Washington's armies are shadowing them along the shore. He needs couriers to carry messages back to New York in case Howe decides to turn back and reinforce General Burgoyne in New York."

Andrew's heart raced. Jenny was sailing right into that armada. How could they sit here talking when he could be gaining miles on his trip to Jenny? He started to rise.

Randy yanked him back to his seat. "Steady, lad. You will leave in the morning ..."

"Morning? Immediately. We're wasting time, Randy."

"You need a plan. If you run off now, you'd be captured for sure and you would never get to Jenny." He squeezed the young man's arm. "Steady. Now let's look at this route."

Andrew sucked in a deep breath and studied the map. Waiting was agony. This route would take weeks. He shook his head.

"No. I can't take this long to get to her. You'll have to find someone else."

CHAPTER THREE

G

RAY STORM CLOUDS SMUDGED THE northeast horizon, stirring the crew of the *Destiny* into action. Jenny jumped as the bosun piped Jonathan's terse orders to the crew, who ran up rigging to trim sails and secure any items that were not battened down. The men's movements were swift, decisive, like an army preparing for battle. Perhaps a nor'easter was exactly that. She pressed against the ship's hull, trying to stay out of the way as the men dashed about, intent on their duties.

The wind picked up and waves swelled, tossing the ship. Her stomach churned and heaved, her nausea worsened by the acrid sulfur odor that accompanied the lightning that danced around the ship. Apprehension charged the air in addition to the shifting atmosphere from the storm. The *Destiny* pitched, throwing her against the railing. She stumbled, trying to maintain her footing, but her skirt caught in her leather slipper. Toppling like a rag doll, she reached for anything that would stem her fall. Her hands found a taut line and slid along it, her flesh ripping away, triggering stinging burns. The wind carried her cry out to sea as she tumbled to the deck.

Mr. Gates hurried to her. "Are you all right, Miss Sutton?" he shouted over the sound of the gale.

In too much pain to answer, she simply nodded. Pulling herself up, she clasped her hands to alleviate the smarting.

Gates took her hands in his, turning them over for inspection. "I have a balm that will soothe these rope burns. Come below with me. You'll want to be down there during this storm in any case." Taking her elbow, he led her to the quarterdeck.

After helping her navigate the ladder, he escorted her to her cabin. Though tiny, space was used as economically as possible. A small armoire stood against the bulkhead next to a table and chair. Opposite, a bunk covered with a neatly tucked quilt nestled against that bulkhead. With only one small porthole, the room was dark as the storm clouds gathered. Though a lantern hung above the table, Mr. Gates did not light it.

"With a storm, it's better not to have any flame," he explained. "The ship will be tossed quite a bit, and a lamp could be unsafe. You had best simply lie on your bunk and try to ride out the storm, Miss Sutton. I will return in a moment with salve for your hands."

After he left, Jenny scrutinized the cabin. Her trunk had been stowed beneath the bunk and secured with ropes. She had unpacked her clothing and personal items, but leaving them packed probably would have been wiser. She knelt and reached toward the handle, but the ship lurched, hurling her forward. She leaned on the trunk for support, causing her hands to slide along the edge of it. She gasped with pain as her skin passed over the rough wood.

"That was unwise," she scolded herself.

"Pardon me?" Mr. Gates asked from the doorway.

"Oh … nothing. I must get accustomed to coddling my hands." Her skin pulsed in pain from the fiery heat, as if she'd picked up scorching bricks from the hearth.

Mr. Gates set a lantern and a leather case on the table. "Here, let me examine them."

Taking her hands, he studied them. Lightly running a finger along one palm, he stopped when she winced and shrank back. Even his gentle ministrations increased the pain.

"I apologize for any discomfort I may cause," he said. Opening a jar, he dipped his finger into it and rubbed the salve into the burns. Though she instinctively wanted to pull her hands away, Jenny forced herself to sit still, sucking in her breath and holding it until he was finished. The scent of lavender and comfrey drifted up to her and the pain ebbed.

"Thank you."

He smiled. "Those are nasty burns on your hands." He nodded toward the bunk. "I think it best if you climb under the quilt and tuck it in as tightly as possible. The ship will be rocking for the next few hours."

"I will do as you say, Mr. Gates. Though I would be happy to assist in any way possible."

"That is very generous, but I think you will be most helpful tucked into that bunk." He winked at her, picked up his leather case and lantern, and left, leaving her in the shadowy cabin.

The ship rolled, knocking her to the bunk.

She could not bear to remain in this cramped cabin. Better to be tossed around on the deck than in this dark cell. Rising, she lurched to the door, matching her steps to the rolling and pitching of the ship. She took her time climbing the ladder to the deck since grasping the wooden rungs was agony on her throbbing palms. Losing her balance, she wrapped her arm around a rung to steady herself, sparing her aching hands.

When she reached the deck, the salty mist from the storm shrouded the scene before her. The wind caught her hair, flinging it in stinging tangles against her face. Men scrambled to tie lines against the gale, their faces grim and determined. The ship swooped up against a monstrous wave, then slammed down, jarring her spine. Nature's fury would have its way with her—with all of them. Did she want to die locked in a darkened cabin? Or facing her fate head on?

Perhaps even helping to stave off that fate?

She huddled against the rail, trying to stay out of the sailors' way as they slid by on the slippery deck. One stopped to yell something to her, gesturing toward the ladder, but she couldn't hear him over the roar of the wind and the sea. He gave up and continued to his task. Rain pelted, blowing drenched hair into her eyes, blinding her.

Suddenly, arms encircled her, lifting her off her feet.

"Jenny—get below," Jonathon raged.

"I can help—." She gulped as the wind captured her breath.

He plunked her down near the top of the ladder, pointing down toward the cabins. "Now," he bellowed.

Lightning flashed.

"I can help, Uncle Jonathon—." She stood with her feet spread wide to balance against the swaying ship.

"You will be in the way. I can't be worried about you while I'm trying to navigate this storm."

"But ..." Her words were swallowed by a roar of thunder.

"This is an order! You must do as I command." He loomed over her. "I told you this voyage would be dangerous—God's blood, I don't know what Constance was thinking to call you back."

"She didn't."

He stood, gaping at her. It was as if nature continued her fury all about them, but they were locked in a silent, endless space. His eyes blinked. He blinked again. "What?"

She couldn't contain the lie any longer. "Mother didn't beg me to join her in New York." She had to shout to be heard over the crashing waves, the teeming rain.

His eyes narrowed, growing darker. His nostrils flared.

"I'm sorry I lied to you. But I need to go to Father. If I don't, he'll die." Memories of a rushing carriage, of Kathryn's scream, of the crashing hooves flooded her mind. Thunder clapped nearby, and she covered her ears, cowering. She straightened, resuming her stance. "I must be there."

Jonathon's face was as stormy as the skies. "Go!" He jabbed his finger toward the ladder.

She scrambled back down and stomped to her cabin. *I could help. Surely, I could manage some task up there.* After stripping off her leather shoes, she flipped the quilt back, yanked it over herself, and tucked it in tightly. She lay on her back looking up at the wooden beam above her. *I cannot die down here. I must reach Father.*

The pitching of the ship increased as the afternoon darkened. She was barely able to discern the objects in her cabin in the faint light. While the throbbing in her hands waned, the discomfort in her stomach increased and she reached beneath the bunk for the chamber pot. Her stomach retched as she emptied its contents. Lying back, she closed her eyes, trying to stem the dizziness, but it only worsened. The ship undulated with the surging waves, tumbling her back and forth in the bunk. Her stomach heaved again. She longed for a drink of water, but she would have to go topside to get it.

The ship's violent swaying and lurching lasted for an hour, during which time Jenny was sure she had emptied any trace of food from her stomach. Gradually, the pitching subsided and she could lie flat on her back in stillness. Grateful for the reprieve, she dozed off. With the fear of death subsiding, her thoughts turned to Andrew. What was he doing at that moment? She threw one arm over her closed eyes. Thinking about him sharpened her misery. She had to accept he was gone from her life.

She finally submitted to sleep.

☾

Jenny woke to a soft tapping on her cabin door. Disoriented, she slowly opened her eyes and scanned her surroundings. Her stomach ached with the distress of her seasickness but still managed to send out sharp hunger pangs.

The tapping sounded again.

"Miss Sutton?" Mr. Gates's voice was quiet, and she suspected he was trying to balance checking on her with not wanting to wake her if she were asleep.

"Come ... *cough* ..." Her throat flamed with dryness. She tried to clear it, but she was so parched she couldn't raise any moisture. She tried again. "Come in." As she rolled over on the cot, she was assaulted by the stench of her vomit. She covered her mouth and nose with the quilt.

The door slowly opened and Mr. Gates peered around it. If he noticed the stench, he made no sign. "I wasn't sure if I heard you or not." He smiled as he entered carrying a basin and ewer, a flannel cloth draped over one arm.

She had never seen such a beautiful sight. She edged up on the cot to receive the welcome offerings.

Mr. Gates took a pewter mug from a cupboard built into the wall. The water sloshed as he poured it. She relished the sound. When he handed the drink to her, it was all she could do not to seize it and guzzle it down.

He read her mind. "You'll want to sip it for a while, missy. Too much too fast will have you heaving into this again." He picked up the chamber pot and carried it to the door where he handed it off to a cabin boy. Ridding the cabin of the odor was a blessing, and Jenny sent up a silent prayer of gratitude for this man who so reminded her of Father. She sent up another silent prayer that Father was all right ... and that no more storms would delay their arrival in New York.

Returning to her side, Mr. Gates dipped the flannel cloth in the water and patted her face. Too weak to protest, she surrendered to his ministrations. He dabbed water on the blisters on her palms and applied the ointment he'd used before. The sweet smell of the herbs soothed her, amazing her at how quickly she improved.

"Here, lass. Eat this slowly." He handed her a biscuit.

She took it gratefully and nibbled a small bite. Her stomach protested but then settled. She smiled her thanks.

"If you are up to a stroll on the deck, it might help you gain your strength faster," Mr. Gates said.

Jenny nodded, sipping the last of the water. He assisted her to standing, and she took his arm. Light-headed, she swayed, but he steadied her, waiting for her to regain her balance. Slowly they left her cabin, heading for the deck. The onslaught of fresh sea air invigorated her, and she inhaled deeply, relishing the cool, salty air. Mr. Gates cupped her elbow with his hand as they wandered the deck. She gaped in shock. Men were lying in various states of distress. A man with a white cotton cloth wrapped around his head was curled in a fetal position, moaning, as seeping blood streaked the fabric scarlet. Several voices merged in an eerie chant of "water" and "please help me." Another man sprawled on the deck, with his leg twisted obscenely in the wrong direction, his eyes glazed with pain. Two crew members tended them, tying tourniquets, bandaging wounds and applying splints. Ropes that had been neatly coiled were now tangled together. Barrels that had lined the deck had tipped and scattered, some still rolling back and forth.

"Mr. Gates, you are needed among these men much more than escorting me for a stroll." She edged her elbow from his hand, feeling foolish. "Please, return to your crew. I will be fine."

Mr. Gates beamed with gratitude. "Aye, missy. That would be a fine thing—if you're certain."

She stood taller. "I am certain."

He tipped his hat and hurried off.

Jenny perused the men near her. These were the less injured who didn't require wounds stitched or splints applied. She crouched beside a crewman bandaging an arm.

"How can I help?"

He looked at her in surprise then nodded. He showed her how to wrap the bandage to keep it in place. She learned quickly and followed him along the line of injured. Little did these men realize how much they were helping her. She was able to stop worrying about the two men she loved most—for a while at least.

☾

Andrew hefted the saddle onto Shadow's back. Jonathon had often allowed him use of his finest horse, and since Jonathon was at sea with Jenny, Shadow was his surest chance to make the trek to New York. He checked his saddlebags one last time before leading his mount out of the stable. He halted.

Randy leaned against a tree.

Andrew snugged the cinch strap. "I made it quite clear last night …"

"Aye, you did, lad. And I wondered if your conscience bothered you enough to change your mind."

Andrew resisted stretching against his weary muscles caused by lack of sleep for just that reason. "No." His voice cracked. He swallowed. Then the image of Jenny sailing away on the *Destiny* came to mind. He knew she would not return. If he didn't find her, they would be parted forever. And the damn British were not going to keep him from the woman he loved. His blood grew hot at the thought and he clenched his fists.

Throughout the colonies, the stronghold of Parliament had ruined many lives. People he knew were so indebted to Britain that they'd committed suicide. Taxes were high and representation of colonial interests, nil. He had been fighting for the Patriot cause, and this journey would allow him to do more. It could also cost him his life. But what was life without Jenny? Randy's plan was solid. Following it, he could help the cause and get to Jenny safely … he hoped.

"Do you remember the lobsterbacks in your home, what one almost did to your sister, Emily? Didn't you lie abed with a bullet wound from a British rifle while they took over Brentwood Manor?"

"I'll do it." His throat was dry, the words quiet.

Randy studied him.

He cleared his throat, standing taller. "I'll do it. I'll follow the route you've planned."

Randy pushed off from the tree and unrolled the piece of parchment, revealing the map. "Here's the route to Alcott's farm. Any questions, lad?" Randy couldn't hide his concern, making Andrew more nervous than he had been. He would be riding through British-held areas carrying information that would prove him a traitor.

"No. I have all of your instructions."

Randy retrieved a saddlebag propped against the tree. He tucked the map into a secret pocket. "Good man." He slapped Andrew on the arm, which, delivered by any other man would have been a tap, but Randy almost knocked him off his feet. "You'll be fine, Andrew. Keep to the roads I mapped out, and if you hear someone approaching, slip into the trees."

Andrew nodded. Turning, he mounted Shadow.

"Godspeed," Randy said.

Andrew touched the front corner of his hat and galloped off.

The sun beat down on his back as he rode, his linen shirt already damply clinging to his skin, but a refreshing breeze cooled him against the humid July air as he flew down the road leading out of Yorktown. The obstacles ahead would not deter him. He had to find Jenny. He had to keep her safe.

❦

Wispy clouds streamed past the full moon as Jenny finished helping with the wounded crewmen. Her black hair hung in ringlets, clinging to her face and neck. As she stood and stretched, her spine cracked with released tension.

Because the deck was wet from the storm, it was safe to light the firebox for cooking, and the scent of a wood

fire and sizzling pork drifted to her. Her stomach ached
for food, and she salivated at the aroma. The biscuit she'd
nibbled earlier was all that had filled her since being seasick.
She removed the white cotton shawl from her shoulders,
or what was left of it. She'd ripped half of it into strips to
bind up wounds and create splints. Taking the jagged remnant, she wiped her neck and face, her tired arms feeling
like lead weights. She tucked the damp fabric in at her waist.

"Jenny, you must eat something." Jonathon stood behind
her. When she turned, he handed her a pewter plate filled
with pork, potatoes, peas, and a hardtack biscuit. Carrying his own plate, he took her arm and led her to a row of
crates. They sat down to eat dinner.

She leaned over the food and inhaled the sweet aroma.
Her stomach growled mightily. Her hand flew to her mouth
as her face grew hot. "Excuse me."

Jonathon threw her a half smile. "That's the most beautiful sound I've heard all day."

She looked down at her plate, mortified.

"We all shall get to know one another quite well on this
voyage. It is the cost of sailing in close quarters. You'd best
get used to the natural rhythms and sounds of our bodies.
None of us will notice because we're so used to it. And the
crew will be far less discrete than you."

She smiled, relieved at his words. "Thank you, Uncle
Jonathon." She looked down at her plate. "I'm sorry I lied
to you."

His silence was more difficult to bear than any rebuke.
She poked at the food, her appetite gone. After several minutes, she couldn't endure it any longer.

"I'm so sorry …" She choked then swallowed.

"To say I'm disappointed in you would be an understate-
ment. Your actions above deck today diverted me from a
dangerous task. Having to make an extra stop to deliver you
to safe guides delays my mission."

Now she was silent. Save for sneaking a sweet biscuit or

pulling Kathryn's hair, she had never lied—never about something of such great consequence. But she felt she had no choice.

"I must help Father."

"And so you shall. But you have put others at risk. You need to know the ramifications. Now eat. Keep up your strength, for you have a long journey ahead."

A crewman approached and handed them each a tankard of ale. She resisted the urge to guzzle hers to assuage her parched throat. They ate in silence for a while. She barely tasted this simple fare. Guilt could do that. In the absence of a proper napkin, she retrieved the remains of her shawl. Jonathon took it from her and studied it.

"Perhaps you can atone for your deception. You've ruined your shawl. I shall fetch you another."

She looked around. "Do you keep a supply of fresh shawls on the *Destiny*, Uncle Jonathon?"

"No. But I do have one I would like to give you. Wait here."

She wiped the remaining gravy with the last of her hard-tack and sipped the last drop of ale. As the ship gently swayed, she was lulled into drowsiness. Leaning against a burlap sack of beans, she dozed for a moment. Voices carried on the cool night air, and from the opposite end of the ship, a deep bass voice rose in the darkness singing a sea chanty.

The song pierced her heart with its sweet melancholy. Tears stung her eyes. Her time together with Andrew been so brief—just the months she'd lived at Brentwood Manor with Uncle Jonathon and Aunt Emily. But they had fallen in love quickly. Andrew always swore he thought she was an angel when he first saw her. It had been a drenching rain the day she'd arrived at Brentwood Manor, and he had braved the storm to sprint out to her carriage with an umbrella. She smiled at the memory, but the smile dissipated. She would never see him again.

"Jenny."

Jonathon towered over her. She scrambled to sit up, knocking her plate to the deck. Jonathon stooped to retrieve it.

"Thank you."

He nodded and unfolded a shawl the shimmering periwinkle color of a peaceful sea. She gasped as it reflected beams of light from the lantern above them. When she touched the fabric, it was like running her hand along a warm stream, smooth and silky. Ivory and gold threads ran through the blue silk like waves lapping the shore.

"Uncle Jonathon, it's beautiful,"

"I'd like you to have it. But with it comes a favor. A favor for a favor, if you will." His gaze burned into hers, punctuating the significance of his request.

She fought down a flutter of apprehension.

"Your father is under suspicion by the British now, and so will you be when you arrive in New York. But you can be of great service to the Patriot cause if you are careful. What I ask you to do is simple but of great import. Do you understand?"

She nodded. Crossing her arms, she hunched in to ward off the chill that ran through her. She remembered standing with Father on King Street in Boston when British soldiers fired into the crowd. Five people were killed and the soldiers were acquitted. From then on, Father had cautioned that British power would grow in the colonies, and he'd vowed to work against it. Now he lay seriously injured because of his stance. "I will do whatever I can to help the Patriot cause. It was a British sympathizer who injured Father."

"Since you are willing to risk this journey, I will ask this of you. The first Sunday you are in New York, wear this shawl to your church service. A man named Laurence Montclair will introduce himself and inquire as to your father's health. He will say that your shawl is as blue as the water off the cape. If he does not comment on your scarf, simply answer his inquiry about your father." Jonathon paused, allowing her time to digest this. "If he does comment on your shawl ..." He paused again, scanning the deck of the ship.

"What, Uncle Jonathon? What do I do if he comments on this shawl?" Part of her didn't want to know. Deep inside, she sensed that what he was going to ask of her would have significant consequences, not just in her life but in the life of a young country fighting for its freedom.

Jonathon looked back at her. "You do not have to do this."

"Well, first I must know what 'this' is, mustn't I?"

He inhaled deeply, then nodded. "If he comments on your scarf, you are to give him this." He reached into his long coat and drew out a letter. Made of parchment, it was folded in thirds and sealed with scarlet wax imprinted with a "B." He looked to the west. "There will be another as soon as I have information on the armada. The *Despatch* sails to New York ahead of us, so we will rendezvous with them. I will send word to Montclair to expect you ... if you are willing." He didn't give her the letter, merely held it for her to see ... to decide.

She didn't want to take it, didn't want to take this step that might lead to others, surely to risk. Should she be caught delivering this letter, or even caught in possession of it, she would be guilty of treason. But isn't this what Father had been fighting for when he was injured? Isn't this what Jonathon had been fighting for, almost died for? People were risking their lives for freedom.

And didn't she owe Uncle Jonathon for how she had deceived him?

Jonathon returned the letter to his breast pocket.

"I will do it. I will deliver the letter." Jenny's voice was firm.

"Are you certain, Jenny? It's the only thing I'll ask you to do. I promise."

She took the blue silk shawl and the letter.

CHAPTER FOUR

(

ANDREW HAD RIDDEN FOR THREE days to reach Fredericksburg, Virginia, the first destination on his journey. Having eaten the last of his food ration at noon the day before, his hollow stomach felt stuck to his spine. Loud rumbles protesting hunger had accompanied him through the night. Twice he'd hidden in woods alongside the road as other riders approached, and once it had saved his life as a troop of British soldiers galloped past. Seeing the landmark for the Pembroke property, he urged Shadow to a faster pace.

Andrew cantered into Cyrus Pembroke's yard, the full moon lighting his way along the drive. Pulling up on the reins, he slowed Shadow to a trot as they neared the house. Sweat poured from horse and man as the humid summer night closed in around them. Andrew gulped the last drops of water from his leather canteen.

Cyrus Pembroke had been a courier for Jonathon, but the British threatened him and his family when they caught wind of his sympathies. Andrew had to be careful even approaching the property lest British troops be in the area watching. Randy had instructed Andrew to arrive in dark of night, but they both agreed haste took precedence over caution if Andrew was to connect with Jonathon in the northern colonies … and get to Jenny as soon as humanly possible.

A swath of amber light fell across the porch as the front

door opened. Cyrus hurried out to greet Andrew. Snatching Shadow's reins, he stilled the horse to standing, stroking the steed's forehead, whispering soothing words. Andrew threw his leg over the horse's back and dismounted. When his feet hit the ground, Andrew stumbled from exhaustion and thirst. Cyrus grabbed his arm to keep him from falling. "Thank you, sir." Andrew rasped, his throat raw. "I come from Brentwood."

"Go inside. Quickly." Cyrus scrutinized the property, no doubt searching for prying eyes, before he looped Shadow's reins over the porch railing then helped Andrew into the brick house.

Aromas of beef stew and fresh biscuits floated from the back of the house when he entered the hall. Cyrus held his arm as their boots clattered along the hardwood floors. Andrew squinted against the harshness of the candlelight, so bright after his ride under the night sky. When he entered the dining room, his vision adjusted to the glow of the lantern on the table and the small flames in the fireplace. With the warm humid night air, a small flame would keep the stew cooking but not heat the room too much. Still the heat was enough to make Andrew feel his remaining strength ebb, and he stumbled. Cyrus eased him into a chair and poured a tankard of ale, setting it before him.

A woman was ladling a hefty portion of stew onto a pewter plate. She picked up two steaming browned biscuits from a platter set on the hearth and quickly tossed them beside the meat and vegetables, shaking her hand then licking her fingers. As she set the plate before Andrew, she reached for a pitcher and poured honey over the biscuits.

Andrew stared at the food before him for a moment, too weak to lift his arm and pick up the fork. Willing his arms to move, he placed his forearms on the table, clasped the tankard and lifted it to his lips. Though it was warm, the full-bodied liquid was sweet balm to his dry throat and he gulped half the tankard.

"Easy, boy," Cyrus said. He laid his hand on Andrew's arm to slow his slaking. Nodding to the woman, he said, "This is my wife, Eleanor."

Andrew set the tankard down.

"Thank you, sir. Ma'am." He wiped his sleeve across his foamy mouth.

Eleanor smiled.

"I'll tend to your horse while you eat." Cyrus clomped out into the night.

Andrew jabbed the fork into a chunk of beef so tender it split into strands that soaked in the gravy. Chewing the first bite, he moaned in appreciation. He didn't pause even when Cyrus returned. Once he had eaten enough to regain some strength and sampled enough ale to allow speech, he nodded at them

"This is a feast fit for King George." His fork stopped halfway to his mouth. Growing up in London, this had been a common compliment paid the cook.

Cyrus scowled; Eleanor chuckled.

"A poor choice of words, son," Cyrus said.

"Excuse me, sir. This is a feast fit for General Washington." Despite his faux pas, he continued eating, settling into the chair, comforted in the validation of Cyrus's sympathies.

Cyrus grunted and left the kitchen. While he was gone, Andrew finished the stew and biscuits and a second tankard of ale. Eleanor busied herself with the fire, then settled down with her embroidery. Too tired to make conversation, Andrew rested his head in his hands and closed his eyes, listening to the soft crackling of the embers and the steady poking and pulling of her embroidery needle.

Soon Cyrus returned with Andrew's saddlebags.

"You have something for me?" His rough voice signaled impatience ... and fear. "I don't want the British arriving to find a courier possessing information for the Sons of Liberty in my home."

"Yes."

Cyrus slung the saddlebags on the table, and Andrew unlaced the leather straps and reached inside, slipping out a parchment folded in thirds. A red seal impressed with a "B" secured it. He slid it across the table.

Cyrus didn't touch it; he simply stared at the ivory paper, bold against the deep walnut table. He looked up at Andrew. "The British have been here." Cyrus's voice was hollow against the muggy air.

"I know."

A crackling broke the silence as a log collapsed into the embers. Eleanor had ceased the movement of her fingers against her linen sampler. She did not look up but sat in rigid expectation.

Cyrus inched his hand along the table, tapping his finger on the corner of the letter. Breathing deeply, he tugged it back to sit before him. Gently, he lifted the missive, slid a knife under the seal, and unfolded the letter.

His wife stood and left the room.

He retrieved a piece of cowhide from a cupboard, laying it flat atop the letter. Small rectangular holes were scattered through the leather. Cyrus adjusted it, exactly matching the corners to the parchment. As he read the revealed message, he nodded. When he finished, he stared into the fire. Emotions played over his face—one minute indecision, the next fury, and finally determination. He rose and paced the room.

"You will need to start early in the morning …"

"No, I will leave tonight. I must get to—"

"You will be no good to anyone if you ride yourself to death."

"I need to get to Jenny—she'll arrive in New York before I can get there."

Cyrus turned, his face a mask of rage.

"Do you put your trivial desire to see a girl before the cause of freedom?" He pounded the table, rattling the pewter plate. "Lad, what we are about is more important than your small heartache. Grow up, boy." He lowered his voice and resumed his pacing. "Besides, I must compose the instructions to be delivered to your next stop."

"But, sir, I must …"

"You will sleep tonight to regain your strength, and at dawn you will set off. The ride will be as long as today's. If you don't consider your own health, think of your horse's. Neither of you is good to us dead. Let the girl go, lad; there'll be plenty more in your life."

That's where you are wrong. Jenny is my life.

ℭ

The *Destiny* lay low in the water, cannon loading her down more than when she had simply been a merchant ship. Now that the nor'easter had passed and repairs had been made, all attention was once again on General Howe's armada sailing past them only miles away. Apprehension was heavy in the air as they pulled farther out to sea, every crewman stealing glimpses toward the west.

Please, don't delay our journey any more. How would she find Father when she arrived in New York? Would she arrive in time to help him?

And now there was this disquiet she sensed from Jonathon and the crew. He'd explained their need to sail out into the Atlantic to avoid a confrontation with the British—a confrontation they surely would lose. She didn't know how much more she could bear.

She pulled herself up. She must not let these feelings defeat her. She would face whatever came in New York, help Father regain his health. She could do this. She must.

"How are your hands healing, Miss Sutton?"

She turned to look into the kind face of Mr. Gates. Extending her hands palms up, she smiled.

"Your magic healing salve seems to have sped up my recovery, Mr. Gates."

Taking her hands, he examined them. In the days since

the storm, they had healed well. While her skin was still rough and reddened from the blisters, no signs of infection were evident. "Excellent. We should arrive in a safe harbor in due time. I look forward to seeing you safely to our friends who will take you to your father."

Jenny's stomach tightened. She didn't know what to expect, and that made her more uneasy than anything. She liked order and control, and she had neither right now. She nodded.

Mr. Gates smiled at her, still holding her hands. Could he feel her trembling? Squeezing her hands, he winked. "All will be well."

Another promise made. Could it be kept?

☾

Rough hands shook Andrew awake.

"C'mon, son."

Andrew lurched up, pawing his bed for his pistol. Looking around, he didn't recognize the room he'd slept in, then he spotted Cyrus. The man shook his shoulder, urgency in his expression.

"You must leave now—before dawn."

Andrew nodded, rubbing the sleep from his eyes. Yawning, he stood and recovered his breeches and boots, donning them quickly. He tucked in his shirt as he followed Cyrus downstairs. Cyrus continued out the door and Andrew entered the dining room, its door open to the kitchen house out back. He rubbed his head trying to clear his sleep-muddled mind.

Eleanor packed biscuits and fruit into a burlap sack. When she finished, she handed it to him with a mug. Andrew blew across the steaming black coffee, its smell bringing him to full awareness. As he sat down, he nodded his thanks, then tucked the sack into his saddlebag. She handed him a warm biscuit drizzled with honey. The bun was soft and warm in his mouth, the honey sweet on his tongue, dripping, so he licked his fingers after he gobbled it down. Chuckling, Eleanor wiped his hands with a damp linen cloth.

"Take care, Andrew. Godspeed."

He nodded. He could have used another four hours of sleep. Stiffness claimed his back and shoulders, and his legs were still rubbery from yesterday's ride. Yawning, he stretched his arms above his head then scratched his belly. Even another two hours of sleep would have helped.

Cyrus returned, urgency in every movement. Handing a letter to Andrew, he patted the younger man's arm. His eyes were bloodshot; he'd probably been up all night preparing this document. On another sheet was a map showing the location of Andrew's next stop. It would be another hard day's ride. Andrew massaged his lower back and buttocks, dreading another day in the saddle—until he thought of Jenny. He focused, listening carefully to the instructions Cyrus gave him.

Shadow snorted a greeting, groomed and fresh for another day's ride. Mounting, Andrew leaned down to shake Cyrus's hand, but he stiffened at the sound of hoofbeats growing closer.

"Ride, Andrew." He pointed toward the woods. "That way. You will not be able to make it back along the drive. Hurry."

"But, sir …" How could he leave Cyrus and Eleanor to face down British soldiers alone?

"Hurry, son."

Pounding hooves sounded just around the curve of the drive. Cyrus slapped Shadow's flanks and Andrew sped toward the trees. Small branches stung as they slapped his face. He crouched low in the saddle, trusting Shadow to find a path through the woods. Suddenly, a musket blast … and Eleanor's shrill keening.

CHAPTER FIVE

ℭ

JENNY WOULD HAVE WELCOMED THE cramped quarters of the *Destiny*. She huddled beneath her blue shawl, a woolen blanket stretched across two tree limbs in a vain attempt to keep her dry. Mr. Gates and two other crew members sat beneath the leafy canopy, their coats drenched, hats pulled down to shelter their eyes. The rain intensified until thick drops ricocheted off the ground and bit into her legs. This downpour seemed eternal.

Sleep had been useless, and they had missed a good night's sleep the night before, trying as quickly as possible to get inland from the cove where the *Destiny* sheltered. Like New York, New Jersey was rife with British troops. Perth Amboy might have been a safe harbor, but travel up Sandy Hook Bay would have been too close to British-held Staten Island. Their only choice was to land farther south and make the rest of the trip on foot.

As a gray ribbon of dawn lightened the eastern sky, the rain eased. Mr. Gates handed out strips of dried beef and hard tack. She had gotten used to this fare aboard the *Destiny*. If she paid no attention as she ate it, the food was easier to consume.

"Eat hearty—we have a long trek today. I'd like to reach our first stop by sundown." He shook out his jacket, took off his cap, and wiped his drenched hair with his handkerchief.

Jenny rose and wrung out her shawl and the wool blanket.

Though her back ached and her stomach still longed for food, she hurried along. The faster they made this trip, the sooner she'd be with Father.

The sky cleared to brilliant blue with a scattering of clouds that billowed along from the west. The humidity clung to them like a cape, inviting flies and mosquitoes to feast all day. By the time they reached the farm that was their goal, she had scratched her arms and legs to bleeding.

The farmhouse door opened upon their approach, the barrel of a rifle all that emerged.

"State your business." The voice carried across the small pond in front of the house.

"We seek shelter on our journey to Perth Amboy."

The rifle lowered a bit.

"We seek liberty from our suffering along the road."

The rifle disappeared. A short man with hair like straw and pale blue eyes emerged, a toddler girl with matching features clinging to his leg. He beckoned them, scanning the yard as they approached. Even though they stood before him, he moved closer.

"We quarter two lobsterbacks here. They've ridden to town for the day but will be returning before long. You'd best be on your way."

Mr. Gates's shoulders sank. He glanced at Jenny.

"Could you spare some victuals? We've nothing left to eat." Mr. Gates looked at her again.

A slender woman with a gaunt face joined them. She held an infant who stared at them but made no noise.

Jenny wanted to take the baby—the woman looked too weak to hold the child.

"I got nothin' to give you. The soldiers have taken over our home. They've confined us to a small room at the back, and they've eaten all our stores. I can't even feed my wife and babes."

Mr. Gates laid a hand on the man's shoulder. "God be with you, sir. I will try to send help."

The man blinked back tears and pulled back his shoulders. "In all times, I've always been able to take care of my own …"

"But these are different times." He patted the man's shoulder. "Come. Let's depart before the soldiers return. We don't want to bring this family any more suffering."

They trudged through the woods, avoiding the road lest they meet up with the soldiers. Jenny's legs trembled, and she wobbled along the path. The image of a baby too weak to cry filled her mind. How could soldiers take the home and food away from a family? From babies? Father had been fighting against exactly such injustice. What if he was too weak to recover? Her body ached, and the urge to drop to the ground and simply surrender overwhelmed her. She gritted her teeth. *I must go on. Please, give me the courage to go on.*

☙

Heading for his next stop, a farm north of Annapolis, Andrew skirted a small town. Though he'd been able to stay on the main road most of the time, he thought it prudent to duck into the forest whenever riders approached. The British were thick in some areas, and a few close calls urged him to greater caution. Shadow sensed when it was imperative to be silent, standing motionless among the trees.

Every mile he traveled took him closer to British occupation and possible capture. No matter how many times he shook his head, the sound of Eleanor's scream reverberated in his ears. And his mind's eye imagined the scene: Cyrus lying dead at his wife's feet. Eleanor collapsing beside him. Cyrus had paid the ultimate price in the fight for freedom, and Eleanor probably would as well. Every time he acknowledged that Cyrus had sacrificed his life for him, Andrew shivered, though the August night was hot and muggy. Randy and Cyrus were right. This was bigger than he and Jenny being parted. Oh, God, how he missed her, but he had a mission to complete before he could give in to his own desires.

He nudged Shadow to a quicker pace.

Now windows flickering with lanterns and candlelight lit his path around the perimeter of the town. The door to a public house burst open, spewing a drunken man who swore oaths at the innkeeper. Something to do with the owner's daughter. Andrew dipped into the trees, giving wider berth to the buildings on the outskirts.

As he headed out of town, the woods fell away to farm-land. Corn planted on either side of the road rustled in the breeze, but was too short to allow concealment should he need it. Nudging Shadow with his heels, he cantered down the road, hurrying toward the spot ahead where the forest resumed.

Behind him, hoofbeats thundered. As if on cue, Shadow broke into a gallop, and Andrew hunched forward, leaning against the horse's mane. The hoofbeats grew nearer. Had they spotted him?

"Halt." A voice rang out against the midnight air.

Andrew urged Shadow on, and the horse complied. They flew toward the wooded stretch of road.

"In the name of King George, HALT."

A bullet zinged past them on the left.

Shadow sped up, horse and rider moving as one, smooth and swift. They reached the trees and Shadow veered into the forest. The steed had an uncanny awareness of where to run, zigzagging among the trees. Andrew simply gave the horse its head, lying low against it. Shadow vaulted over a fallen tree and halted. The horse's breath gusted through its flared nostrils. Andrew held his breath, listening.

His hand encircled his throat. What would it feel like to hang? Gulping, he loosened the stock about his neck. He had seen a man hanged once, riveted by the fear in the man's eyes, how his legs trembled. Andrew had trembled with him. Someone had thrown a rope over a sturdy branch then, low enough to reach, but high enough for a man to swing. Would they place a black cloth over his head as they had done to that man that day? Through the material, he had heard the man's weeping mixed with gasps for the breath that would soon be choked. The crowd had been boisterous until that moment. Then, as one, the people quieted.

Andrew had wanted to run, to look away, but he had been transfixed, rooted to the ground. The knot of the rope had been skillfully placed just at the jaw—an easier death than strangling. The ladder was kicked out from beneath the man. *Snap.* His legs kicked, a stain spread over his breeches, and a woman and young boy nearby wept softly. Then his legs were still, and the people who had been frozen in grotesque curiosity moved as if they'd just come alive. Some of them laughed as they drifted away, some were silent. Andrew had vomited.

Was that what hanging would be like for him?

No, he must banish these thoughts and see his mission through. He must reach Jenny. He shook his head to rid his mind of the gruesome scene. He would not hang. They would have to catch him first.

The troop was on the road beyond where Shadow had left it.

"Search the woods. Find them." The command sliced the night.

The soldiers dismounted, clambering into the trees. Andrew crouched as they slashed their sabers into branches and bushes, hacking through any hint of the direction Shadow had taken. He hunched against the horse, his legs moving with the rhythm as Shadow's sides expanded and lowered, a bellows of breath, slowing as they stood, waiting. The soldiers searched either side of the road, advancing even farther along than Andrew and Shadow had traveled.

"Find them!"

The sounds grew fainter as the troop moved on. Finally, the sound of men mounting horses floated back to Andrew.

Hoofbeats echoed then faded into the distance. Shadow snorted; Andrew chuckled.

"Was that a comment on the efficiency of the king's troops, Shadow?"

The horse whinnied softly. They waited until all was silent on the road. Then, weaving into and out of the woods, they continued to the next stop.

C

The sharp light of the noonday sun reflected off the window panes of the house Jenny had been searching for in Manhattan. She ran her hand across her midriff, feeling the loose cloth of her dress. Traveling for four days on foot with little to eat had taken its toll. But somewhere there was a mother cradling her thin baby. Jenny would be hungry for only a few days. Their fate was unending.

The farmer who had sheltered them the night before had offered a hearty meal of roasted rabbit and corn, but her appetite had dwindled, and what she'd eaten lay like a lead ball in her stomach. She'd had a good night's rest on a straw mattress that was opulence compared to the hard ground that had been her bed the previous nights.

The same farmer brought her the final miles to this house where Mother and Father stayed. At last, she would see for herself how Father was doing. So why was she hesitating?

Was Father in good health? Was he still ailing? Was he even alive? She held her stomach attempting to stem the fluttering that threatened to disgorge her breakfast.

No sense standing here wondering.

She mounted the steps and lifted the brass knocker, rapping it hard three times. A young black boy eased the door open, peeking around to see who was there.

"Isaac? Is that you?"

The boy's face lit up. "Yes, Miss Jenny."

"Why, you've grown a foot since I left."

He grinned at her. "Yes, ma'am."

She waited, but he continued to beam at her.

"May I come in?"

"Yes, ma'am." He swung the door wide just as a tall slender woman entered the hall from the parlor. Her gray eyes mirrored Jenny's, but her hair was flaxen.

"Isaac, who is at the—oh, my gracious." The woman froze, her hand flying to her heart.

"Mother, I've returned."

She collapsed into Mother's arms. All the fear and discomfort she'd felt melted into Mother's warmth. She was home. She was safe. She slumped a bit, legs trembling, and smiled at Isaac as he moved a chair closer, but Mother would not release her.

Isaac closed the door and slipped to the back of the house. Jenny clung to her, then stepped back. "I am travel-worn and dirty. I will soil your clothing."

"Jennifer, I told you to remain at Brentwood Manor," she scolded, hugging her tighter.

"I know, but I could not resist coming to see Father. How is he?"

Mother wiped her tears with her handkerchief. Lines creased the corners of her eyes and mouth, lines that had not been there when Jenny had left the previous year.

"Your father ... is still ailing."

Thrilled, she hugged Mother again. Father was still alive.

"What have you endured, child, to arrive here so quickly? I sent the letter only a month ago."

"Uncle Jonathon was coming to New York anyway ..."

"He cannot. They will arrest him—"

"He did not sail into port here in the city."

"Then how did you arrive? Are you alone?" More lines creased her forehead.

"No, Uncle Jonathon would never abandon me." Jenny laughed, brushing her fingers along the furrows etched in Mother's brow.

"Of course he wouldn't." Mother smiled, erasing at least

the new creases. "Forgive me for such thoughts, it's just that times are so different now, so treacherous ..." She pulled her wrap closer as she gazed toward the window. She shook herself and looked at Jenny. "I forget myself. Let me ring for tea, and then you can tell me of your adventure since departing Brentwood Manor." She pulled a rope bell, and a slender woman with silken brown skin hurried in.

Seeing Sarie was like a warm, soothing balm. She had served the family for years, but Jenny loved her like an older sister.

"Miss Jenny," she said, her voice breaking. "You've come."

Jenny drew her into an embrace. "Yes, I've come, Sarie." Pulling back, she searched the servant's eyes—striking blue eyes, brimming with tears, bright against her mocha skin.

She wiped at her own tears.

"This is what Mr. Sutton needs. Your presence will surely bring him 'round," she said, squeezing Jenny's hand.

Mother reached for the back of the chair where she stood.

"I'm sure it will." She turned to Mother. "I'll do whatever I can."

"Let me fetch tea for you ladies," Sarie said over her shoulder, having already turned toward the back of the house.

"How serious is Father's injury?"

"It is probably good that you've returned after all."

"I want to see him."

"After tea, you can take a nap. I'm sure you're exhausted after your voyage."

"No. I want to see Father now."

Mother nodded slightly. "Of course, dear." Her brows drew down. "It is good that you are here."

❧

Little of the golden afternoon sunlight peeked through the partially closed shutters when Jenny entered Father's room. Mother's arm encircled her waist. A foul odor permeated the air, and she paused. It took all her strength not to press her handkerchief to her nose to block the stench. Swallowing, she continued into the room. For a moment, she couldn't make out the figure in the bed. As her vision adjusted to the dimness of the room, she gasped at Father's emaciated form. Edward Sutton's face was as pallid as the pillow he lay on, his jaw set against the pain. Seeing her, his expression brightened and he attempted to smile, though it was more like a grimace.

"Father," she whispered as she rushed to his side, fighting her repulsion to the odor.

He reached up to stroke her cheek, but the effort was too much. His hand fell back to the bed.

"My Jenny." His voice was soft and raspy.

She took his hand, kissing it, cradling it against her face. "I'm here, Father."

"It gladdens me." He stopped, the effort to speak too much.

She looked up at Mother, standing tall, shoulders back, holding a damp linen cloth. A single tear escaped before she could wipe it away.

Sarie entered carrying a pitcher of water. Placing it on the bedside table, she opened the shutters on the window closest to the bed. Father winced, turning away from the bright light, and Mother placed the damp cloth over his eyes.

"You may want to leave while I tend to your father." Mother's voice was soft.

"No, I will stay."

Sarie picked up the pitcher and held it for a moment, as if deciding what she must do next. Her gaze shifted from Mother to Jenny.

"Miss Jenny, I don't mean to tell you what's best, but it would pain Mr. Sutton to have you see him in distress."

Jenny wavered for a moment; the stench signaled a gruesome wound. She could be here to lend emotional support and leave the repugnant task of dealing with the wound to Mother and Sarie. Did she have the fortitude to face this task? Did she have a deep enough love? She tightened her hand around his. "I will stay."

Mother nodded.

Sarie poured water into the basin and handed Mother the towel. Dipping the towel in the basin, she wrung it out and carefully drew back the blanket covering Father's leg.

The putrid odor surged up. Jenny reeled, letting go of Father's hand to cover her nose. The stench intensified when Mother slowly pulled back the compress that covered the wound.

"Oh my God." Jenny jerked back.

An ugly gash stretched from Father's knee up his thigh. Yellow pus oozed out even as Mother wiped it clean. One area was an ugly blackish-green.

Jenny's stomach lurched. The smell invaded her nose and throat. She gulped down bile, willing herself not to be sick.

Though Mother worked slowly, taking great care not to hurt him, Father moaned in pain, gritting his teeth.

Jenny reached out and took his hands in hers, trying to comfort him. "Shhh, Father. I am here with you." Her words rang hollow. What could she do to help him? She laid her head beside his on the pillow. "I am here, Father. I am here." Tears burned as her hollow words became a hollow pit in her stomach.

You will not do your father any good by feeling sorry for yourself.

"What can I do?" she asked.

Mother wrung out the cloth.

"Pray, Jennifer. You can pray."

Reaching into her apron pocket, Sarie took out a fresh linen, fragrant with comfrey, thyme, and lavender. She gave it to Mother, who applied the compress to the wound, securing it with strips of cloth tied around Father's leg. Finally, she pulled the blanket up, covering his legs and dulling the odor. Picking up a vial from the bedside table, she gently propped him up with one arm and placed the bottle to his lips. She tipped it to allow him to swallow a small dose of the elixir. She replaced the vial but continued to hold him in her arms. She kissed his forehead.

Sarie closed the shutters, casting the room into twilight. She picked up the basin, pitcher, and old compress. Her usually brilliant blue eyes were slate with sadness when she glanced at Jenny as she left.

Jenny studied Father. Her arms were leaden; her mind muddled. Memories of him played in her head: Father swinging her and Kathryn into the air, making them laugh with glee. She and Father riding horses, galloping over fields, him laughing as she vaulted over fences and hedges. The authority he exuded when he strode across a room, strong and commanding. Now he shrank into the bedclothes, his eyes as pained as when he had carried Kathryn to the house. When her eyes were lifeless.

How could this have happened to him? When Jenny boarded the ship for Williamsburg, he had cautioned her to be safe and sensible. Had he not listened to his own words?

Mother still held him in her arms. Her face was drawn and pale, and she stared ahead as if she, too, had been remembering her lively, robust husband.

"We must pray for him, Jennifer. We must have courage."

"Tell her."

Mother jolted at her husband's voice. Whispering gently, she eased his head back to the pillow, but he tried to rise.

"Tell her." His voice was strong, then it faded to a whisper. "You must." He searched Mother's face.

She nodded in understanding. "I shall tell her if you rest."

He nodded, Jenny thought more in exhaustion than compliance. He drew in a deep breath and sighed. His chest stilled. Mother's face paled, and she leaned toward him, her body tense. But her shoulders relaxed upon hearing his slow, even breathing, and her panicked expression returned to sorrow. She stared at Jenny as if she were not there, almost transfixed. Then, as if waking, she nodded at her.

"He is resting. Now I must keep my part of the bargain."

Pulling the blanket up on his chest, she kissed his cheek and patted his hand. "Come, Jennifer. There is much to tell you."

CHAPTER SIX

C

"WHAT YOU ARE TELLING ME is that Father has been spying? For General Washington?" Jenny whispered, glancing toward the door to the back of the house.

An imperceptible nod.

She tried to sort through the questions that tumbled through her brain. How had she not known this before? She tried to find her voice, but words would not form. Leaning back against the winged chair, she stared at the ceiling. Heaviness closed in around her. Finally, she spoke.

"And that is why he was attacked by a British soldier?"

"Not a soldier. A Ranger. One of Rogers's men."

Jenny frowned. "Roger who?"

"Robert Rogers. He earned his reputation during the war against the French, who were aided by the Indians. Their tactics were … unusual. When the colonies decided to break from the crown, he tried to join the Continental Army, but General Washington did not trust him. As suspected, he had British sympathies and is now an officer in the Queen's Rangers, though everyone calls them Rogers's Rangers, for he is the undisputed leader."

"How did Father encounter him?"

"He was on a mission from Boston to Manhattan. At a stop at an inn, he encountered this Ranger, disguised as a minister, who engaged him in conversation. The 'minister' expressed views in support of the Patriot cause, and they talked until late into the evening. When all other patrons had retired, this man removed his robe, revealing his green uniform and allegiance to the king. Brandishing a hatchet, he attacked your father." Swallowing, she paused.

Jenny waited for her to continue. Outside, silence was cloaked in darkness. Only one candle, glowing on the table before them, lit the room, its flame still in the summer air.

Mother stirred in her chair.

"Your father had sensed something amiss, and the attack was not a complete surprise. He was able to fend off the first blows, but the Ranger hacked at his leg and then delivered a blow to his temple. Your father did not lose consciousness." Her voice dropped. "He was aware enough to feel the Ranger pull his hair back ... he was about to scalp him ..." Mother was shivering despite the warm evening temperature.

Jenny ran to her side. Kneeling beside her, she took Mother's hands in hers. "Hush. You do not have to relive this."

"You must understand the importance of this cause to your father, Jennifer. And the peril." She took a deep breath. "The innkeeper heard the commotion and came into the room. He fired a shot toward the Ranger but did not hit him. He told him to leave, and the Ranger ran out. The innkeeper saved your father's life. He tended to his wounds and sent word back to me in Boston. When I arrived ..." She shuddered. "I thought he was dead.

"When he could be moved, we brought him here. Your father often stayed here when he traveled to Manhattan. The house belongs to his friend in Boston who comes here when he has business on Wall Street."

"Is this what Father wanted you to tell me?"

Mother stroked her ebony curls. "No, Jennifer. He wanted me to tell you that there is work that must be done. I cannot leave him, and I believe he wants you to complete it."

Jenny stifled a shiver as a chill snaked down her back, the same sensation as when Jonathon handed her the blue shawl.

The blue shawl that was tucked in her wardrobe upstairs. Just as with Jonathon, she knew there was no turning back once she complied.

❦

Timothy Morley brought Andrew a slab of rye bread and a tankard of ale. With seven children, the Pennsylvania farmer had little food and no room to shelter Andrew in the house, so he would sleep in the barn. Andrew was grateful for the bread and ale and whatever shelter Timothy could afford.

He didn't mind the solitude of the barn, for he sorely missed Jenny tonight and would rather think of her than make conversation. How he longed to hold her. Perhaps he would very soon. With luck, he would reach New York in a few days.

He lay back, hands tucked beneath his head. Through a window high in the loft, stars dotted the pitch-black sky. Jenny loved lying in the grass, gazing at the stars. He would lay on his side to drink in her face, lit in the moon's glow as she pointed out constellations. All the time she spoke, he had one thought: to kiss her soft, full lips. The dimple that faded then showed itself as she spoke drove him to madness. Finally, he would cover her mouth with his, tasting her sweetness, hearing her laugh.

These thoughts aroused him rather than bringing the rest he desperately needed. Lying on his side, he wished Jenny were beside him. He must have drifted off, but suddenly his senses were alert. Something or someone was moving along the exterior wall of the barn.

He rose slowly so as not to cause the hay to crunch. Creeping toward the window, he hunched beside it and listened. Night sounds met his ears—crickets, peepers, the breeze through the leaves. He waited. There it was. A low *pssst*. Someone was out there, and he was signaling a companion—or two. Andrew eased up to standing and peered out into the darkness. He cursed the crescent moon, which offered so little light. Squinting, he focused on the house, but all was quiet. Did he see movement under the tree near the barn? Yes. One man crouched there. Andrew scanned the rest of the yard. Nothing moved. Slowly, he crept back to where his saddlebags lay, slipped the flap back, and eased out his knife. He picked up his rifle from beside the blanket he had been sleeping on and returned to the window. The man under the tree was waving his arm, motioning to someone. A shadow moved away from the barn, from just below the window where Andrew stood. The hunched figure scuttled to the protection of the tree.

"Drop your rifle."

Andrew froze at the voice behind him. Slowly, he bent down, placing his rifle on the dirt floor. He tucked his knife up his sleeve.

With his toe, the man behind him pushed Andrew's weapon across the dirt floor. The cold metal of a pistol pressed against his head. A cool circle that could end his life in a second. He swallowed. Perhaps he would never feel the hangman's noose after all.

In that moment, Jenny's face came to him, a look of horror on her face at the sight of his head blown away. He couldn't desert her. He had to find a way. Ducking quickly, he pivoted, grabbed the man's hand that held the pistol, and brought his right hand up, driving the knife into the man's neck.

The man gaped at him, startled, eyes bulging. His mouth formed an "O" as if ready to speak. Then he crumpled, a ribbon of scarlet trickling into the hay beneath him.

Andrew's throat stung with bile. He had never killed anyone. He trembled, unable to take his gaze from the man. *Move! This is not the time for self-pity.* The family that had sheltered him was in grave danger, for these men were obviously planning an attack. If he did not act immediately,

Timothy, his wife, and his children would be murdered.

He wiped the blade of his knife on the man's pants and yanked the green jacket from his body. A Ranger. He picked up the Ranger's hat, a Scottish tam with a red band and tuft. Placing it on his own head, he took the man's hatchet and pistol. Retrieving his own rifle, he propped it just inside the barn door.

Sweat beaded on his upper lip. What he was about to do could cost him his life. He glanced out the window at Timothy Morley's farmhouse, where seven children lay sleeping. Tucking his knife into his belt, he grasped the hatchet in one hand, the pistol in the other, and took a deep breath.

The shadows shifted. One looked back, scanning the barn.

Andrew had to emerge. Now he was grateful for the crescent moon that hid his face from the men ahead. The man he'd killed had been his size, so he didn't need to slouch. He slipped from the barn and stood against its wall, scanning the yard as if doing reconnaissance. The first man motioned him to join them, but Andrew signaled for quiet. He pointed toward the house. Both men turned to check what he was pointing at. As they did, Andrew reached back into the barn, retrieved his rifle, and put a bead on the first man. They turned back, puzzled, until the first man caught on and raised his pistol. Andrew fired. The man lurched up, clutched his face, and dropped to the ground.

A dog barked in the night. Shadow snorted, his hooves stomping in the stall.

Andrew leapt back into the barn, never taking his attention off the second man, who stared down at his companion in confusion, then glared at Andrew.

"Are you mad? What have you done?" he cried in a hoarse whisper.

A light flickered in an upstairs window of the house.

"Stay inside. Stay inside," Andrew whispered.

The second man walked toward the barn, arms outstretched.

"What are ya' doing?"

Andrew lifted the pistol and fired. The man was tossed up off his feet, then crashed to the ground.

The door to the house opened. Timothy ran out, brandishing his rifle aimed at Andrew's head. Andrew dropped the pistol, held up his hands, then snatched the tam off his head, throwing it to the ground.

"Timothy, it's me, Andrew."

Timothy held the pose for a moment. Andrew shrugged out of the jacket. Timothy lowered his rifle and gazed about, baffled. Seeing the Rangers' uniforms, his shoulders sagged as Andrew approached. Despite the darkness, Andrew caught fear in the farmer's face.

"They will come for me again," Timothy's voice quavered. He caught sight of the hatchet. "My wife and children ..."

Behind Timothy, a woman and several children huddled at the door. Andrew clapped Timothy on the arm.

"Let's take care of these bodies." He lifted his chin toward the house.

Turning, Timothy nodded. "Indeed."

"There's one more in the barn," Andrew said.

The two of them put the bodies in a wagon and drove it into the woods north of the house. They spent the rest of the night digging and filling a large grave. As sunrise lit the edge of the eastern horizon, they tossed their shovels into the back of the wagon.

Andrew had never felt so tired.

❦

Jenny stood before the looking glass. Raven curls swept high on her head with two ringlets teasing her neck, resting against the blue shawl that wrapped her shoulders. Something about this simple errand made her tremble, perhaps the knowledge that there was nothing simple about it. While she did not know the purpose of her task or the contents of the letter, she presumed getting caught would be deadly.

She had selected a pale yellow dress of lutestring, the light silk comfortable on this sultry morning. Smoothing her skirt, she took a deep breath, her hand moving up to the stomacher of her dress, behind which butterflies flitted. Another deep breath. She must do this. For Jonathon. For the fledgling nation. For Father.

Picking up the letter, she turned it over in her hands. Jonathon had combined both messages into one to facilitate her transfer to Laurence Montclair. The crimson seal imprinted with "B" stared back at her. What did it contain? What consequence lay in her simple act of responding to an inquiry and handing over this letter?

She had not confided her mission to Mother, for she suffered enough tending to Father day and night. While Sarie helped with his care, Mother remained with him as much as possible, and Jenny did not want to add to her burden. But, this morning, she had informed Jenny that she would accompany her to church that day.

"I have missed you, Jennifer. Any moment I can spend with you is a gift." She had kissed Jenny's forehead. "Your father will be fine for the hour we will be away. Sarie will sit with him." She'd fluttered her hands, arranging Jenny's curls.

Was she trying to convince me or herself?

She adjusted the scarf in the mirror.

Mother's presence would complicate the mission. Would this Laurence Montclair even approach her then? Of course, she needed a chaperone to attend the church service, but she had assumed one of the household staff would accompany her. Wandering from one of them would be simpler, but not from Mother. While she was grateful to be back with her parents, Mother had circled around her like a bee around honeysuckle since her return. Discretion, perhaps artifice, would be required today if she were to fulfill her promise to Jonathon.

At that moment, Mother swept into the room. Jenny

slipped her hand through the opening in the side seam of her skirt and tucked the letter into the pocket in her under-petticoat.

"You look lovely this morning, Jenny." Mother lifted the corner of the blue shawl running the fabric through her fingers. "This is charming. Did you acquire it in Williamsburg?"

Feeling exposed, Jenny snugged the scarf closer. "Uncle Jonathon gave it to me."

Mother's fingers stopped moving. "Uncle Jonathon?"

"Yes."

She held Jenny's gaze. "How kind of him." She fingered the fabric. "How very kind."

Jenny studied her own hands, her face flushing. "Well, we must be off if we're to be punctual for the service."

Mother took her hand. "We need to pray for your father. We need to pray for many things, especially in these times."

As they rode to the church, Jenny turned over several options to escape Mother for a moment to allow Laurence Montclair to approach her. She didn't know anyone in Manhattan, so she couldn't pretend to meet up with a friend. She could drop her glove in the pew and return to the church to retrieve it. But, most likely, Mother would accompany her. Oh dear, this was complicated.

"Serious thoughts hold your mind," Mother said.

Jenny reached for her hand. "These are serious times. I worry about Father."

Mother nodded, pursing her lips. For a moment, the fear held, then her brows drew down, two fierce lines above her darkening eyes, as a line of British soldiers marched by. Composing herself, she adjusted her skirts and lowered her gaze. Their carriage stopped to allow the soldiers to pass.

One young man caught Jenny's attention. His posture was more erect, more rigid, than any other soldier's. His face was intent, jaw set. Upon seeing her, he smiled, and touched the brim of his cocked hat. Shocked at his boldness, she turned away.

Mother tapped her knee. "It would be best to be civil, if not kind, daughter. There is much to lose by defying the king's troops."

"More than a father who lies near death because of a British sympathizer's hatchet?"

"We do not want to draw any more unfriendly attention to the Sutton family. Not if we are to escape arrest." Mother nodded slightly toward the young man. Taking a deep breath, Jenny turned back to him and nodded. She was rewarded with a broad grin.

"Lieutenant Ashby, mind your path," shouted the captain.

Lieutenant Ashby turned to see where he was going just in time to avoid running into a cart full of vegetables. The angry farmer cursed and waved a rake at him. The lieutenant seized the farmer's arm and shoved him to the ground, tipping the cart and spilling produce along the road. Sitting forward, Jenny leaned out the window, ready to call out to him, but Mother pulled her back.

He glanced back at her, his face as crimson as his coat, and nodded curtly.

When their carriage arrived at St. Paul's Episcopal Chapel, they stepped down and were greeted by the priest. Mother introduced her.

"Welcome, Jennifer. I am sure your presence brings great comfort to your parents." Pastor Farr's gray hair and kind blue eyes reminded Jenny of Mr. Gates. His easy movements belied his burly size, and Jenny's hand was enveloped in his welcoming handshake.

"Thank you, Pastor Farr." While she smiled at him, she desperately wanted to search the people entering the church in an effort to identify Laurence Montclair. But the priest held her gaze while he held her hand, and etiquette dictated she keep her attention on him.

"How is Edward, Mrs. Sutton?"

His shift in attention to Mother allowed Jenny a surreptitious glance around the yard, but no one fit the description Uncle Jonathon had given her. Would Montclair approach her before the service or afterward? She suspected later, but her entire being was on alert. Finally, Pastor Farr graciously swept his arm toward the church, ushering them in for the service.

Jenny fought the urge to fidget throughout the service, her nerves jumping like frogs hopping through her body. Sitting still was agony, and Mother placed a hand on her knee more than once to still her feet from jiggling. Finally, the refrain of the last hymn echoed and faded. They joined the others as they departed down the aisle.

Outside, the August sun beat down on the congregation as they visited in the church yard. Several people approached Mother to inquire about Father's condition and wish him well. This was the perfect opportunity for Jenny to slip away from Mother's side. She strolled to a leafy elm, seeking its shade.

"Miss Sutton?"

Jenny turned. A middle-aged man with thick, white hair and lively, hazel eyes smiled at her. He was not much taller than she, his clothes meticulously tailored. The layers of his white cravat cascaded between the double-breasted, russet long coat, the brass buttons gleaming. His tan breeches were tucked neatly into shiny leather boots. She detected a faint aroma of cloves.

"I do not believe we have met. I am Laurence Montclair." He bowed. "I am a friend of your father's, and I would like to inquire as to his health."

Dear God. Did the earth just tremble?

She thought she was prepared for this, but her stomach churned with fear. She did not know the ramifications of this meeting. She did not know what information she was passing or what would be the result. But deep within, she suspected it would involve life and death decisions and events. All she had to do was hand over a letter and she would be finished—that is, if he added the words Uncle Jonathon had related. If he did not say the second phrase, she was to go home and burn the letter immediately.

"Thank you for your concern, Mr. Montclair. Unfortunately, Father is not faring well. His wound has become infected and he suffers for it. Thank you for your kindness." He had not said it. Perhaps he would not. Perhaps she would simply walk away and be done with this favor she had promised to fulfill.

"May I be so bold to say your shawl is lovely? It's as blue as the water off the cape."

Jenny stiffened, staring at him. His gaze scanned the yard then returned to her. He nodded slightly.

Jenny's hands trembled. She fumbled as she tried to find the slit in the seam of her skirt. Finally, she reached into the pocket for the letter. Her palms perspired, so she handled it gingerly. As she was about to extract it, he raised his hand.

"Patience indeed is a virtue, but it must be a difficult one to embrace when you so fervently hope for your father's recovery."

Jenny stopped. This was not part of what she had rehearsed with Uncle Jonathon. Each muscle throughout her body felt stretched to its limit, as though, if she moved, she would shatter. Her hands froze in place. Then she understood. A couple walked past them, the man tipping his hat. She smiled and nodded and Laurence Montclair bowed.

His gaze returned to hers; again, an imperceptible nod. She withdrew the letter, keeping her shawl draped over her hand to shield the exchange. He efficiently took it while bowing over her hand then slid it into the pocket of his long coat. Tipping his hat, he turned and left.

"I see you've met Mr. Montclair." Mother was beside her.

Jenny continued to stare in his direction, hoping Mother would not detect the flush that heated her face.

"He is a good friend of your father's … and your Uncle Jonathon's. He is a brave man, but you must be careful."

Mother linked her arm through hers as they strolled to their carriage. Jenny felt the tightness of Mother's grip. Mother's fear was palpable.

☾

Lieutenant Ashby stood, as if at attention, beside their carriage. His crimson coat cast a robust aura to his face; his crisp white breeches accentuated long, muscled legs. Removing his hat, he bowed.

"I am your most humble servant, madam." Though he addressed Mother, his gaze never left Jenny. Steel-gray eyes below his white powdered wig lent a coolness that reminded her of an icy January day.

"Good day, sir," Mother said, her fingers pressing into Jenny's arm.

"Pray, good madam, if I may be so bold to present myself. I am Lieutenant Nigel Ashby in service to His Majesty, King George III."

Jenny wanted to blurt that he stated the obvious, but she bit her tongue.

"Good day, Lieutenant. I am Mrs. Constance Sutton, and this is my daughter, Miss Jennifer Sutton. How may we be of service to you?"

"By allowing me to help you into your carriage and escort you home."

Mother shuddered, but her smile never faltered.

"You are very kind, sir. We would accept your offer of assistance, but we have our driver to see us home."

Mathias, Sarie's husband, turned in the driver's seat and nodded at the soldier. His expression was blank.

Ashby ignored him and stepped forward, extending his arm to her.

"I insist." He glanced at Jenny.

"You are very generous," Mother said as he assisted her into the carriage.

He pivoted and held out his arm to Jenny. His gaze held

hers, as if daring her to look away. With one hand, he held her elbow as she climbed into the carriage, his other hand resting on the small of her back.

The spot burned.

Turning to him, she forced a smile. "Thank you, Lieutenant."

He bowed then clambered up beside Mathias.

"We must play along, Jennifer." Mother whispered above the noise of the horse's hoof beats. "I am unsure of the lieutenant's intentions. He seems quite taken with you, but it could be a ploy."

"I will comply with his wishes, Mother. At least, as long as I am able. My blood boils at his closeness."

"Keep that humour under control. Our lives might depend on it."

When they arrived at the house, he jumped down and opened the door. Offering his hand to Mother, he braced her step from the coach. Turning to Jenny, he held out his hand. She wanted to slap it away, but she forced down her anger and accepted his help. *I can get out of this carriage myself, you ass.* She smiled, and dropped his hand.

"May I call on your daughter, Mrs. Sutton?"

His words were a bolt of lightning striking her. Her eyes widened as she caught Mother's gaze. A steady gaze, a polite gaze. Not a gaze that said, *my husband is grievously injured because of one of you.* She stood erect, a smile pasted on her lips. The picture of serenity.

"Of course you may, Lieutenant Ashby."

Jenny began to speak, but Mother placed a hand on her arm, pressing firmly. Almost pinching.

"Good day, madam. Miss Sutton." He tipped his black hat, his smile broad as he turned and retreated toward the southern end of town.

"Mother, how could you …?" Jenny crossed her arms.

"Come inside, dear."

Sarie met them at the door, taking their parasols and

shawls, folding Jenny's sea-blue shawl over her arm. What a day this had been, and it was just noon. She followed Mother into the parlor. Finally, alone, Mother took her hand.

"We must act with utmost caution, Jennifer. We cannot afford to offend Lieutenant Ashby, nor can we allow him into our confidence. But he seems quite enamored with you, and that could work to our advantage. We can trust no one."

"Even Mr. Montclair?"

Mother stared out the window, silent. She finally said, "Be very careful of Mr. Montclair."

Mother had not answered her question.

CHAPTER SEVEN

C

DESPITE FATHER'S GRAVE CONDITION, MOTHER insisted on a morning carriage ride every day. Jenny enjoyed sitting beside her, taking in the scenery and the bustling activity of the city. Carts and carriages bumped along on the cobblestone roads, or carved deeper ruts into the earth on rainy days. As much as possible, pedestrians walked along the wooden plank walkways in front of the shops.

No matter where their ride took them, they always slowed as they drove past the apothecary shop. Jenny was glad, for the window display of blue and white porcelain jars from China captured her imagination. Today, she craned her neck to observe the display—what was life like in the Far East?

"Stop, Mathias," Mother said, interrupting her daydreaming.

Mathias pulled the reins. "Whoa, Aggie. Whoa, girl."

The carriage rolled to a stop. Mathias hopped down to assist Mother. She turned to Jenny. "I'll just be a minute. We need more elixir for your father."

Jenny protested, but Mother swooped into the shop. Hadn't there been more than half a bottle when she'd administered the tonic that morning? She studied the front of the white clapboard shop with its muntin-paned windows and neatly swept front step. Above the door, the British flag snapped in the breeze. Swinging next to it, a wooden sign read "Apothecary" above a picture of a mortar and pestle. She wanted to alight from the carriage and yank down that flag. How could Mother do business with a Tory? Although, with the British occupation of New York, she had little choice.

Jenny remained seated, studying the window display. Something was different. The largest of the porcelain jars had been removed. That was her favorite, as it depicted a serpentine dragon breathing fire. Perhaps the owner needed to store herbs in it. She glanced at the other pieces displayed: two smaller jars, several plates of different sizes and three mortar and pestle sets.

When Mother appeared, her cheeks were rosy, and she was a bit out of breath. Mathias helped her into the carriage and they continued home.

Jenny took Mother's hand, not commenting on the fact that she held no new bottle of elixir.

𝖺

Finally reaching New Jersey, Andrew halted Shadow in front of a roadside tavern marked on the map Randy had provided. Purple dusk cloaked the western sky, the east already embracing the ebony night. Road-weary and sweaty, he desperately wanted to sleep in a bed.

A grizzled man with wispy white hair that flared out on either side of his head emerged from the inn, a rifle in his hands. "Kin I help ya'?"

"I need a room."

"Got no rooms."

Andrew scanned the windows on the second floor, then the yard with no carriages or horses. His bones ached. His muscles screamed. He had no time for this.

"I'll pay a good price."

"Got no rooms."

"Sir …"

"Git now. No place for ya here."

"I've ridden from Williamsburg. I'm riding for the Sons

of Liberty."

If he had miscalculated and this was not the correct tavern, he could have just signed his death warrant. But he had checked and rechecked the map. This had to be the inn on the map.

The man stared at him. He raised his rifle, aiming it at Andrew's face.

"Gimmee a name."

"What?"

"A name. A name. Anybody can ride up here and spout, 'I'm with the Sons of Liberty.'"

"Randy O'Connor."

The rifle remained pointed at him.

"Jonathon Brentwood."

The rifle slowly lowered. The man continued to squint with one eye as if still sighting the gun. He coughed up phlegm and spit it at the ground.

"Ya' named two of the finest." He motioned for Andrew to alight. "Mighty nice horse." He patted Shadow's flank and got a neigh in return. "Howey Doone." He held out his hand.

"Fine, thank you." It took Andrew a moment to realize the man had just introduced himself. "Oh. Andrew Wentworth. Jonathon's brother-in-law."

Howey shook his hand, then beckoned Andrew to follow him inside.

The faint aroma of what had been cooked for dinner welcomed him, causing his stomach to answer with a loud growl. The black stewpot was hooked on a cast iron rod that swung into the hearth. Sitting on a brick on the edge was a pan of fresh corn bread. Andrew's mouth watered.

Howey pulled out a chair and grunted.

No sooner did Andrew sink into the chair than a tankard of ale sat before him. He took a hearty swig then held the cool tankard against his face. His whole body sank into the comfort of a chair, a welcoming fire, a cool drink, and what he hoped would be a bowl of stew. He was not disappointed. Howey plunked a pewter plate with hunks of venison swimming in herrico sauce before him. A piece of corn bread sat beside it, soaking up the excess gravy.

While he ate, he told Howey about his journey thus far.

"Bah. Ya' need water."

He might be in need of a bath, but thought it rather rude that Howey would point it out so bluntly.

"The sea, boy. The sea. Ya' hain't going ta get to New York from here in less than two weeks by horse. Ya' shoulda been at sea all along."

Andrew's spirits sank. Up until now, the food and drink had lifted him from exhaustion and he'd been feeling optimistic.

"I'll git ya' where ya' need ta be. Leave your fine mount with me. Ya' can reclaim him on yer return. In the morning, we'll see about a boat. It be the only way."

Andrew wiped up the rest of the gravy with a chunk of warm bread. Now energy seeped from his body like sand through fingers. He longed for a soft bed.

Carrying a lantern, Howey led him to a room on the upper floor. He wrapped his arms around one side of an armoire and slid it out, allowing him to access a half-door hidden behind it. After pushing it open, he gestured to Andrew to enter. A straw mattress and chamber pot furnished the nook. Andrew bent down, practically crawling into the space. He frowned at Howey.

"Ye'll thank me later, my boy." He hooked the lantern on a nail sticking out of a beam, grunted, and left. The sound of the armoire sliding back into place caused Andrew a moment of panic.

With no window, the air was stagnant, the space stuffy and hot. His linen shirt clung to his skin, rivulets of sweat running down his sides. He brushed back the strands of hair that had crept out of his queue and now hung about his face. He wanted to strip out of his clothes, but the necessity of a quick escape was always on his mind. Ruefully, he extinguished the lantern flame since even the little heat it let off added to his misery.

As the evening progressed, the public room below him added heat from the hearth and smoke from the patrons. Between the smoke and the dust in the nook, Andrew cleared his head with two hearty sneezes. The noise of the boisterous patrons below would cover any sound he made. The rough burlap he lay on covered straw that crunched and crackled each time he moved. As usual when laying down to rest, he thought of Jenny. How he longed to run his fingers along her silken skin.

Achoo!

He wiped his nose with his sleeve and tried to find a comfortable position.

He imagined the sweet sound of her voice, the soft glow of her smoky, gray eyes. As exhausted as he was, his body stirred with thoughts of her, with memories of lying beside her, their bodies pressed together. They had not consummated their love yet, both agreeing to wait until marriage. Now he cursed that decision, as one or both of them could be dead within the month. Perhaps she …

"My friends," a baritone boomed from below. "Raise your glasses and drink with me. Long live King George."

Voices resounded. "Long live King George." Metal against metal clanged as pewter mugs met in the toast.

Achoo! Blast—had the men below heard him?

From the sound of their merrymaking, his sneeze hadn't been heard over the din. The noise had been increasing as the evening wore on and ale flowed freely.

Now he understood the innkeeper's words.

"Who owns the fine black steed in the stable?" the baritone voice demanded.

Andrew went cold. Sweat broke out in prickles on his skin.

"He was left in me care by a boarder, Cap'n." The innkeeper's voice rang clear.

Cries of disbelief rose from the group.

"What man in his right mind would leave such a mount? For you, old man, to care for?"

Derisive laughter floated up to Andrew. He had wondered the same himself, but had little choice. And Randy had vouched for this man. This man who had put him out of harm's way.

"I will search for the owner." The noise of a chair sliding over the roughhewn floor. "And you will remain here while I do so, old man."

The soldier's boots clomped across the wooden planks as he inspected each room on the main level. Then the footfalls moved up the stairs and into each room in the second story. Finally, the boots were on the other side of the wall. The doors of the armoire were flung open. The soldier stood just a few feet away.

Andrew held perfectly still, for the crackle of the straw surely could be heard. Another sneeze tickled his nose. *Oh, God no.* He pressed his finger beneath his nose.

The doors of the armoire banged as the soldier slammed them shut … just as Andrew was overcome with the sneeze. *Chooie.*

It was soft, more like a swish than a sneeze. No sound came from the other side of the wall. He imagined the man standing there, head cocked, listening. He held his breath. The armoire door creaked open again, and a soft tapping—hands exploring the interior of the piece—sounded through the wall. Finally, the door was closed and the sound of footsteps headed toward the stairs.

Bawdy laughs greeted him.

"What were you doing up there all alone?" someone called out.

"Next he'll head out to the stable to be with the horse he finds so fine," said another.

The joviality continued into the night until the troops

stumbled out the door to return to their camp.

Andrew stared into the darkness. He shifted from one side to the other, trying to get comfortable enough to sleep. But now it was the memory of the man swinging by his neck that would not leave his mind.

C

From her seat within the carriage, Jenny saw people moving along the city street. Some ambled, chatting amiably, some hurried, obviously intent on an errand. She bolted upright at the sight of a man striding along the road. Her heart thudded as she studied his gait—could it be Andrew? Beneath his three-cornered hat, tawny hair was tied back in a queue that lay against his tan coat. Her heart beat a tattoo as the carriage closed the space between them. But her hopes were dashed when he turned to greet a companion, revealing his profile. Every time a man resembling Andrew came into view, she'd had the same reaction.

She collapsed back in her seat. Of course it wasn't Andrew. She had left him in Virginia. Now that she had reunited with her parents, she would never return to Brentwood Manor. She would never see Andrew again. Stinging tears blurred her vision as she recalled the warmth of his embrace. She must banish all memories of him; she couldn't bear to think of him and be strong for Father. Her shoulders sank with the burden of her grief. And with the burden of what Father and Uncle Jonathon had asked of her.

British troops made quick work of suspected spies. Though she had not witnessed any, death sentences were being carried out throughout the city. Even her own actions—accepting the letter from Jonathon and delivering it to Laurence Montclair—were enough to arrest her for treason.

She shivered. Well, she had kept her promise to Jonathon, so she was finished with suspicious activity. Tories would call it seditious activity. She snuggled deep into the velvet seat in the enclosed carriage. As if that would hide her. As if that would protect her.

Now she could concentrate on helping Father to recover. Was it her imagination that he seemed improved since her arrival? She prayed it was so. Watching him lie in such pain and distress, however, was unbearable. Her errand today was to get more of the elixir that alleviated his suffering. This would be her first visit inside the apothecary.

Jenny looked across Broadway Street, where the charred remains of burned houses were black against the summer sky. Jonathon had told her about the fire that had destroyed houses and buildings along the western edge of Manhattan almost a year earlier. Many said Patriot rebels had set the blaze and fanned it to deny the British shelter should they take the city, but even British General Howe had said the night had been windy, sweeping the fire from building to building. In any event, almost a third of the city had been razed, leaving thousands of families homeless.

Among the charred ruins, ragtag urchins dressed in tatters ran, playing among the burnt-out buildings. Standing among the blackened facades, women in bold makeup stared at her as she passed. One beckoned with an obscene gesture to Mathias as he drove the carriage by.

Jenny dragged her scrutiny from the destruction and despair.

When they arrived at the apothecary, she studied the window display, looking for the tall blue and white porcelain jar depicting a dragon. Yesterday morning as they'd driven by, the jar had been missing again. She'd looked for it carefully while Mother had stopped into the shop, again returning with no new bottle of remedy for Father.

As the carriage came to a halt, she gathered her gloves and parasol. Alighting quickly, she checked the window. The dragon jar was in its usual place. She hurried to the entrance. The sooner she obtained the tincture, the sooner Father would find some relief. When she opened the door, tangy, spiced aromas greeted her.

"Good day, miss," said a plump woman from behind the counter. The smile on her face looked permanent, as if she had been born with it and never had to exert herself to make it appear. Beneath her cap, light brown hair curled alongside her face. She stood before shelves filled with more blue and white porcelain jars from the Far East labeled with exotic names like "flora stigma crocus" and "caryophylla." Lower shelves held brown glass bottles, and beneath them were drawers labeled with more familiar names like "flora sulphur" and "lavender." She worked a pestle crushing fennel seed in the mortar. The rich scent of anise filled the air. "May I help you?"

"Yes, you have been mixing a tincture for my father, Edward Sutton. He is in need of more, please."

The woman's hand stopped moving. She shot a puzzled glance toward the window display and then toward a door to the back room. "You will need to speak with the apothecary, Miss Sutton." She placed the mortar and pestle on the counter, wiped her hands on her apron, and adjusted her cap … which was perfectly placed already. She nodded at the door. "Please follow me,"

Jenny smoothed her hair, trying to dispel her creeping unease. Her hand paused mid-air then she looked back at the window. During their daily carriage rides, Mother only stopped for unneeded elixir when the dragon jar was missing from the window. Goosebumps rose on her arms, and the floor seemed to tilt a bit. Perhaps it was the potpourri of aromas that made her a bit lightheaded. As they walked toward the back of the shop, Jenny noticed a young towheaded boy working on his books in a small room off to the side. The woman swung a door into a neat office where a man sat, working on a ledger. He looked up as they entered.

"Mr. Montclair!" Jenny gasped.

The steady grate of the pestle from the front of the shop ground into the silence as Jenny sat opposite the apothecary. Her lightheadedness had increased. What Mr. Montclair told her echoed Mother's revelation about Father's covert activities gathering intelligence for General George Washington. As she listened, she rubbed her temples, trying to ease the pulsing blood rushing through her veins. How had she not known this all the time she had lived in Boston?

"We have sorely missed his expertise," Montclair was saying. "We have an urgent need to pass along information, and your father had set up a seamless process in the home in which you are currently residing."

She nodded slightly, trying to absorb his words. The pestle scraped along the stone mortar. Jenny pictured the spice reduced to powder. Then, silence.

"Ideally, we would continue to ... relay intelligence in the same way."

The words hung in the air, the implication clear. Uncle Jonathon's voice echoed in her mind: *It's the only thing I'll ask you to do. I promise.*

"Of course, I understand if you are unable to continue your father's mission. His wounds are proof of the gravity involved."

"I ... I don't know ..." The ramifications of what he asked whirled in her mind. This would be considered treason by many.

Montclair steepled his fingers and pressed them to his lips. "I understand, Miss Sutton. I would never pressure you into doing something distasteful."

She sat up. "It is not that it's distasteful, Mr. Montclair ..." She swallowed. "It's ..."

"Dangerous. Yes, it is. I will not deny that."

"But Father has suffered so for his commitment to the Patriot cause, so I cannot simply dismiss your request."

"His valor is renowned. But to ask you, a young woman—"

"Do you think I am incapable?" She tilted her chin up.

"Not at all. In fact, I see your father's fire in your eyes."
He smiled at her. "But if you were my daughter—or my
son—I would be hesitant to request this of you. Menace
increases daily. Shall we allow this conversation to rest for a
while? I think you are wise to be cautious."

Her head spun with confusion. Was she betraying Father's
commitment to the cause of liberty? He'd sent her to Brentwood Manor to shield her from the violence taking place in
Boston during its British occupation. Yet he insisted Mother
tell her about his involvement in these perilous ventures.
Did he demand that so she could continue in his stead until
he was able to resume the work?

Could she continue his work? Was she capable, without
Andrew beside her, of risking her life for the cause of freedom? She could say no and life could continue as it was, her
only worry caring for Father. But did that mean Father was
suffering for nothing? Had risked his life for nothing? Oh,
God, what should she do? She clasped her hands, squeezing
her fingers as though she could tease out an answer.

Mr. Montclair rose, his chair scraping against the floor.
Jenny noticed the sound of the pestle pummeling the contents of the mortar again. Opening the door to the front of
the shop, he called out, "Mrs. Carter?" The young boy with
tousled blonde hair and freckles sprinkled across his nose
ran up, almost bumping into Montclair in his haste.

"Mother is finishing with a customer, Mr. Montclair. She
will be here in a moment, sir."

"Thank you, Zachary." He returned to his seat.

"Mr. Montclair, I—"

He raised his hand, shaking it gently. "No need. All will
be well."

Mrs. Carter entered with a vial and a letter.

Mr. Montclair studied Jenny.

She looked down at her hands.

"Just the tincture, Mrs. Carter."

"Oh," she said, clasping the letter to her ample bosom.

"Of course." She handed the vial to Jenny, arched an eyebrow at Montclair, and left, closing the door behind her.

Jenny's stomach flipped. Had she made the right choice? Was she betraying Father's work by refusing to become a part of this? Could she muster the courage to agree to Montclair's plan? Her gaze rose to his, seeing only compassion.

"Do not doubt your choice. Even the bravest man out on that street," he nodded toward the front of the shop, "would make the same. Please wish your father well for me, Miss Sutton."

CHAPTER EIGHT

C

B EFORE JENNY COULD OPEN THE front door, Sarie
threw it wide, beckoned her to enter, and snatched Jenny's shawl.

"Your mother is waiting in your father's room." Her voice
broke.

Jenny tingled with apprehension, and she forced her wobbly legs to navigate the stairs. She paused outside Father's
door. Whatever the news, she had to be strong for Mother.
Taking a deep breath, she grasped the vial, pressed her hands
against her skirt to hide their trembling, and blinked back
threatening tears. As she opened the door, her nose was
assailed by the pungent smell of the putrid wound. Even the
lavender sachets could not mask it anymore.

Mother rose from her seat beside Father's bed and stood
before her.

"Jennifer."

The tone of her voice revealed the truth. She need say
nothing more.

Jenny handed her the vial.

Together they walked to the bed, and Jenny took Father's
hand. It was cold, though beads of sweat dotted his forehead. She took the cotton towel from the basin and wiped
away the sweat. He moaned, then turned to look at her.

"My Jenny." His voice rasped against a deeper rattle in
his chest.

She took his hand again and sat beside him.

"The doctor said his only chance is to ..." Mother stopped. She took a deep breath. "He must amputate your father's leg."

Perhaps Father did have a chance to live! That was more than she'd believed when she entered. She studied his face, drawn with pain. How could he go on like this? How could they bear to watch him?

She took Mother's hand. "It is our only hope."

Mother nodded.

With a feeble tug, Father pulled her close. "Jenny."

"Yes, Father?" She bent to hear his thready voice.

"You must take your mother to safety. She can't remain here. They know ..." He swallowed, the effort too great.

"Rest, Father. You are going to be well soon."

His rheumy eyes blinked at her. "Do not humor me, child. Promise me you will save her. Take her ..." Agitated, he tried to sit up.

Jenny gently pushed his shoulders against the pillow. She bent her head to his ear. "I promise. I love you, Father."

He nodded and lay back on the pillow. The creases on his ashen face smoothed out, and a peace settled over him.

Jenny slumped back against the chair as the weight of her promise settled over her. In order to keep her promise to save Mother, they must return to the safety of Boston. But perhaps Father would recover. Perhaps he would regain his robust health and return to Boston with them. She studied his face. She mustn't give in to despair. The three of them would return to Boston. Ever farther away from Andrew. But right now, she couldn't afford to indulge herself in sweet memories. For with Andrew, that's all she had.

₡

The drizzle inching down the windowpane matched Jenny's mood. For her, the light had gone out in her life. Too many people she loved were lost to her forever. Numb, she stared ahead as another drop of water hit, then zigzagged down the glass. What determined which direction it would slide? What forces made a drop go left or right? What determined which direction a life would take? Forces beyond her control.

The doctor had been speaking with Mother in low tones, murmuring in the gloom of the day. A hand touched her shoulder.

"Jennifer, Dr. Ramsey is leaving."

Jenny looked up through her tears. She rose, extending her hand.

"Thank you, Dr. Ramsey."

He shook his head.

"You did everything you could." Jenny stifled a sob.

"I am so sorry for your loss, Miss Sutton." He turned to Mother. "Mrs. Sutton. It was the only hope to save him …"

"We know that. You did what was necessary."

"He fought to live longer than I thought was possible. He was a strong and intrepid man." Dr. Ramsey bowed then left the house.

The women sat on the parlor settee in silence, holding hands. Her tears spent, Jenny was exhausted; her ribs ached from weeping. After a while, Sarie came in to light the candles, and soon the room was wrapped in a warm glow—a protest against the steely rain outside and the sorrow within the house.

Mother rose, picked up a candle, and took Jenny by the hand.

"Come with me, Jennifer."

She followed her into Father's office.

Mother checked the rooms at the back of the house then closed the door. Raising the candle high, she stood before the tall escritoire.

"This is what your father wanted me to show you."

She handed the candle to Jenny, motioning for her to bring it close to the upper part of the desk. Gingerly running her hands along the molding at the top, she stopped. Suddenly, the front piece of the molding fell forward, revealing a recess. Jenny gasped and stepped back.

Mother pulled a letter from the dark opening, handed it to Jenny, and replaced the molding. Grasping the front desktop, she swung it down, revealing six drawers, three on either side of a locked cabinet. She selected a key from her key ring and unlocked the cabinet. Pulling out the two small drawers, she pressed her hand against the back and slid the false panel to the side, revealing yet another nook. From this she pulled out a piece of leather with small, rectangular holes cut into it.

The room spun. What was this about?

Mother held the items in each hand. She took the ivory parchment folded in thirds, a red wax seal with a "B" once having secured it. The same seal that had protected the letter Jenny had given to Mr. Montclair. Gently unfolding it, she laid the letter flat on the desk. Then she placed the piece of leather over it, allowing only certain words to be visible.

Jenny looked at the letter, then at Mother. She rubbed the crease between her brows. Could this day get any worse? Was Mother losing her mind?

"Jennifer, this is what your father wanted me to show you." Mother repeated her earlier words. "He is … was … working with the Sons of Liberty against the British. This was another reason he sent you to Brentwood Manor, to keep you safe. The British suspected him …" She glanced toward the window. She removed the leather cover. "Read it."

Jenny scanned the letter. It appeared to be a love letter written to someone named Felicity. It was simply signed, "The One Whose Heart You Captured." Puzzled, she shook her head. "Why do you have this?"

Mother placed the leather fabric over the letter. The holes allowed only certain words to be visible. A cryptic message including a number, which had been the number of kisses he would bestow upon their next meeting, a direction, and someone being captured.

What she held in her hand was a message. Treason. She stepped back, dropping the letter on the table. "Mother, you are in danger. We must leave this place. Tonight. I promised Father."

Mother returned each item to its place, locked the cabinet, and shut the escritoire. "Not yet, Jennifer. We must see your father properly buried." She frowned. "Did you speak with Mr. Montclair when you stopped at the apothecary shop?"

Jenny nodded. Was Mother so stricken with grief that her mind suffered? This was such a sudden change of topic.

"Did Mr. Montclair ask you to do anything … unusual?"

"Actually, Uncle Jonathon did. He asked me to deliver a letter to Mr. Montclair while we were at church my first Sunday here."

"I see."

"When I stopped in at the apothecary, Mr. Montclair asked me to deliver another letter." Jenny felt sick. "I refused. I'm sorry, Mother."

Mother embraced her. "Hush, Jennifer. How could you know?"

"I could have been helping all along." She glanced at the ceiling, picturing Father's body lying in the room above them. She pressed her fingers against her eyes to stem the burning anger searing within. Perhaps she could not have saved Father's life, but she could have continued his work—his mission. He died for the cause of liberty, a man of courage and dedication, and she had cowered. Her cheeks burned with shame. She lowered her head.

Mother placed a finger under her chin and lifted her face. "There is no shame in good sense, daughter." She smiled, her gray eyes soft with kindness.

Jenny hugged herself trying to still her trembling. She could not deny the fear that ran through her body, an itchy, tingling prickle that set her skin afire. Father was dead because of his beliefs. Was she willing to follow his path?

🌙

Tears slid down Jenny's face onto the pillow, dampening the crisp linen. She pressed her face into her handkerchief to catch her tears. Her misery at failing to save her twin, Kathryn, was as sharp as it had been when she was a child. Now, her heart ached from losing Father, too—and from missing Andrew. How she wished he were here now to hold her and comfort her in her sorrow. Her body felt like a wet rag, wrung out and limp.

Pressing down the sorrow, she fought the waves of fear that flooded her. Fear for Mother, fear for herself. Were the British watching this house even now? Mother had said they suspected Father—would she and Mother be safe here in New York?

She sat up. Perhaps they could flee back to Williamsburg … to Brentwood Manor. Surely, Uncle Jonathon would welcome them. And she would be with Andrew. But how could she arrange such a journey? All the ships in the harbor were British, and the trip was impossible for their household by land. Father's last wish was for her to keep Mother safe, not find a way to reunite with Andrew. They must return to Boston. Her promise was sacred.

She slipped out of bed and went to the window, open to the suffocating August evening. Leaning against the side of the deeply inset window, she pulled aside the curtain and studied the street. A candle burned in a glass lantern in front of their house. With the soft breeze, trees whispered through their leaves, and in the distance, a dog barked. But no people were about. More important, no one was standing across the street watching the house.

Climbing back into bed, she blew out the candle on her bedside table and stretched her body its full length. She pulled a light sheet over herself and turned on her side. Running her hand along the mattress, she longed for

Andrew to comfort her. Her skin tingled deliciously as she imagined him lying beside her. He would pull her into his arms, cradling her against his warmth, pressing her to him. Soft kisses along her neck, across her breasts. Loving him would be the source of her strength. Then she would have the courage to do as Father had hoped she would.

Courage to save Mother. Courage to take on the cause for liberty.

☾

"You are a fine horse." Andrew patted Shadow's neck.

Shadow neighed and tossed his head in agreement.

Andrew laughed. "Sometimes I believe you understand exactly what I'm saying."

Another toss of the head. One alert brown eye studied him.

"I will be back for you."

"C'mon, lad. Got to make haste." Howey's voice echoed down to the stable.

Andrew brushed his hand down Shadow's nose, turned, and walked out into the soft dawn light.

"Git a move on now." The innkeeper beckoned with his arm. "That horse'll be here when ye return."

Andrew glanced back at the stable then climbed into the rickety cart beside Howey.

"We'd best make good time or we'll miss the ferry." He gee'd and slapped the reins against the slump-backed mare.

They rumbled along a two-track path into the woods beyond the inn. Once in the shelter of the trees, Howey relaxed. Pulling out a pipe, he handed the reins to Andrew. He dug into his coat pocket for a leather tobacco pouch, untied the strings, and scooped the pipe in, then brought it out brimming with dark shreds. He tamped the tobacco down with his thumb before he snapped together the ends of a flint striker to light the pipe.

Andrew enjoyed the sweet, charred aroma that encircled

his head. He inhaled, remembering Jonathon smoking a pipe on quiet evenings spent at Brentwood Manor. Laughter filled the room at a lively game of whist. Jenny would seek his hand beneath the table, stroking it until he could barely sit still.

Jenny. Where are you now? Are you well? Andrew sighed deeply.

"I'm figuring it's not just business that keeps ye moving, son."

Andrew said nothing.

"Ah, a lass." Howey sent a sideways glance. "Could be yer undoin'. Keep yer senses about ye at all times."

They rode in silence for half an hour until the lush forest gave way to flat, marshy land. Andrew batted his hands at the onslaught of flies.

"Ouch!" He smacked one that bit his thigh. But there were too many for him to keep up with.

"Yer ripe." Howey laughed, a wheezing, hoarse sound. "They like ya."

Andrew wanted to jump off the slowing cart and run into the river ahead to fend off the flies. When his feet touched the ground, it was springy and moist. As he neared the river, his boots sucked loudly as he pulled them out of the mire. He finally shed them, opting to carry them instead.

"Not far now," Howey said.

Andrew was too busy swatting flies to respond. Though the river wasn't cold, compared to the heat of the August day, the contrast of its coolness shocked him. He tossed his boots on the shore and waded in, enjoying the chill that covered his skin. He splashed water on his arms and head, then dipped in to his shoulders to escape the flies. Flexing out his muscles, cramped from the night spent in the crawl space, he swam to where Howey stood puffing on his pipe.

At the river's edge, Howey pulled out a small rowboat that had been hidden in the marsh grasses along the shore. Andrew helped him slide it into the water, and both men hopped in. Despite his age and small stature, Howey's muscular arms worked the oars quickly, gliding the boat down the river.

Eventually, they came upon a small wooden dock that leaned precariously toward the water. Two men stood on a raft, one balancing a long pole, the other holding onto a post on the dock. They squinted against the sun glinting off the river. Howey whistled, sharp and shrill, and the two men whistled back. As the rowboat neared them, the men prepared to help pull it to the dock.

The boat rocked as Andrew stood to step onto the raft.

"Whoa, son. Take it slow. That lass of yers can wait a few minutes more."

The two men laughed, one offering a hand to Andrew.

"A randy boy, eh?" said the one who held the pole.

"Aye. But he's about the Sons' business, so take good care a' him." Howey shoved off, waving as the rowboat headed back up the river.

"We can get ya' to the mouth of the bay, but yer on yer own from there. The coast is crawlin' with British ships." His voice dropped to a hoarse whisper. "You'd best take care, son."

The sun dipped behind a cloud, turning the river a stygian green. Andrew looked toward the east and swallowed. Had he been a fool to think he could outwit trained British troops? Was it just luck that had kept him safe so far?

Jenny. His objective had been to save Jenny. He thought of Cyrus and Timothy. Of the burdens and punishments visited upon colonists by the British and the suffering about to ensue as General Howe's armada reached its destination. He shook his head. He had to risk all and continue.

For Jenny. For all of them.

CHAPTER NINE

⸙

JENNY STARED AT THE GAPING hole at her feet. Pastor Farr's voice droned on, the indistinguishable words flowing over her like a cold stream. Soon they would lower Father's body into the earth. Never again would he tease her. Never again would his strong arms embrace her, chasing away her fears. No tears moistened her face, for she was beyond shedding them. She stood tall, determination a sturdy rod running through her body, solid and resilient.

Mother's soft weeping brought her back to the present. Two men lowered the coffin into the ground as Pastor Farr recited the final blessing. Mother picked up a handful of dirt and tossed it in. The clump broke up into recoiling bits that scattered along the top, sounding like the skittering paws of mice.

Jenny shuddered then pulled herself more erect.

The people who had attended the service murmured their condolences as they stood with them in the heat of August. Now their friends began to shuffle off. She followed as Pastor Farr took Mother's arm and escorted her to their carriage. Jenny stopped. Standing beneath a tree, Laurence Montclair stood, watching.

Of course, he couldn't attend the service. He flew the Union Jack above his door. He had to maintain the appearance of a Loyalist. But he could linger nearby, for Father was his patient. He risked his life with every message he conveyed, with every Patriot contact he allowed. Just as Father had. She scanned the people in the churchyard. And who else here was taking such chances?

If she and Mother fled to Boston, a chain would be broken. Father left her with a dilemma: protect Mother or continue his work.

A group of British soldiers approached carrying rifles and bayonets, Lieutenant Ashby among them.

"You people must disperse," shouted the captain.

Pastor Farr moved to the front of the crowd. "Please, Captain, this woman has just buried her husband."

The captain looked past the minister. "Move along now." He nodded and one soldier shifted his rifle from his shoulder to present arms.

People moved apart and walked away. Mother stared, mouth slightly open, eyes glazed. Pastor Farr gently guided her to a bench.

Jenny seethed. How dare they interrupt Father's funeral? The soldier angled his rifle in her direction, just an inch or two, just enough. Ashby stared straight ahead, never meeting her gaze. Eventually, the mourners dispersed, so the troop moved on.

She approached Montclair. "I will do whatever you ask."

He studied her, his hazel eyes boring into hers. He nodded, put on his hat, tipped it, and left.

She stood motionless and let the sun soak into her skin. There was no warmth.

☙

Jenny sat in the dark parlor, the shutters closed and tied with black crepe. Neighbors had brought food enough to last the week, and Sarie once again encouraged her to eat something. Jenny picked at some fruit, cutting a melon into smaller pieces, to mollify her, but she soon gave up that pretense and Sarie cleared the plates.

How could she eat? She was hollow. Father was dead,

and Andrew was gone from her life. She sighed and sank back into the cushion, resting her head. She didn't have the strength to worry. She didn't have the strength to hope.

The sharp rap of the knocker at the front door startled her. She moaned. *No more food, please.*

But it wasn't food that Sarie brought in. It was Lieutenant Ashby.

Good God, no.

He bowed. "Good day, Miss Sutton. May I offer my condolences on the death of your father?"

Did his eyes glint?

"Thank you, Lieutenant." She held out her hand, and he bowed over it. Though his lips did not touch her skin, his warm breath did. She forced herself not to flinch. "Please, have a seat."

She rose and pulled the bell cord signaling Sarie, who appeared immediately with a tray of tea and cakes. Ashby ignored the servant as she poured his tea. She kept her gaze downcast, but her lips were drawn taut. She glanced at Jenny as she filled her cup. Jenny sent a faint smile.

"Thank you, Sarie."

Sarie curtsied and left.

"I also wanted to apologize for the misunderstanding at your father's funeral. I, that is, my captain, was under orders to disperse any crowd of … people. It was most unfortunate. I hope you will allow me to offer any assistance you may require." Sitting on the edge of his chair, spine rigid, Ashby sipped his tea.

Did he ever relax? Was there a pole thrust through his body that prevented him from easing back into the chair?

"Thank you, Lieutenant …"

"Please, call me Nigel."

"Thank you, Nigel."

Silence fell as he waited for her to reciprocate.

"How long have you been in Manhattan?" Jenny asked.

"Four months."

"So, you were not here when the fire burned much of the city?"

"No." His eyes flashed. "I wasn't here when the rebels set torches to many buildings to prevent the king's troops from having housing and food." His nostrils flared.

She sipped her tea to hide her trembling. His disdain for the Patriot cause was evident in his sneer. The cause Father had just died for.

"Do you know the circumstances of my father's death?"

Nigel frowned. "I assumed he was ill."

The crease between his brows and his puzzled look lent veracity to his statement. *How naïve does he think I am? He may appear innocent, but surely, he has been informed about Father.* She stood.

"Thank you for stopping by to convey your sympathy. I feel a need to rest now."

He clambered from the chair, tipping the small, three-legged table beside it. Reaching out, he caught it before it toppled, but the teacup and saucer crashed to the floor, shards of blue and white porcelain shattering against the dark, pine floorboards.

His scarlet face matched his coat. He fumbled, trying to brush the slivers of the tea set into his hands. Jenny knelt beside him, stopping his hands. At her touch, he halted and met her gaze. Dark eyes sprinkled with golden flecks held warmth, perhaps passion. Whether or not he was sincere in his sympathy about Father's death, she was certain he was sincere in his interest in her.

She stood. "Please don't bother. We will clean this up."

"My deepest apologies for the destruction of your china." He looked at the floor, still flushed. He bowed. "I can show myself out." Donning his hat, he hurried to the front door.

Despite his earlier comment about the rebels, a tinge of sympathy for his distress stilled her antagonism, at least for a moment.

"Do not be fooled, daughter," Mother said from the door

leading to the back of the house. "He knew exactly what he was doing."

Mother had never been cold. This cynicism was an attribute that she wore like a cloak ... like the cloak of grief she wore for her husband.

Jenny shivered.

☾

Once again Jenny slipped her hand into her skirts to ensure the letter was still in her petticoat pocket. Satisfied, she hurried her steps to the apothecary. Casting her gaze about, she studied the street looking for anyone who seemed interested in her movements. Satisfied, she willed her heart to halt its pounding. Her promise to Montclair had set into motion activities that now included her in the fight against Parliament's oppression. New York was a mix of Tory and Patriot sympathizers. She must be extremely cautious, because she did not know who was friend or foe.

Whenever possible, she stole glances to the right and left, scanning the street for anyone particularly interested in her destination. Just last week two men had been arrested, one because he lingered too long outside the British battery, one because he bumped into a passing British guard. Both were in the gaol, awaiting trial. The jeopardy mounted every day, making Jenny extremely cautious.

She surveyed the street once more before she entered the apothecary and was enveloped in the spicy aroma of herbs and oils. She inhaled, relishing the smell.

"Good day, Zachariah," she said, greeting the young boy who was sweeping the floor.

"Good day, Miss Sutton." The boy finished his task. "I'll get me mum." He disappeared into the back room.

In a moment, Lucy Carter appeared, accompanied by a man who stood a half-foot shorter than she and sported a day's grizzled stubble on his face. Smiling at Jenny, she introduced him. "Good day, Miss Sutton. May I introduce

Mr. Ephraim Carter, my dear husband?" She beamed at him.

He smiled warmly as he bent over her hand. "I am your most humble servant, Miss Sutton. My sympathy for the loss of your father. He was a brave man."

Jenny detected the aroma of rum as he spoke, but his twinkling eyes gave no hint of its influence.

"Thank you for your kind words, Mr. Carter." She couldn't help but return his warm smile.

As they spoke, Lucy crushed herbs, sending out a pungent aroma of lavender that covered any scent of rum. "Miss Sutton, I thought perhaps my latest delivery had arrived, but I see I must wait until next week. Have you come for your elixir?"

Jenny nodded, hearing the words that signaled Lucy was ready to receive the letter.

"I'll leave you ladies to your business, then. Good day, Miss Sutton." He disappeared into the back room.

She chose her words carefully. "Yes, Mrs. Carter. I'm here to pick up my mother's elixir. Father's death has been extremely difficult for her."

Lucy blinked in recognition. As she turned to reach for the bottle on the upper shelf, the door to the apothecary opened and Lieutenant Nigel Ashby entered. She froze, her hand stopping in midair.

Jenny swallowed down her panic. She had to think quickly. Lucy stood still as a statue behind the counter

"Good day, Miss Sutton." Ashby bowed slightly. "Mrs. Carter." He touched the brim of his tricorn.

Lucy simply stared at him.

Jenny held out her gloved hand. "Good day, Lieutenant Ashby. How nice to see you again."

Ashby bent over her hand. As he did so, Jenny lifted her foot, catching the leg of a table near the entry. Sweeping her foot to the side, she toppled the table, which sent the silver snuffboxes that had been displayed on it tumbling before his feet.

"Oh. My word," she exclaimed, stooping to retrieve them. As she did so, she reached into her pocket and grasped the letter.

"No, let me, please." Ashby bent to gather the containers.

"My goodness. You and I seem to have difficulty near small tables," Jenny said.

While he was thus engaged, Jenny slipped the letter across the counter to Lucy, who tucked it into her apron. In turn, Lucy retrieved the amber bottle from the top shelf and handed it to Jenny. Lucy's eyes were bright with fear, her cheeks flushed. Jenny wanted to warn her, to calm her, but there was no opportunity.

"Thank you, Mrs. Carter. Your elixir eases my mother's sorrow. You mix the most effective tinctures in all of New York." Hopefully, her praise would be cause enough to explain Lucy's heightened color. She glanced at Ashby, who had completed his task and was observing this exchange. He looked from one woman to the other then nodded toward the bottle in Jenny's hands.

"Perhaps you would allow me to sample this renowned curative."

She faltered. "Oh, that I could, Lieutenant Ashby. But it is *most* potent. I must return immediately, for my mother worries when I am about town, and she is in need of her afternoon dose. Since we are in mourning, we cannot receive guests at present." The bottle burned in her hands. Did it send out a signal that hidden within was a message … a message that could bring her to the end of a rope?

He bowed. "Of course. At the least, let me escort you to your home."

"You are most kind." Jenny nodded slightly. "Good day, Mrs. Carter."

Lucy stood mute, gaping. Jenny widened her eyes at her.

"Oh—good day, Miss Sutton." She stirred as if waking from a dream.

Ashby opened the door, and Jenny swept out of the shop. He turned to look at Lucy once more before he followed Jenny out into the street.

Jenny stilled the trembling in her arms as she carried the bottle.

"Allow me." He took it from her. He offered her his arm, and she slipped her gloved hand through to rest lightly on his forearm. "How is your mother?"

"She is—" Jenny stumbled, and he steadied her.

"Are you all right, Miss Sutton?"

She nodded. "Yes, thank you, Lieutenant Ashby. I just caught my heel on a stone."

And caught sight of Andrew slipping around the side of the building. There was no doubt in her mind.

Andrew was here.

CHAPTER TEN

ANDREW DUCKED INTO THE BACKDOOR of the apothecary, almost knocking the mortar and pestle from Mrs. Carter's hands.

"Excuse me! So sorry." He folded his trembling hands around hers to steady the set. But her hands were trembling, too.

He saw her. He saw Jenny.

She glanced at his hands then his face. "You're as shaken as I am. I'm mixing this for my nerves, and I have enough for two. You look as if you've seen a ghost."

"Not a ghost—an angel." He kissed her cheek.

"Get away with you." Her giggle followed her to the front of the shop.

"So. You've seen Jenny. Has she seen you?"

Montclair stood behind him.

Andrew slowly turned to face him. "Yes, I'm certain she saw me."

"Well, you've been here all of three days, and finally got what you were seeking."

No, I've been seeking to hold her, to be with her, not simply see her from a distance. Every night since he'd arrived, he had been watching the house where Jenny and her mother were staying. Seeing Jenny move past a curtain, wondering if it was she who lit a lantern or a candle when a soft glow illuminated a window, was driving him mad. His body ached to hold her. His heart swelled at any sight of her or even a hint of her presence. But he had to be cautious. He could not put her at risk by simply walking up to her front door.

"The Suttons are under suspicion. You can't go to her, for any connection between you could alert the British." Montclair's gaze bore into his.

Andrew ran his hands through his hair. Hiding in the back room of the apothecary shop allowed him too many hours of thinking, of longing. Today when he heard Jenny's voice in the front room, he almost burst in … but then that British officer appeared.

Instead, he listened at the door, pressing his finger to his lips to signal silence to Zachary. The boy saluted and sat quietly. Then the table crashed, again Andrew wanted to run into the room. Was Jenny all right? Had the officer accosted her? A tug on his sleeve pulled him back. Zachary stood with his finger to his own lips. Andrew grinned. He slipped out the back door and stood at the corner of the shop, waiting for the door to open. Waiting for a glimpse of his Jenny. To be this close was deliriously painful.

When she came out of the shop, she was smiling at the officer. Andrew's heart dropped. She put her arm through the man's and they turned in his direction. She caught sight of him, her eyes widening in recognition. She stumbled and the officer caught her, steadying her with an arm around her waist.

Though he hated seeing her with the man, he supposed she was trying to throw off any suspicion she was under. But having that officer around was going to make it almost impossible to meet with her. Which he intended to do despite Montclair's warning.

❧

Jenny paced the room. Stopping by a front window, she eased back the shutter and peered into the evening. Surely, Andrew was out there. Right now. Watching for her. It was all she could do to resist running out into the night, her roiling impatience a prod for action. But she had promised Father she would take Mother safely away. If Andrew were here, how could she leave him again?

"Child, what is the matter with you?" Mother's fingers stilled over her embroidery.

"Nothing, Mother. Nothing."

Mother dropped her handiwork to her lap. "I believe there is something. What is it?"

Jenny took a seat in the chair beside Mother. How could she burden Mother any further? Her face was pale and drawn with grief. She moved through the day like a ghost, ethereal and slow. Sometimes she didn't respond to Jenny's conversation but stared ahead, eyes misted with sorrow. They hadn't even discussed fleeing to Boston yet as she had promised.

How could Jenny leave now?

"Do you remember my mentioning Uncle Jonathon's brother-in-law? A young man named Andrew?"

"I believe you mentioned him in every letter."

"Of course I did not." Jenny's face warmed with her blush.

"I've saved the letters. Shall I show you?"

One corner of Jenny's mouth lifted in a smile. Mother softly pressed a finger to her cheek.

"Oh, that dimple, Jennifer. An angel poked a finger there to see if you were done."

Tears sprang to Jenny's eyes. "That was what Father always said."

"Yes. He also said that dimple would be the undoing of many a young man."

Jenny felt the heat deepen as she remembered Andrew kissing said dimple, claiming it melted his heart.

"You miss Andrew?" Mother's voice was soft.

She nodded. Now the tears were not for Father. She leaned forward, dropping her voice. "I saw him. Today. At the apothecary shop."

"He was in the shop?"

"No. I saw him outside. He was hiding along the side of the building. I think he knows I saw him." A small cry escaped from her throat. "He'll be imprisoned if he's caught."

Mother's gentle smile had disappeared. A crease formed between her brows, her lips drawn with apprehension. "Laurence must know he is here. Did he say anything to you today?"

"No. I didn't see Mr. Montclair today, just Mrs. Carter. Oh, I'm so sorry. In my confusion in seeing Andrew, I forgot to give you this."

She rose to retrieve the amber bottle. Uncorking it, she pulled out a small piece of parchment. Puzzled, she turned it over and over. It was blank. Handing it to Mother, she started at a knock on the back door.

Mother pocketed the paper and motioned for her to remain in the parlor. She hurried out to the hallway, which led to the back of the house.

Jenny's heart raced. Could it be Andrew calling at this hour? She dared not hope, but her heart betrayed her, leaping in her chest, blood rushing through her veins. Was that voice his? Unable to restrain herself, she ran to the door and peered down the hall. Her heart dropped. This man was shorter than Andrew, and his hair was dark. His clothes were dark. He could easily disappear into the night unobserved.

He glanced at Jenny, pulling his hand back into his cloak.

Mother patted his arm. "Mr. Gordon, may I introduce my daughter, Jennifer? Jennifer, Mr. Daniel Gordon."

He bowed. "I am your servant, Miss Sutton."

Jenny approached, hand extended. He bent over it then shifted his gaze to Mother.

"Jennifer is aware of our mission."

He hesitated then drew a folded letter from beneath his cloak. Mother exchanged the parchment Jenny had just passed to her for his letter.

Gordon tucked the paper into his cloak, tipped his black cocked hat, and opened the back door, a murky shadow slipping into a velvet night.

Mother grasped the letter and took Jenny's hand, leading her into the small office across from the parlor. A desk sat diagonally in one corner, positioned to catch the morning sun from windows on either wall. This was the room from which Mother ran the household. Stores of dry goods and spices lined the shelves that ran to the height of the high ceiling. She pulled over a stool, climbed on it, and reached for a leather box tucked into the highest shelf. Placing it on the desk, she drew out a key ring from the petticoat pocket hidden beneath her skirt. With a small brass key, she unlocked the box and revealed jars containing the most expensive spices used for cooking their meals.

Jenny inhaled the blended aromas that transported her back to the apothecary shop. Then she recalled applying salve to the ugly wound that took Father's life. She took a ragged breath. Mother's touch brought her back to the present.

"This is what we need," Mother said softly as she lifted out a small glass bottle. Laying the parchment on a metal tray, she tipped the bottle over it, letting a few drops spill onto the paper.

Neatly written words emerged as the liquid spread over the once-blank paper.

Mother pursed her lips as she studied the message. "This is most urgent. I must get this to Laurence immediately."

Jenny peered over Mother's shoulder, reading the text. It made no sense. It was a combination of numbers and letters that appeared to be a recipe for a curative.

Mother glanced at the darkened windows, shutters pulled tight. "I must go out tonight."

"Mother, you cannot leave at this hour. It is much too hazardous."

"Jennifer, we must put fear of our own safety aside. Powers

are at work here that will decide the future of our nation."

"You sound like Uncle Jonathon."

"This is what your father sacrificed his life for."

Jenny's face flamed, heat spread through her. "I will go."

"No." Mother shook her head, a lock of hair escaping from her cap. She grabbed Jenny's arms.

"As Father's wife, you are already suspect. I am newly arrived and fairly unknown. Please let me run this errand. Let me do it for Father."

Mother was silent.

"Do I take this to Mr. Montclair?"

"Yes."

"Then I have a perfect excuse. You are in desperate need of more elixir. If I am questioned, I am the frantic daughter of an ill mother. What reason would you have for being out at this time of night?"

Mother nodded, still holding her arms. She lessened her grip and her hands fell away. "You are right." She inhaled deeply, letting out a sigh. "Yes, it must be you." She rolled the paper up and placed it in the amber bottle. "You must keep this safe. The message is revealed now." Handing the vial to Jenny, she smiled. "You are fiery and spirited, like your father."

"And my mother." Jenny kissed her cheek.

☾

Andrew jumped when the shutter opened slightly in the front window across the road. A glimpse. Just a glimpse of ebony hair. Jenny. His pulse quickened. He mustered all his restraint to keep from sprinting to the house. She was a matter of yards from where he stood, yet she might as well have been an ocean away.

Though Montclair had directed him to stay away, he had to see for himself that Jenny was safe. But he couldn't put her in peril. If Jenny were caught, like her father, she, too, would die. He squeezed his eyes, shut trying to block the image of Jenny in gaol, or worse, hanging from gallows. Digging his fists into his eyes to banish the thought, he backed into the shelter of an ancient oak.

He scanned the windows, hoping for another glimpse, another reassurance that Jenny was inside and safe. Hearing someone approach, he ducked behind the tree. Two British officers walked along the other side of the road. He couldn't hear their conversation until they were in front of the lantern that lit Jenny's front door.

"This is the one that bears watching, Lieutenant Ashby," said the shorter man.

"Yes, sir." The younger officer studied the house. He was taller than Andrew, slender, with erect posture, as if constantly standing at attention. He looked familiar. Of course—he had escorted Jenny from the apothecary shop that afternoon. How unfair that this cur could walk with Jenny out in public and he had to stay away from her.

Andrew wasn't sure he could disarm both men and prevent them from entering Jenny's house, but he was willing to try if necessary. He raised his rifle. If he fired at them, other soldiers would apprehend him. That would also draw attention to Jenny's house. He lowered his rifle and his hand slid to the knife tucked in his boot.

"Sutton was a rebel sympathizer. We have reason to believe his wife will carry on with his seditious dealings."

Ashby shifted from foot to foot. He glanced around, then back at the house.

"Don't be nervous, Lieutenant. We keep a watchful guard on those who oppose us."

"Yes, sir."

They continued walking. Lieutenant Ashby looked back at the house. Soon they were out of sight.

Andrew paced as bile churned in his gut. He returned the knife to his boot. The British were watching her mother's every move. Soon, they would suspect Jenny of possible treason as well. He had to get her away from here. Quickly.

He leaned against the enormous trunk and prepared to spend the night guarding the house. He pushed off the tree at the sound of a soft neigh, then a whispered, "Shhh." Someone leading a horse was skulking along the side of Jenny's house. Andrew crept along the roadside until he was directly across the road from the horseman.

His heart stopped.

CHAPTER ELEVEN

T HE AUGUST NIGHT SHROUDED JENNY with a
dark, sultry coolness. Her heart slammed in her chest as
she led the mare through the yard and into the road. Here she
was, living another lie, pretending to be something she was
not. How could this end well?

Just a few lanterns lit the street. Since most of them flickered near the front doors of the houses lining the road, she
led the horse to its center where shadows held the rutted
ground in darkness.

She tucked a lock of hair up under the slouch hat Sarie
had given her and tugged its sloping brim down over her
brow. Isaac's trousers fit her waist but were snug about her
hips and too short to stay tucked into her boots. Father's
jacket drooped at the shoulders and was folded twice at the
cuffs. Anyone seeing her would think she was a servant running an errand.

Perspiration ran in rivulets along her neck and dampened
her shift as she walked the horse toward the busier road a
quarter-mile ahead where she would mount and hurry to
the apothecary shop. The sound of a racing horse's hooves
along this quiet street at night might draw curious observers
to the windows, and if she were discovered ... Her trial for
treason would be brief, the hanging briefer.

Well, then I must not be discovered.

"Come along," she quietly urged Aggie, the mare that

had been comfortably settled for the night and was not inclined to travel now. "Gee up," she whispered, pulling on the bridle.

A hand clamped her mouth, an arm encircled her waist, lifting her off the ground. In panic, her feet kicked out, and she swung her arms trying to escape. She didn't scream. That would mean discovery. She at least had enough wits about her to realize that. She fought her attacker the best she could.

"Jenny. Jenny, it's me. Andrew," a familiar voice whispered.

Her limbs went weak as she slumped against him.

He released her and stepped back.

"Andrew," she cried. Turning, she leapt into his arms. Her pants allowed her to wrap her legs around him, and he laughed aloud. She silenced him with a kiss fierce with desire, and he answered in kind. Their lips were desperate to taste; their tongues danced a passion of joyful reunion.

Then she pulled back, studying the face she had seen every night in her dreams. But his face had changed. His soft features had more of an edge, his cheeks ruddy, his jawline firmer. His azure eyes glowed softly but held a seriousness that had never been evident before. His smile didn't come instantly as usual, but as she beheld him, slowly, his lips broke into a broad grin. When a strand of his tawny hair blew gently in the night breeze, she reached up to brush it back. Hot tears burned her cheeks as laughter bubbled up. "Andrew." Her face grew warm, her smile her widest ever.

With her legs still wrapped around him, she felt his desire, and she moaned. She slid down, standing before him. Andrew bent his head to hers, his lips brushing hers softly, then with an urgency that matched her own. His tongue probed her mouth, and she gave in to the request, deepening the kiss, clinging to him. Finally, she pulled back.

"It's not safe for you here," she whispered.

"Nor for you." He pulled her into the shadow of a tree.

Aggie moseyed behind them.

"I saw you today ... at the apoth—"

He stifled her words with an impatient kiss. Then he held her, cradling her head against his chest, his heart wild, matching the beating of her own.

"Where are you going? Why are you dressed like this?"

His voice was music.

She quickly told him about her involvement with Laurence Montclair.

"Montclair told me that you had agreed to work with the Sons." He ran his hands up and down her arms. "But you must not. It's too risky."

"My father was part of the group."

"I heard he died. I'm so sorry."

She took a deep breath. *Would the pain of losing Father ever go away?* "But I arrived in time to be with him for a short while." She explained his run-in with the Ranger, the resulting wound, and the amputation. "Mother explained about the Patriot group working for General Washington. Before he died, Father insisted she do so. Our house has been a drop-off site for information. A courier arrived this evening with a message, which Mother decoded. She said it's urgent. Since she may be under suspicion, I must deliver this message to Montclair immediately."

"Your house is being watched." He related what he'd heard from the British officers. "You were with one of them this afternoon."

Jenny nodded. "Ashby."

"Yes, that's what the older man called him."

Andrew peered down the street where the two British officers had walked—where she was headed. "Had you come outside a few minutes earlier, they would have met you in front of the house."

Jenny stared into the darkness that led to the main street. She chewed her lip, her mind churning with fear, but then the image of Father's agonized face floated before her, enraging her. Inhaling deeply, she reached inside for strength. Determination obliterated her fear.

"I must go. Mother depends on me to deliver this to Mr. Montclair tonight."

"I'll take it. You return to the house."

Jenny looked up at him, giving him a half-smile. "We'll go together, just as we did when we rescued Jonathon."

Andrew kissed her. Right on her dimpled cheek.

☾

His knees buckled at Jenny's smile. That damned dimple reduced him to schoolboy flutterings ... and desire. He kissed her cheek, then moved to her lips, tasting her sweetness. He wanted to stay there forever, but Jenny pushed him away, laughing softly. How he delighted in the lilt of her voice.

"We must go. Now." She pulled on his hand.

At the end of the quiet road, they searched in both directions. To their left, one lone carriage trundled along in the opposite direction. He helped Jenny mount the horse and flushed hot when she threw her leg over the horse, straddling it as a man would. Taking a deep breath, he swung up behind her. Not wanting to draw attention, he nudged the mare to an inconspicuous trot.

The cool air rushing over his face helped to temper his rising desire. If only he could detour into a grassy field and lie beside her, hold her and let her know the depth of his love. He shook his head. He needed to keep his wits about him. He needed to protect Jenny.

He studied the road and scanned the side streets they passed, looking for any sign of Lieutenant Ashby and his superior. Nothing. They neared Fraunces Tavern where raucous laughter and fiddle music spilled out the front door into the night air. Andrew urged Aggie to the other side of the road as they passed in front of the pub. Most likely, at this hour, patrons would be tipsy and in good spirits, but he did not want to chance that either of them might be recognized.

They continued, avoiding any sign of people about. Finally, they reached the apothecary shop and rode into the backyard. He dismounted and reached up to help Jenny alight. As she leaned forward, her jet-black hair tumbled from beneath the hat, cascading over his upturned face.

"Ohhh ..." He fought the passion stirring within. "How you tempt me."

Smiling, she pulled back her hair and tucked it up beneath the hat. "Temper your lustful desires, Mr. Wentworth. We must see our task through."

He reached up for her again. Just touching her was like being bucked off a wild stallion. Not that he had ever experienced that, but he imagined it was the same. Perhaps her effect was even more intense.

One candle glowed through the window of Montclair's office. They climbed the steps to the back door and Jenny rapped lightly. No movement came from within. She rapped harder.

"Turn around. Slowly."

The *click* confirmed that a flintlock was pointed at his head. Raising his hands, he stepped in front of Jenny as he turned.

"Good God, Wentworth. What are you doing stealing about at this time of night? And who is that young buck with you?" Laurence Montclair released the half-cocked gun as he lowered his arm. "Come in. Come in." He opened the door and ushered them in. Once inside, Montclair poked his head back out the door to check the yard. Closing the door, he bolted it, went into his office and closed the shutters, dropping the clasp to lock them. Then he motioned them into his office.

"Guarding the Sutton house again, eh, son? You're a randy young gentleman with a mind full of that beauty ..."

Jenny stepped into the glow of the candle on his desk.

Montclair's expression shifted like moonlight on a lake, from perturbed to confused to amazed.

"Miss Sutton. Excuse me … I didn't mean to use such vulgarity in front of a young lady." He took in her clothing, quickly glancing away from the trousers.

Jenny laughed. "Please do not concern yourself, Mr. Montclair." She stepped forward. "Mother received this missive this evening. She thought it imperative you see it immediately."

Montclair took the letter and held it near the candle.

"Damn. Hewlett is aware of the planned attack." He glanced at their faces and waved the parchment. "General Samuel Parsons is planning to lead Continental troops in an attack on the British holed up in Setauket. Lieutenant Colonel Richard Hewlett is on to him. He'll have his British troops ready and waiting for the Continentals. How in hell did they find out?" He rubbed his eyes. "Andrew, you will need to travel to Setauket at first light."

"But, Mr. Montclair, I've only just …" He looked at Jenny.

"Confound it, Wentworth. You and Miss Sutton must not be seen together. If Mrs. Sutton is under suspicion, they will be watching Miss Sutton as well. If she is seen with you, it will confirm her involvement. You are to stay away from her. If you love her, keep her safe—safely away from you."

How in God's creation could they be parted again? Andrew slammed his fist onto the desk. "I must protect her."

"You will have her hanged? That's how you'll protect her?" Montclair's voice was hoarse with restraint. He leaned across the desk, glaring at Andrew as the clock on the wall ticked off minutes.

All the joy of finding Jenny drained from Andrew, sapping his energy. His exhaustion from a weeks-long journey overtook him as he sank into a chair. Resting his elbows on his knees, he dropped his head into his hands. It was all he could do not to break down and cry like a lad.

Jenny rubbed his shoulder. She stooped beside him, taking his face in her hands, her soft skin against his cheek like a balm, restoring him. He gazed into her eyes, gentle and smiling in the candle's glow.

"We will be together soon, Andrew. For over a year, liberty is what you and Jonathon have been fighting for. Liberty is what my father died for. Our sacrifice is not too great." She stroked his cheek.

He took her hands in his, kissing her palms, and nodded. Looking up at Montclair, he nodded again. "Yes, I'll go. Give me my instructions."

❦

The breeze had picked up while they were in the apothecary shop. Jenny cherished Andrew's embrace, for it could be their last. She held him close, her head resting on his chest, listening to his heartbeat. *Please, God. Keep him safe.* He kissed the top of her head then stepped back.

"I must leave, Jenny." His hoarse voice mirrored her sorrow.

"Yes. But we will be together again, I know—"

He swept her into his arms, his kiss desperate, ravenous. She met his lips with a passion that burned, taking his lips, hungrily. When at last they parted, hollowness replaced the passion. Her hand slipped away from his, and she turned and mounted the horse. She committed to memory every detail as she looked down at him. His face, turned up to her, smiling gently. His shoulders, strong and broad. The detail that haunted her as she rode away was the grief in his eyes.

She reined Aggie to a walk. The horse nickered her approval. This pace would give Jenny time to regain her composure before arriving home. Leaves rustling in the trees above her covered the sound of the horse's *clomp, clomp* on the cobblestones. She neared Fraunces Tavern. While lantern light still glowed in the windows, the noise had settled considerably. She decided to ride by on the road.

As she passed, the door flung open and three men staggered out.

"You there. Boy."

A fourth man rode out from beside the tavern, blocking the road.

Keeping her head down, she pulled the mare to a halt. Perspiration prickled against her skin.

The shortest man stood on the top step, almost tripping as he descended. "I'm talkin' to you, boy." He approached her. She tugged at the reins, but the man on the horse moved in to block her again.

"Evenin', sir. I'm just headin' home." She deepened her voice, hoping to convince them she was a young man. She touched the brim of her hat and tugged the reins to direct the horse around the man obstructing her.

"We'll shee wha … where yer goin'," the short man slurred as he squinted at her. He seized Jenny's leg.

She jerked back on the reins and the horse bucked. The man held tightly to her, yanking her off the horse. As she tumbled, her hat fell off, spilling her jet-black hair across her shoulders.

CHAPTER TWELVE

"OOOOFFF." AIR BURST FROM JENNY'S lungs as she hit the ground. She shook her head, trying to erase the blackness with its dizzying bursts of light. For a moment, all she heard was buzzing, as if a swarm of bees surrounded her. Then, her vision cleared.

And her panic rose.

The other two men had descended from the porch, their faces twisted with drunkenness and lust. She glared at them. Suddenly, one of them lurched backward, shock clear on his face.

Andrew appeared from behind him and pummeled him until the other seized his arms. His gaze met hers, his brows drawn together as they pulled him away.

She stared at him, puzzled.

He followed me.

The dazed man beside her staggered sideways then stared down at her.

"What have we here?" The short man teetered as he leered at her, then at Andrew. "On yer way home, eh? On yer way to a bit of a tumble, I'd wager."

The other men laughed. The injured man clambered up, helping to hold Andrew, but the two were barely able to stand, let alone restrain him.

Andrew twisted away and ran to Jenny. The drunk beside her swung then twirled when his fist missed Andrew.

Andrew brought his fist up, catching the man in his gut. He doubled over, moaning. The other two men each grabbed one of Andrew's arms again.

The man on the horse held her mare's reins. "Let's make him watch."

"I found her, so I get the first go." The short man unfastened the top button of his breeches.

Jenny stirred. Sitting up, she scrambled backward, but the drunk caught her by her feet. She kicked furiously, but he only laughed. She clawed at his hands. He captured her flailing wrists, heaving her up to stand. When they were face to face, she froze. She stood an inch taller than him. She thrust her face into his.

"Shall I tell Mrs. Carter about our little tryst?"

Gasping, he staggered backward. "Miss Sutton?"

Ephraim Carter's eyes were not twinkling tonight. Instead the rheumy effect of too much rum clouded them, and he squinted, trying to focus on her. He dropped her wrists and stepped back. "Miss Sutton. Excuse me. I thought you were a …"

"And if I were a whore, would that excuse what you and the other men were about to do?"

He hung his head. The other men released Andrew and stepped away.

"Leave them be." Ephraim's voice was low. "They work for the Sons."

One man picked up Jenny's hat, returning it to her with a jerky bow. "Sorry, miss." The man on horseback handed the reins to Andrew, tipping his hat. Andrew helped Jenny mount the horse, then swung up behind her.

Jenny glared at the men. "Is this what we're fighting for? For you to attack a woman—any woman? My father gave his life to fight for your liberty. Shame on you."

She tapped her heels against the mare, giving one disdainful look back as they rode away.

When they were a safe distance, Andrew slowed the horse to a walk.

"Are you all right?"

She nodded, resting a shaky hand on his. "Yes. You followed me, didn't you?"

"I had to make sure you arrived home safely before I left." He buried his face in her hair. "Jenny." The heady, familiar aroma of lilac filled him with desire. He was unable to tame his body, their bodies so close, moving in rhythm with the horse's gait. Was she aware of his longing?

"It will be like this for us now, Andrew. Living in fear, unsure of who we can trust." Her voice was serious.

Perhaps she *wasn't* aware of his desire.

They reached her road and turned toward the house.

"Remember our peaceful nights at Brentwood Manor?" she asked.

"Mmmmm." He nuzzled her neck.

"Andrew." She laughed softly on the night air.

"I want you, Jenny. Now."

They had reached her yard.

She half turned toward him. He slid off the horse and reached up to her. As she leaned forward, his hands brushed against her breasts. Her breath caught, fueling the fire in his belly. She stood before him, her breathing fast, but she wouldn't look up at him.

Tilting her chin up, he repeated, "I want you, Jenny." His mouth covered hers, moving, hungry. He ran his hands along her back, down to her buttocks, pulling her into him. She melted against him, a soft moan driving him on. Her arms looped up around his neck, her hands running through his hair.

He would soon explode. A rush of pleasure pulsed through his body. He kissed along her neck, burrowing into the crook. She was trembling, her breath hot against his ear.

"Jennifer?"

She pulled away.

"Is that you, Jennifer?"

Mrs. Sutton rushed out the back door, her voice strident with fear. "Jennifer? Please … are you there? Are you all—" She stopped a few feet from them, lifting a candle up to see more clearly.

Andrew moved away as Jenny tried to tame the curls wildly dancing about her head. She wiped at a tear that ran down her cheek. He pulled his longcoat forward, hoping to hide his present state of arousal, but it didn't fool her mother.

"I have been sick with unease, Jennifer. And you have been out here … dallying with this young man?"

"No, Mother—"

"Did you at least deliver the message to Laurence?" Her voice shook with anger and, he suspected, fear.

"Mother, please. Let's go inside."

Mrs. Sutton scowled at them, then led them toward the house. Turning, she pointed at him. "You see to the horse."

Jenny cast a half-smile at him, and even in the candlelight that damned dimple assailed him.

❦

Jenny poured a glass of brandy. "It is not what you think, Mother." She handed her the drink. "I did deliver the message to Mr. Montclair, immediately."

"Jennifer, I have been worried sick all night."

"I'm sorry, but so much happened." Should she explain the incident at the tavern? She didn't want to add to Mother's distress, but she had always been honest with her. Mother needed to know about the occurrence. She poured two more glasses of brandy, trying to form an explanation. The back door closed. Her heart skipped. Andrew was here. In her house. He would meet Mother. Oh, that he could remain safely here.

He stood at the door. The sheepish look on his face melted

her heart. Reaching for his hand, she drew him into the room and handed him a crystal snifter.

"Mother, this is Andrew Wentworth." She couldn't control the smile that covered her face.

"Well, I should hope so. After all your talk about him in your letters, I would hope you wouldn't be dallying in the night with someone else." She rose, extending her hand. "Mr. Wentworth."

He bowed over it. "I'm so pleased to meet you, Mrs. Sutton. Jenny's affection for you has come through every story she has told me. May I offer my condolences on the passing of Mr. Sutton?"

She returned to her seat on the settee and indicated the chair beside it. Jenny smiled at him. Andrew returned her smile, glanced at Mother, then studied the hearth as he sat down.

Together they explained the events of the evening, starting with their meeting with Montclair. Jenny's throat tightened as she recounted his command that they not be seen together. How could she stay away now that they were finally united?

"He is very wise. It is protection for both of you." Mother looked from one to the other. "I know it's difficult, but the risk is too great."

"You are right. As I was watching your house this evening …"

Mother arched one brow.

Andrew cleared his throat. "Well, yes, I have been watching every evening since I arrived." He shifted in his seat.

Mother patted his arm. "It's all right, Andrew. I appreciate your concern for our safety." Jenny caught the twinkle in Mother's eyes and the gentle tone of voice she used when teasing.

"Well, when I was out there tonight, two British officers happened by. One told the other, named Ashby, that your house was under suspicion."

Mother set her snifter on the side table and nodded slowly. "I wondered if he had ulterior motives for his attentiveness to Jenny. Even more reason for you two to stay apart." She looked at her daughter, her voice soft. "I know that's not what you wish to hear, but it must be so."

"But for tonight …" Jenny folded her hands as if praying, pleading.

"Alas, especially tonight. For if you were seen on the street by anyone other than Mr. Carter and his cronies, they will come for us."

Andrew rose. "Your mother is right. I must go."

Mother stood. "I must see to preparations for breakfast. I will return in a few moments." She raised one brow at Jenny before she swept out of the room.

Jenny smiled. "I believe we have a few precious minutes alone." She craved his touch, his nearness.

He shifted in his seat but did not move closer.

She reached out her hand, inviting, beseeching.

He remained where he was.

"Andrew?"

"I don't know. Here in the light, you look like a lad." His lips twitched up, his eyes danced.

Her gaze darted to the door. "We have precious little time together." Reaching up, she swept off the hat, freeing her black curls to tumble and swirl around her shoulders. "I am no lad."

He was up and beside her in one swift movement. He wrapped her in his arms, leaning her back against the pillow. "Jenny," he whispered. His soft, warm lips moved over hers. He traced kisses along her cheek, along her throat. Never in her life had she tingled with such an agonizing need that started in her belly and suffused her whole body. She clung to him as if these were the last moments they would ever share.

They could be.

"Andrew." Her arms tightened. His lips found hers again,

and he nibbled along her neck, pausing in the crook. She thought she would shatter with the joy of holding him, tears streaming down her cheeks. He stroked her back, sliding one hand forward along her side, just tempting her breast. She shuddered. His hand moved forward.

"Jennifer." Mother's voice from the next room was like a splash of cold water.

They sat up, but he kept one arm around her shoulder.

Mother entered. "Mr. Wentworth."

He dropped his arm.

Jenny brushed her hair back as if that would hide the flush of pleasure on her face.

"I'm afraid you must leave now." Mother's voice was gentle. "No matter how safe you think you may be, there are too many who cannot be trusted. If only one person sees you …"

Jenny shivered. She took his hand.

He stood. "I will do whatever is necessary to keep Jenny safe, Mrs. Sutton."

"Thank you. I'm sorry it must be this way."

He nodded. Taking Jenny's hand, he helped her rise from the settee. Despite Mother's presence, he kissed her long and full. She stumbled back a step when he released her.

"I cannot say farewell, Jenny. I will only say, 'Until we meet again.'" He kissed her hand, bowed to Mother, and disappeared.

Tears streamed down Jenny's cheeks. *Would his words prove true?*

CHAPTER THIRTEEN

C

AFTER ANDREW HAD SEEN JENNY safely home from Montclair's, he'd returned for instructions for his mission to Setauket. Montclair got him to the wharf, where they'd met a whaling crew that sailed him across from New York to Long Island. He'd traveled on foot the remaining distance to Setauket.

He now crouched behind a bush, watching British soldiers drill in front of the white clapboard church in the early morning sun. A mounted officer shouted instructions as the troop pivoted sharply, avoiding the gravestones standing at attention along the lawn. Suddenly, at the officer's instructions, they dove behind the markers, aiming their Pattern rifles at an imagined enemy.

He swallowed against the sickening feeling in his stomach. Their actions confirmed the message he was carrying to Major Benjamin Tallmadge. The British already knew of the planned attack.

He crab-walked away, not rising until he was well beyond view of the mounted officer. Then, he broke into a run. He had to reach Tallmadge before General Parsons launched the raid. Heart racing, feet pounding the earth, he sprinted along the road leading to the Tallmadge house. His lungs screamed against his labored gasps, but he would not slow down.

He wiped at the sweat that stung his eyes and blurred his

vision. A farmer driving a rickety cart loaded with his harvested vegetables meandered along the road, blocking the center, so Andrew had to skirt it by running into the field. He leapt over small shrubs and tree roots, doubling his pace once beyond the farmer. How long could he maintain this? His heart felt as if it would explode.

Up ahead was a large, brown, saltbox house. Slowing, he ducked into the trees. Bracing himself with one arm against a sturdy maple, he doubled over, gasping. As his heartbeat slowed, he scanned the yard and noted a young boy just inside the stable door. His dark skin contrasted with the brilliant white shirt and straw hat he wore. Andrew approached him carefully.

"Is this the home of Benjamin Tallmadge?"

The boy looked at him, his large brown eyes wary. "Who you?"

"My name is Andrew. I have a message for Major Tallmadge."

The boy stared at him.

Andrew wanted to shake him. *Just let me know if I'm in the right place.* "Please, it's important that I see Major Tallmadge immediately. Is this his home or do I need to look elsewhere?"

A rifle cracked in the distance, and the young boy jumped at the sound.

"You there. State your business." Behind him, a voice resounded.

Andrew turned to see a man a few years his senior aiming a rifle at his chest. One quick shot and he'd be dead. The man's nose looked too large, his forehead too high for his pale face. He wore the blue wool jacket of an officer in the Continental army. Silver buttons gleamed along the white trim of his coat and his white vest.

"Major Benjamin Tallmadge?"

"Who is asking?"

More shots echoed from the direction of the church. The

man jerked in the direction of the noise, then turned back, again aiming his gun at him. "Quickly," he said.

"I am Andrew Wentworth. I've come from New York City with a message for John Bolton."

At the name, the man lowered his rifle. He glanced to the left and right. "And just in time—I am about to leave for ..." He glanced in the direction the shots had come from. "Come inside. Quickly."

The interior of the house was refreshingly cool, making Andrew's sweat-soaked shirt clammy against his skin. Grasping the cotton material, he pulled it away, fanning it in an attempt to dry it. It immediately stuck to his body again.

Tallmadge led him to the dining room and pulled out a chair, inviting him to sit. He poured a glass of cider and set it before him.

Andrew scanned the room. Resting on the sideboard was the plumed helmet signifying Tallmadge's rank of major in the 2nd Continental Light Dragoons. Andrew studied him with a deeper appreciation. *His looks must belie his abilities.*

"How do you know of John Bolton?" He cocked his head, reminding Andrew of an inquisitive bird.

"I've never met him. My orders were to ask for him."

Tallmadge nodded. "Well, where is this message for John Bolton?"

"I was told to give it to him directly. He would request it with a specific phrase." Andrew broke out in a sweat again.

"Culper requests the message."

Andrew started at the exact words he was to listen for. So, Tallmadge was John Bolton. He pulled a letter from the leather pouch he carried, relieved to see that it had remained dry despite his dripping perspiration. Handing the letter to Tallmadge, he sank back against the chair. His body shook as his muscles relaxed and his mind calmed. No longer was he solely responsible for this message. His legs trembled from his exertion, and he rubbed them to try to still the tremors.

Gunfire in the distance reverberated in earnest now.

"I'm afraid my message arrives too late. The battle has begun. I hurried here as soon as Laurence gave it to me."

"Montclair?"

"Yes. Leaving the city was not difficult, but navigating the sound proved almost impossible."

"Yes, the British guard it well." From his breast pocket, he took out a piece of leather and unrolled it, revealing rectangular cutouts. Placing it over the parchment, he quickly read the message. "Damn. How did they discover our plan? Their spy network is as good as our own."

They both looked at the window as gunfire filled the air. Tallmadge rose.

"I'm sorry. I tried ..." Andrew spread out his hands.

"It's not your fault. The British had this information long ago. Parsons was hell-bent on this raid after the success of Sag Harbor. Once a general gets a plan into his head, it's difficult to change his mind. Knowing the British were aware of the raid might not have made a difference. Rest easy."

Andrew crossed his arms on the table and laid his head on them. His arms, sticky with sweat, stuck to the table. He sat up and fought to stay awake.

"There is a stream just behind the stable. Cool yourself off there while I prepare a message for Montclair." Tallmadge patted his shoulder. "You did your best, Andrew. We are grateful for your effort."

Rising slowly, he wasn't sure his legs would carry him as far as the barn. His first steps were wobbly, but he gained his footing and shuffled toward the river. He thought he heard his feet sigh in delight when he tugged off his boots, then he peeled off his clothing.

The cold water shocked him as he plunged into the stream. Still able to hear the gunfire, he took long strokes, diving as deeply as possible. Tallmadge said it would have made no difference, but it might have. If the British had been taken by surprise …

He lay on his back, head in the water, looking up through the leafy maples. The water covering his ears blocked any sound of gunfire—it blocked any sound at all. He relaxed, floating. The sky was a brilliant blue, the leaves etched green against it. He had completed the mission Montclair sent him on. Now he just wanted to return to Manhattan as quickly as possible. He needed to know that Jenny was safe, and that Lieutenant Ashby was nowhere near her. He wanted to stand guard outside her house every night and protect her.

He wanted to hold her. To inhale her scent of lavender and lilac. To kiss her. To make love to her. Despite the cool water, his body stirred. But he had to stay away. That was how he could protect her.

Another gunshot. This one very close. Too close.

&

Jenny's eyes burned from lack of sleep and crying. How many times did she get up to look out the window toward the oak tree, wondering if Andrew had returned from Setauket and stood guard there? How many times did she start to put on the disguise she had worn, planning to sneak out and see for herself if he was watching outside her house? But just as he promised to keep her safe, she must take care to not endanger his life.

Where was he now? How long would the trip to Setauket take? With the British presence there, he would be in grave danger. Pressing her hands together, she sent up a silent prayer for his safety. She should have ridden with him as she did when they rescued Uncle Jonathon. But, no, that would have put him in more jeopardy.

She hadn't been able to eat since Andrew left, and this morning she picked at her breakfast, stirring the suppawn until the thick porridge absorbed the maple syrup Sarie had drizzled over it. Breaking off a hunk of the warm, rye bread, she nibbled at it for a moment, then abandoned it on the plate. The rich, dark coffee soothed her throat, hoarse from muffling her sobs through the night.

"You must keep up your strength, Miss Jenny." Sarie poured more coffee into her cup. "Your mama needs you to be strong. She don't need another sick person to care for."

Jenny took a spoonful of porridge, but she couldn't swallow it.

Sarie stared at her. "Miss Jenny …"

Jenny swallowed. The porridge slid down like a lump of mud. She snatched her coffee and took a hearty gulp.

The front door knocker sounded. She looked up, her heartbeat quickening. Could Andrew have returned from Setauket? Would he brazenly appear at her front door in daylight? No. Her heart sank.

"I'll get that. You jus' keep eatin'." Sarie shot her a stern look.

Jenny sighed and forced down another spoonful. Sarie was right—Mother didn't need another person to nurse. Caring for Father had taken its toll on Mother, and now, taking over the system of messages was further draining her strength. Jenny nibbled at a bit of bread as she contemplated the magnitude of what they were about. If the British discovered … She jumped at Sarie's voice.

"Lieutenant Ashby is callin', Miss Jenny." Sarie stood at the door, her brilliant blue eyes guarded with fear.

"Thank you, Sarie." She toyed with the porridge remaining in her bowl as if lost somewhere in the clotted gray mass were answers for to how to handle Lieutenant Ashby's attentions. Ashby had been kind when he'd come to pay his respects after Father's funeral, but just the sight of his red uniform made her stomach squirm. Maintaining a pleasant composure in front of him took all her reserve. She started as her reverie was interrupted by the sound of the dining room door opening.

"Do you want me to tell the lieutenant that you are indisposed?" Sarie asked.

"No, I'm coming." As she passed Sarie, she squeezed her arm gently. "Everything is fine," she whispered.

Sarie's wide eyes revealed her doubt.

Jenny stopped outside the door to the parlor, brushed her hand over her stomach to quell the butterflies, and took a deep breath. Squaring her shoulders, she opened the door and swept into the room.

Lieutenant Ashby rose. "Good day, Miss Sutton." He bowed over her hand. As usual, his posture was erect, his spine ramrod straight. The perfect British officer.

"Good day, Lieutenant. To what do I owe the pleasure of your visit?" She tried to breathe evenly and dispel the quaking in her legs. The idea of this man standing outside her house a few nights ago at almost the exact moment she'd emerged shook her to her core. She forced a smile and indicated a chair as she took her own.

Sarie carried in a tray set for coffee. The blue and white porcelain cups rattled against the saucers, and the rich, fragrant liquid sloshed out of the spout of the silver coffeepot. She set the service before Jenny, meeting neither her gaze nor the lieutenant's. She bobbed a curtsey and left.

Jenny lifted the pot, spilling a bit more of the steaming liquid. She forced her hands to be steady as she poured and served Ashby's coffee. *I must be strong. I cannot let him see my fear.* She stared directly into his eyes and smiled, knowing her dimple would likely catch his attention.

He shifted in his seat and crossed his legs.

"Forgive my clumsiness." Taking a napkin, she wiped up the spill. "I'm still affected by my father's death. My grief often takes hold when I least expect it."

He shifted again. "No apology necessary, Miss Sutton. I understand completely. The loss of your father surely must be a great sorrow to you and your mother." He cleared his throat. "Do you have ... anyone to watch over you? That is, I mean, to ensure your safety in this city? Every day there is more tension with the rise of the rebellious patriots."

"I'm sure we have nothing to be anxious about." Unable to still her trembling, she reached out to place her cup on the table beside her.

"Oh, but you do."

His harsh voice startled her, and she rattled the cup, almost spilling its contents. She looked up at him, her heart thumping. "What do you mean?" She searched his face for some clue of his intent. Was he here to arrest her? And Mother? They should have left immediately after Father's funeral as she'd promised. But then she would have missed precious time spent with Andrew.

He scrubbed his hands along his thighs. "Forgive me. I didn't mean to speak so curtly." He took a deep breath. "There are subversive elements in the city who are covertly working against the Crown." He looked at the floor as he spoke. "When captured, these rebels are put in gaol until they are tried for treason." He paused as the clock ticked the minutes. Finally, he spoke again. "Most are hanged."

Heat stabbed through her. Her trembling was impossible to still. Could he hear her heart hammering?

"I just want to ensure your safety … and, of course, your mother's."

He was warning her.

Standing, he picked up his hat by one of its corners. She stood, too, extending her hand.

"I will take my leave now." He bowed over her hand. "I am your most obedient and humble servant, Miss Sutton." His gaze bored into her.

With perfect posture, he left the room.

CHAPTER FOURTEEN

(6

Andrew jumped up from his leisurely floating at the sound of the nearby gunshot.

"I don't know what your reverie concerns, Andrew, but it doesn't seem to involve your mission." Benjamin Tallmadge stood on the shore, a rifle resting on his shoulder. "Despite your impetuous nature, you're obviously dedicated to the cause. Just keep your head about you." He turned toward the house and motioned for Andrew to follow.

He did so, hopping into his breeches as he went. Once inside, he sat on a chair in the dining room to don his stockings and boots. His shirt had dried a bit and no longer stuck to his body, and he welcomed the coolness of the shuttered room.

Tallmadge held up a parcel of parchment tied in a leather strap. "Listen carefully." He riffled the edges of the blank papers. "The only sheet that has vital information is the fifth sheet in the bundle. Do you understand that?" He counted from the top of the pile and uncovered the fifth sheet. "The strap is tied in a bow on the top of the pile. You must count down to the fifth sheet. All the others are blank."

Andrew looked at him as if he were daft. "Sir, they're *all* blank."

Tallmadge patted his shoulder. "They're all blank for those who should not see them." He winked. "Montclair will know what to do. But in the event that you are stopped, all you carry are blank sheets of paper, perhaps to write love letters to that beauty who haunts your mind."

He nodded, still not convinced. "Yes, sir."

"Speed is of the utmost importance. I cannot stress the urgency in this missive. Do you understand? No stopping along the way to visit your lass. What is her name, son?"

He swallowed. Should he reveal her name? Tallmadge's clear eyes met his. There was no subterfuge there; he was actually interested. If Mr. Montclair trusted him, he could. "Jenny Sutton."

Tallmadge sat back. "Edward Sutton's daughter?" He toyed with the tankard before him. "I've heard he died from his wounds."

"Yes, sir."

Tallmadge looked at the bundle of paper. "What we are about is a rebellion. Valor is required. If you love her, and I believe you do, you must protect her. She and her mother are probably being watched."

"They are, sir." He related the conversation he'd heard between Lieutenant Ashby and his superior.

"Then you must return at once. I will get you on a safe boat so you can return by Long Island Sound."

☾

Benjamin Tallmadge carried an unlit lantern as he led Andrew through a forest of maples where the air was cool and the lowering sun was less severe. Dried leaves crunched beneath their feet as they walked in silence. While the leather pouch slung over his shoulder carried only the sheaf of parchment, Andrew felt its weight in consequence. He shifted it to lie diagonally across his chest.

They broke out of the trees and walked to the edge of the water where a rowboat was perched on the shore. Seagulls swooped above them and waves gently lapped the sand. The evening sun shot fiery fingers of orange and magenta into the wispy clouds to the west. Andrew shaded his eyes as he studied the water, wishing his insides were as calm. The two men doffed their boots and rolled down their stockings, stuffing them inside.

"Some call these waters Long Island Sound, some The Devil's Belt. To use the current, you'll want to stay toward the middle of the sound, but it could put you in the path of British ships and Tory whaleboats. They patrol for Patriots who sneak across from Connecticut or up from New York City." Benjamin hefted the bow off the sand. "If you see or hear any approaching boats, row hard for the shore." He pushed the rowboat into the water, Andrew hurrying to help.

The water on Andrew's feet and legs sent shivers up his body. He welcomed the relief from the damp, warm air. Once the boat was fully in the water, he tossed in his boots and hopped aboard, spraying water inside. He adjusted the leather pouch over his shoulders, tapping the parchment within.

Benjamin lit the lantern, placing it on the seat and shook his hand. "Godspeed, Andrew."

He nodded his thanks and rowed out into the sound. As he floated away, Benjamin waved a final farewell, turned, and disappeared into the woods. The hollow night sound of the surrounding water engulfed him in loneliness as the sun sank into the horizon. He had been lonely before, but his determination to find Jenny had pushed from his mind the luxury of dwelling on it. Now, knowing where she was, knowing he'd be near her again soon, gave him too much time to think. He swallowed and rowed harder.

❦

In the ebony night, lit only by the rising half-moon, Andrew fought against the current. His shoulders ached and blisters sprouted on his palms. Every so often, he rested a bit, but the rowboat floated too close to the shore.

He took a hunk of bread and slice of cheese that Benjamin

had provided, and sculled with one oar while he munched the food. He slaked his thirst from an oak canteen filled with cider. Refreshed, he resumed his rowing, though the muscles in his back protested. His hands burned as the blisters were rubbed raw.

He stopped, listening. A boat was approaching him from behind. As he turned, the lanterns at the bow of a small whaler flickered in the dark. In panic, he redoubled his efforts, but to no avail. The boat was closing in. The faster he rowed, the closer it came. His arms trembled with the effort.

"Stop. In the name of King George, stop."

A rifle shot cracked, the bullet stinging the water just off the side of his rowboat.

The whaler caught up to his boat and pulled astern. A man balancing on the gunwale pointed his rifle at him. "Ship your oars."

He did as he was told, and another man reached for one of them. Now his entire body quavered. Were these men Tories or Patriots? What could he say to discover their loyalty? Tallmadge had warned about Tories defending these waters against anyone opposing the Crown. But perhaps there were also men sympathetic to the cause …

"Gi' it here."

He lifted one oar so the man could reach it. They hauled his rowboat in, secured it, and pulled him on board. The captain, in dark clothes and a woolen cap, thrust the lantern toward his face.

"Who are ya'? And why are ya' skulking through the waters of the sound at night?" His putrid breath forced Andrew back a step. The captain closed the space. "Speak, boy."

"My name is Andrew Wentworth. I'm returning to Manhattan."

"Ya' look like a rebel to me." He spat on the deck. Other crew members nodded, mumbling in agreement.

They were Tories.

"Let's see what ya' carry, boy." He seized the leather pouch, yanking it over Andrew's head, twisting his neck. Untying the strap, he opened the pouch and withdrew the sheets. "What have we here? Carrying messages to the Sons, are we?" He guffawed, and again Andrew recoiled at his rank breath.

"No, sir," Andrew said, trying not to inhale the cloud of foul air.

The captain pawed through the sheets, turning them over, searching for a message. He squinted at Andrew. He stuffed the sheets back into the pouch and threw it at him. Andrew caught it before it went over the side of the boat.

"Gaw. What're ya' about, boy?" The captain shoved his shoulders.

Grimacing against the pain in his aching muscles, Andrew clutched his shoulder, opening a blister on his hand. He fought light-headedness, regained his composure, and straightened. "I am returning home from Setauket." He saw no reason to lie. They did not know his reason for the journey, and since Setauket was under British rule—as was New York—he would let them assume he was a Tory.

"Setauket? Why were ya' there?"

Thoughts—no, lies—ran through Andrew's mind. Which would be the most convincing? Why hadn't he and Major Tallmadge planned on his being stopped and questioned?

"My uncle owns a farm. He was in need of help with his crop."

A man piped up from the back of the crew. "I'm from Setauket. Who's yer uncle?"

Sweat prickled along Andrew's spine. *Damnation. What am I to do?*

The captain swung the lantern toward the speaker. "Quiet. This isn't a social call." He turned back to Andrew, holding the lantern near his face. Closing the space between them, his foul breath whispered Andrew's fate. "We could turn ya' in to the British, but what fun would that be?" He looked back at his crew.

At that signal, they laughed, nudging each other and exchanging crude remarks.

He turned back to Andrew. "I think tomorrow will be a fine day for a swim."

A roar went up from the crew. Shouts of agreement rang through the air.

"Yes, a fine day for a keelhaulin'."

Andrew's knees turned to rubber. It took all his strength to remain standing. He would not show the captain his fear. He stood taller and glared into the man's steely gaze.

He'd never heard of anyone surviving being keelhauled.

CHAPTER FIFTEEN

"WHAT ARE WE TO DO, Mother?" Jenny paced the parlor. "He was warning me, I'm certain of it."

"Indeed." Mother stared into the cold hearth. "We must prepare to return to Boston." The shutters were still closed against the early August morning, but sunlight slipped through the slats, painting her face with stripes of shadow and light. "I will need to contact Laurence so no further messages are delivered here. Until that is communicated, we must remain." She looked up. "It would be best if you went ahead of me. I can send Sarie and Isaac with you ..."

"No." Jenny rushed to her, kneeling before her and taking her hands. "I will not leave you."

Mother brushed back her hair. "It is for the best, darling."

She shook her head. "No. I will stay with you."

"You have your father's courage ... and stubbornness." She kissed her forehead. "Let me prepare a letter for you to take to Laurence."

Jenny followed her into the office. Mother assembled a sheet of parchment, a quill pen, and an inkbottle. She dipped the quill into the bottle and began to write. Nothing appeared on the paper. She ran her finger along the edge to mark where a new line would begin.

"Mother?" Jenny frowned, puzzled.

"Hush, darling. All is well." She finished writing, folded the parchment in thirds, and laid it on the desk. Taking out a block of red wax, she heated it, dripped it on the fold, and sealed it with a brass seal embossed with a "B." She glanced through the window at the street. "This is not an ideal time to be about, but Laurence must make other arrangements as soon as possible. Are you willing to make this trip, Jennifer?"

"Of course." Picking up the letter, she fought down fear as she smiled at Mother.

☙

Jenny noticed immediately that the large porcelain jar was standing in its place in the window display, so there was no message for her to retrieve. Good. That was one less thing to worry about. Her heartbeat quickened as she entered the shop. The pungent aroma of camphor greeted her as Lucy Carter poured the oil into a small amber bottle.

"Good day, Miss Sutton," she said, concentrating on her mixture.

"Good day, Mrs. Carter." Was Lucy the person in charge of placing and removing the porcelain jar? She glanced toward the office. No, Laurence would manage that himself. Though Lucy was very precise as evidenced by the great care with which she measured the tincture.

"Good day, Miss Sutton." Ephraim Carter stood at the door. He rotated his hat in his hands, his gaze pleading with her.

This was the moment she could reveal his cruelty the night she and Andrew had passed Fraunces Tavern. True, he had stopped and had apologized profusely when her identity was revealed, but what if it had been another woman without such protection? Would he and his group of cronies have attacked her? No, he would never have considered any such action if he hadn't been emboldened by drink. She hoped he'd learned his lesson. Besides, what purpose would it serve to expose him now?

"Good day, Mr. Carter." She couldn't help but give him a

warning glare while Lucy was busy with her recipe.

He gave a half-bow, his shoulders relaxing. He bowed again and returned to the back of the shop.

"Is Mr. Montclair in?" Jenny asked.

Lucy glanced at the jar in the window and frowned. "No, he had to meet with Pastor Farr this morning." She corked the bottle and wiped her hands on her apron. "Is there something I can help you with?"

"No. It is imperative I talk with him immediately."

Lucy nodded. "You may still find him at St. Paul's."

"Thank you," Jenny called over her shoulder as she left the shop.

As the carriage rumbled through the streets, she fidgeted with the hem of her waistcoat, fighting the dread that rose within her like mist over a morning lake. She and Mother must flee as soon as possible, but not until some accommodation was made for the couriers. Plus, she would need to leave word for Andrew to follow them as soon as he was able.

Why did Montclair have to be away today? She wanted to hand this letter over to him and be finished so she could move Mother to safety. And how would she deliver the message in front of Pastor Farr? Something was amiss.

The lace along the hem of her waistcoat unraveled in her fingers. She stared at it, her trepidation seeping throughout her bones. She wanted to sit beside Mathias and whip the horses into a gallop. Her heart raced with a premonition of death. Andrew's face came to her mind.

"Oh my God," she whispered.

&

Jenny welcomed the dim coolness of the church, shrouded in silence. Pausing in the nave, she allowed her vision to adjust to the shadowy interior. She made her way along the aisle, her footsteps echoing on the smooth flagstones, her body tensed with a disconcerting chill. Up ahead, in a pew halfway to the altar, sat Laurence Montclair, apparently in prayer. She did not want to disturb him, but she fixed her attention on the back of his head until she neared. Then she averted her gaze and walked past him, taking a seat in the front pew.

Though the church was empty, save for Montclair, the hair on the back of her neck pricked with the sense of being observed. Perhaps Montclair had just noticed her and would join her in this pew. She waited for him.

Mother's warning about not trusting anyone rang in her ears. But surely she could trust him—Mother did. What if someone else lurked in the shadows of the church? What if it wasn't Montclair she sensed but someone else? A Tory? Or worse, a British soldier? To pass this message to Montclair here might be too risky.

Taking out a prayer book, she tucked the message in the back cover as she bent her head over the text. The words blurred. She could drop the prayer book in the aisle beside him as she departed. He could retrieve it for her and take the letter. Anyone watching would find nothing unusual in the exchange.

The bodice of her dress pulsed with the hammering of her heart. If she was being observed, enough time had passed to signify a heartfelt petition for the repose of Father's soul. She rose and turned to leave. Unable to stop herself, she looked directly at Montclair. His gaze held hers. No. His gaze was unblinking. He stared above her toward the cross over the altar. He did not glance her way. He did not move. A scarlet ribbon oozed down his white linen shirt from the gash along his throat.

CHAPTER SIXTEEN

𝒞

A NDREW STRUGGLED AGAINST THE ROPES that cut into his wrists. After being bound the night before, he had been shoved into a corner of the deck onto a pile of coiled rope. They'd stripped him of all but his breeches, and the captain had confiscated his leather pouch with the secret message for Laurence.

"Sleep well. Ya' will need all your strength fer yer morning swim," the captain had said last night as he'd slipped the pouch over his shoulder. He'd thrown his head back and cackled. "Then ya' can sleep with the fishes." He snorted sending thick, yellow slime out his nose. He wiped it on his sleeve, cleared his throat, and spat right beside Andrew's bare foot.

Andrew hadn't slept all night. He had planned how to escape. And he had thought about Jenny. None of his escape plans had come to fruition, and thinking of Jenny had filled him with a weariness that depleted his strength.

"Andrew, you need to keep trying," her sweet voice encouraged him. *"You can never give up. I am with you, my love. Come back to me."*

Just imagining the lilt of her voice lifted him from his despair. Yes, he had to fight. He had to find a way to return to her. She was in danger, too. He could not abandon her now.

His thoughts were interrupted when two crew members

approached, casting a shadow over him. One held a long rope that weighed him down and dragged along the deck. Another length snaked along the deck, disappearing over the rail.

"Time fer yer swim."

They laughed as they secured the rope next to the one that bound Andrew's wrists. Each taking an elbow, they lifted him to his feet.

He swayed as much from lack of sleep as from hunger. The little food Benjamin had provided him was long gone. Waves swelling on the sound did not help as he tried to steady himself. The sun beat down on him as they led him to the bow of the boat.

"Any last words, lad?" The captain's raspy guffaw frightened the gulls sitting along the bowsprit behind them. They squawked their objection to being disturbed as they flew toward shore.

Shore.

Andrew scanned the coastline. They had sailed closer to land during the night. He had no idea of their location, but the distance to land from the ship was swimmable—if he survived the keelhaul, and if they cut him loose, and if the rope didn't drag him to the bottom of the sound. His heart sank.

Jenny.

He had to survive for Jenny.

The crewmen jerked him from his thoughts as they finished fastening the long rope around each wrist. One of them reached to untie the smaller rope that had bound him through the night.

"What're doin'?" The captain asked, hurrying to stop him.

"No use wasting a perfectly good piece of line, Cap'n." The man smiled, his breath reeking from his brown, rotted teeth.

The captain's face broke into a broad grin. "Aye. A good

plan."

The crewman untied the short rope, but Andrew's wrists were held fast by the long one. The other crewman took one end and walked along the breadth of the deck. Andrew was hoisted up on the ratline, the ropes of the rung ladder digging into his feet. He teetered and grabbed a rung to keep from toppling into the sound. He was directly opposite from the rope that dropped over the rail and into the sea.

All eyes were on the captain, who held his pistol in the air. He grinned at Andrew, cruelty displayed on his face. He would make him wait.

Andrew's heart raced though he fought to breathe evenly. *I must remain calm.* The pistol flashed before the sound registered, jolting him. A hand pushed him roughly and the glistening water rushed toward him as he plunged into it. He gulped as much air as his lungs would take before he broke the waves.

Icy water shocked him, dazing him at first. His arms were jerked out in front of him as the sailors on board pulled the rope, skimming him along the bottom of the hull. Barnacles slashed at his skin, tearing the flesh. Saltwater burned in the freshly opened cuts. The urgency to survive took over, and he kicked his legs, increasing his speed along the hull. The shadow of the ship and depth of the water shrouded him in darkness, disorienting him. Only the pull of the rope guided him to the other side of the vessel.

His lungs ached, and the urge to inhale overwhelmed him. But he couldn't abandon Jenny. The base of the keel cut into his back, shoving more barnacles into his skin. A gasp would fill his lungs with water. He had to stay calm. The water brightened as he traveled up the other side of the ship. He was almost through, but the elation was short-lived as blackness covered his vision. He was losing consciousness.

Hold on. Hold on.

Just as he was sinking into darkness, his head broke the

water.

The crew yelled out "Huzzah!"

He gulped a breath, but a wave hit and he swallowed water as well. Coughing, he tried to clear his throat and harness more life-giving fresh air. The crew's jeers echoed.

He couldn't swim with his arms tied together, and the only thing keeping his head above water was that the crewmen were hoisting him back up to the ship.

"Ungh, ungh ..." The jerking motion of the rope cut into his wrists and pulled his shoulders from their sockets. Blood streamed down his upstretched arms. Blackness engulfed him as they hauled him into the ship and dumped him on the deck. He rolled to his stomach, gagging and coughing up seawater.

"Cut 'im loose, lads." The captain's voice sounded like it came from far away.

Andrew fought to stay alert. They were not finished with him yet. He was supposed to have drowned. Rough hands clawed his arms, cutting away the rope. His arms fell slack against his body and shook uncontrollably.

"Yer a tough one, I'll gi' ya' that." The captain kicked Andrew's side, setting off another coughing spell. Andrew vomited at his feet. The captain bellowed.

"Maybe not so tough, eh? Throw 'im over, boys."

A roar of approval went up from the crew.

Brutal hands grabbed his arms and legs, lifting him over the side. Swinging him above the rail, they shouted, "One, two, three," letting him fly on the end of the count.

Plunging into the depths again, he pawed weakly at the sea. Blood leached into the water around him.

Water where sharks swam.

❧

Jenny collapsed back into the pew, her trembling legs unable to support her. She could not pull her gaze away from Laurence Montclair's staring eyes and gaping mouth.

What was she to do? She cast about into the dark corners of the church. No one was here. But someone had been—someone who knew that Montclair was working for the Patriot cause. Whoever killed him would come back for his body. Why, indeed, had they left him here?

To capture, perhaps to kill, whomever he was meeting.

Summoning her nerve, she slipped her hand into the back of the prayer book and retrieved the letter. As she rose, she slipped it into the folds of her skirt. If someone were observing her, she could not chance tucking it into her bodice. She scanned the church once more, stood, and hurried down the aisle. She dared not look at Montclair again, for she would break down.

Before she pushed open the door, she caught a flash of crimson in the recess of the nave. She ran out into the churchyard. Dizzy, she tried to stem her shaking. She slowed her pace, trying to appear natural. Few people were about on the street ahead, and no one was in the churchyard. Nauseated, she hurried to shrubs near the walkway to the parsonage and vomited into the juniper. Her stomach spasmed, and she clutched it, fighting the bile that rose in her throat.

"Miss Sutton?"

She jumped at the voice behind her. Turning, she faced Lieutenant Ashby, the scarlet of his coat brilliant in the late afternoon sun.

"Are you unwell? May I assist you?" He held out a hand to steady her.

She pulled back. Was it he she'd glimpsed as she left the church? Was it a coincidence that he suddenly appeared? Could he have killed Montclair? Coldness swept over her, overriding any sense of nausea.

"I am fine, Lieutenant." She brushed her hands along her skirt.

He glanced at the pool of vomit she'd just deposited. "I suspect you are not fine." Instead of their usual soft interest, his eyes were flinty and probing. "What brought on this unfortunate illness?" He took her elbow, leading her to a nearby stone bench.

She wanted to resist, but in the event that it was not he in the church, she did not want to draw attention to the scene within—or her knowledge of it. But surely, he would have seen her leave the church, for she was sick almost immediately.

"Perhaps the eggs I had at breakfast did not agree with me." She forced a smile at him, ignoring the repulsion running through her.

"So, you came to church looking for release from that affliction?" He frowned.

"I came to church to pray for the repose of the soul of my father," she shot back.

He started. "Of course. Forgive me. Did you find peace in your time at prayer?"

How should she respond? What would excuse her from witnessing what happened to Mr. Montclair?

"Alas, I felt ill even before I entered. I paused in the nave, but it seemed wiser to return to the fresh air. As you can see, it was the wiser course since the juniper is a much better receptacle than the stone floor of the church." She smiled as if he were the dearest man alive. More lies. When had deception become so easy for her?

He studied her.

If he had witnessed her discovery of Montclair, he would know her lie. She would be more suspect than before, for why would she not run to him for help? If he had not been inside, he might just accept what she was saying as truth. It was a delicate balance.

"Allow me to escort you home." Warmth returned to his expression, and he smiled.

She held back the breath she wanted to expel. Had he believed her?

"Thank you." She slipped her hand through his arm, and

they walked toward the street.

❦

Mother ran to her as Jenny entered the house. She held out her hands in warning before Lieutenant Ashby followed her in, but was too late.

"Jennifer, were you able to deliver ..." Mother stopped at the sight of him. "Oh. Good evening, Lieutenant Ashby."

"Good evening, Mrs. Sutton."

Jenny shook her head as he bowed over Mother's hand.

"Won't you come in?" Mother gestured toward the parlor.

Jenny frowned at her. Her stomach still roiled at the memory of Mr. Montclair. Would she be able to keep up this pretense of calm during a social call? Possibly with the murderer? *God, I just want to scream.*

They took their usual seats, and Mother rang for Sarie. When the servant appeared, Mother asked, "May I interest you in a fruit shrub, Lieutenant? Mathias was able to buy some ripe berries at the docks today, and my husband—" Her smile disappeared, and she brought her handkerchief to her eyes. "Forgive me. His death is so new that I sometimes think he is still with us." She cleared her throat. "He acquired a fine brandy while in Boston."

"I would be honored. But are you feeling well enough for such a libation, Miss Sutton?"

"What is it, Jennifer?"

She frowned at Ashby, but he smiled and nodded as if to say, "Go ahead. Tell your story."

"I was ill at church. I'm feeling better now. How providential that Lieutenant Ashby was immediately present to see me home. I'm feeling better, and a shrub will be refreshing."

Mother nodded to Sarie, who curtsied and hurried to the back of the house to prepare the drinks.

Candlelight glowed in the room against long evening shadows. Despite the peaceful atmosphere, Jenny itched with apprehension. Something nagged at the back of her mind. As he and Mother exchanged pleasantries about the weather, she went over the scene in the churchyard. Wouldn't she have seen him approaching as she ran out of the church? Surely, he must have been inside to have appeared so quickly. Blood rushed through her veins.

"… how much I enjoy your daughter's company." Ashby was beaming at her.

Mother grasped Jenny's hand. What had just happened?

"In this treacherous time, it isn't safe for two women to live alone, especially in a city so full of miscreants … and traitors." He let the word linger in the air.

Jenny shivered.

"I see you are alarmed, and rightfully so, Miss Sutton."

Sarie entered with a tray of tall glasses filled with a soft orange liquid. As Jenny took the last glass from the tray, Sarie barely shook her head. A warning.

Ashby sipped his drink. "Delicious. How fortunate that you were able to purchase fresh fruit. Of course, under the rule of King George, we are able to enjoy many delectable foods." He stood, raising his glass. "God save the King."

Jenny froze, but Mother took her hand and pulled her to standing. As one, they raised their glasses. "God save the King."

They all drank.

Jenny choked and began coughing violently. Would she vomit again, right here on the Oriental rug? She gasped for breath.

"Are you all right, dear?" Mother patted her back.

Jenny nodded. Finally, she squeaked out, "Yes, I am all right, Mother." Catching her breath, she settled back on the settee. "Excuse me." She fanned her face.

"You have had a most strenuous day, Miss Sutton."

"Oh?" Mother arched a brow at her.

The memory of Laurence Montclair, blood soaking his shirt, flashed in Jenny's mind. She took a deep breath to stem the nausea. When she opened her eyes, Ashby was staring at her.

"Which brings me back to my previous point. Many violent occurrences take place throughout the city, some not far from this home." Ashby continued to stare at her.

"Violent occurrences? Jennifer, are you all right? You look pale, dear."

He had seen her. He was telling her that. The question was, did he murder Montclair or just witness her arrival?

"Rest assured, Mrs. Sutton, the only violence Miss Sutton experienced was her illness. Bad eggs, apparently."

Mother sat rigid. She took Jenny's hand.

"I would be most honored if you would allow me to protect you. My feelings for Miss Sutton have run deep for a while now. Perhaps you have been aware of them, for I did not attempt to conceal them from you." His gaze bore into Jenny.

She lowered her lids and clutched her stomach. This could not be happening.

"Of course, it would be inappropriate of me to linger at your house for the amount of time required to ensure your safety. So, I am asking for your daughter's hand, Mrs. Sutton."

The room swayed. Jenny clasped Mother's hand tighter.

"I know it's shocking for me to ask this so soon after Mr. Sutton's death, but these are not normal times. The rebellion of the Patriots has forced us to adapt our customs to the urgent needs of the day. Custom, alas, must fly with the winds."

"Lieutenant, I hardly know what to say. This is so unsuitable. You must give us time to digest your words and contemplate their implications."

Jenny stared at the floor. She already knew the implications. If she said no to his proposal, he would expose them both as spies. They would hang.

CHAPTER SEVENTEEN

A NDREW TRIED TO SWALLOW, BUT his parched throat felt like a rasp. He fought to open his eyelids, but they stuck. He was too tired. Too tired to even make the effort. He wanted to surrender to the darkness that engulfed him.

"Come back to me, Andrew." *Jenny reached toward him.*

Jenny? Are you here? Was he imagining her voice? Her sweet smile?

He needed to keep swimming, keep moving. For Jenny. He kicked, but his legs didn't respond. *Try. You've got to try.* He kicked again, but there was no buoying water carrying him along. Sand billowed up, blowing over his aching body. He was on shore.

He was alive.

He forced one eye open. The indigo sky loomed above him, the sand against his back still hot from the day's unrelenting sun. A wave teased his feet then fell away into the sea. He blinked and his other eye opened. He tried to move, even to raise his arms, but they were leaden, their shape embedded in the sand. How long had he been here?

A wave crept up his calves to his knees. The tide was rising, and if strong enough, it would drag him back into the sound. Groaning, he mustered his strength and heaved onto his side. One arm was trapped below his body, the other flopped in front of him. Sand stuck to the blood that had been streaming from his wrists to his elbows. Placing his free hand on the sand, he tried to push up to sitting, but his strength had been sapped in the effort to survive the swim.

Another wave swept up along his thighs, the tide pulling him toward the sea. He rolled to his stomach and clawed at the sand, trying to pull himself farther up on the shore. Ahead of him, trees lined the edge of the beach, the remnant glow of sunset shimmering through the leaves. He reached one arm up and pulled himself forward. A

wave crashed over him, dragging him toward the water. He scrabbled at the sand, but his effort was useless. The next wave broke over his head.

I cannot...

Another swell pushed him back up on shore, the sand scraping his face and chest, but then pulled him back into the surf. His arms went limp, his hands numb. He couldn't fight anymore. *Forgive me, Jenny...*

Blackness.

Rough hands grabbed him, digging into his armpits, fire against his skin, dragging him along the beach. He tried to fight, but his arms hung limp, impotent, unable to resist the attacker.

"Settle, just settle." The voice was far away, as if echoing down a mountain.

Andrew tried to speak, but his cracked lips moved in silence. He surrendered. He could fight no more.

Voices echoed in the blackness of the night. A cool breeze brushed his body, raising chill bumps. He shivered. He welcomed the roughness of a wool blanket as it covered him. Someone cupped his head, lifting it so he could drink from a leather flask. Water dribbled along his chin as he tried to purse his lips to drink. Catching the flow, he gulped until he choked, coughing and spitting out most of the liquid.

"Take it slowly. You're in a terrible state." A deep voice spoke near his ear.

Andrew glimpsed a fire crackling on the edge of the

woods. His head lolled back, and the man set him down on the sand.

"Someone treated you badly."

Andrew barely nodded.

"Are you in service to the King?"

Andrew stared at him.

"Hmmph." The man considered him. "I suspect you're not. This looks like the work of Tories to me."

Andrew's mind was too muddled to consider whether to trust this man. He was too close to death. At this point, he would welcome its relief. He nodded.

"Good. Then you can live." He lifted Andrew's head again and held the flask. "Now, take it slowly."

☾

"Be assured, I pledge my protection to you both. No matter what happens ..." Lieutenant Ashby stressed those last words, "I will see that you are safe." He stood. "I ask you to take this evening to consider my marriage proposal. I shall call tomorrow evening to hear your answer." He bowed and took his leave.

Mother flew to the door and locked it. She returned to her place beside Jenny.

"What happened today?"

"Oh, Mother, Laurence Montclair is dead." Jenny collapsed against her and burst into tears. She dug her nails into her palms to stem the spikes of fear and sorrow that shot through her body.

"My God," Mother breathed, wrapping Jenny in her arms. "No."

Between gasps, Jenny explained what had occurred at the church. She ended with her glimpse of a scarlet coat as she left.

"So, Ashby knows."

Jenny nodded.

"He is forcing you to marry him ..."

"Or he will arrest us as spies."

"We must leave at once."

A knock sounded at the back door.

They froze.

"He's come back to demand an answer tonight," Jenny whispered.

"Go upstairs. I will tell him you were still ill and have retired for the evening." She gave her a gentle shove. "Hurry, darling."

Jenny sped up the stairs, pausing to listen when she reached the top. Mother unlocked the door and swung it open.

"Good evening, Mrs. Sutton. I'm sorry to call so late, but I must see Miss Sutton."

Ephraim Carter.

"Come in, Mr. Carter. I'll see if …"

Jenny hurried down the stairs. Ephraim's ashen face foretold what his next words would be.

"Mr. Montclair is … I can't believe it … he's dead. Murdered."

Mother ushered him into the parlor.

"They found him in the church. His throat was slashed, it was." He shook his head, slumping into the chair. "Rumors are flying that he was working for the Sons." He shot a look at them. "British soldiers came to the apothecary. Tore it all apart searching for proof. I'm scared for Lucy and Zachariah."

Mother patted his hand.

He looked at her. "I'm worried for you two as well."

She and Mother exchanged looks.

Jenny studied that man who swaggered with bravado the night he intended to rape her. Gone was that swagger now. This was a man who feared for his life, and even more, the life of his family. He took an incredible chance to come here tonight and warn them. And if he had been followed …

Another knock on the back door.

Jenny's blood coursed through her veins. If Ashby had returned after all and found Ephraim here, they would all be implicated in treason. But it was the back door. Where the couriers came. Could it be Andrew? She leapt up and rushed toward the door.

"Jennifer. Stop." Mother blocked her. "We must not be impetuous. Especially now. Let me take care of this." She headed to the back door. "Oh, my God." Her voice was shrill. "In here, quickly."

Two men sidestepped their way into the room. Between them, they were propping up a third man.

Jenny gasped.

Andrew.

She rushed to his side, replacing the shorter of the two men who propped him up. His body slumped against her, his head swinging from side to side as they moved across the room. They eased him onto the settee. Ephraim lifted his legs to rest on the sofa, and Jenny propped a pillow beneath his head.

She swiped away the tears that streamed down her face—he had returned, but bruises covered his face and his cracked lips gaped. He moaned as she stroked the crease between his brows and brushed strands of hair away from his face. Her heart danced when he awoke and a flash of recognition lit his face.

"Jenny." His voice was thready, weak with the effort of speaking her name.

"Andrew, I'm here." Oh, that the depth of love within those words could pour over him with healing. She looked up at the men who had brought him here.

"Thank you."

The taller man nodded. "We found him on the shore of Hart Island. He was in bad shape. Keelhauled." His face darkened as he shook his head.

She had to crane her neck to look at him as he spoke. She had noticed when they entered that they filled the doorway with their bulk. The man who spoke was well over six-foot-four. The shorter man was nearly that.

He jerked a bow. "I'm Martin Wirth, and this is my brother, Abel."

Abel snatched off his hat as he bowed.

"Thank you both." She could barely see Andrew through blurry tears. "You saved his life."

Both men shifted from foot to foot.

Mother appeared beside her with a basin and pitcher of water, a towel draped over her arm. "Please, gentlemen, have a seat."

Ephraim slid two sturdy walnut side chairs toward them and the brothers eased down on them. Martin grimaced as his chair groaned in protest.

Balancing a heaping tray, Sarie stopped before each man, offering a mug of ale and a plate of fruit, cheese, and bread. Both broke out in grins of appreciation. Martin gingerly balanced the edge of a plate, the china dish disappearing into his enormous hand.

Jenny dampened the towel and pressed it against Andrew's forehead. He moaned, twisting his head away.

"Shhh, Andrew. All is well. You are with me now." She caressed his cheek, and he turned toward her, his eyelids quivering with the effort to stay open.

"We checked him over, Miss … Jenny. He kept repeatin' your name from the moment we hauled him outta the swell. He was near ta death, but he could say your name. After we fed him and got him warm, he could tell us where you lived. Once he did that, he … well, you can see for yourself."

Mother offered her hand. "I am Constance Sutton. Jenny is my daughter."

Martin nodded and looked about.

"My husband, Edward, passed away recently." She set her jaw.

"I'm sorry, Mrs. Sutton."

"It was a Ranger."

He jerked back as if she'd thrown cold water on him. "Bastards." He slapped his hand over his mouth. "Excuse me, ladies."

Mother tried to hide her smile. "My sentiments exactly, Mr. Wirth. Thank you for giving them voice."

His laugh was as large as he, and Andrew stirred.

A whisper. "Jenny. It's really you."

"Yes, Andrew. It's really me." Her voice caught between a laugh and a sob.

He moaned, trying to lift one arm. In the candlelight, the fierce gashes in his arms from where he had been bound stood out scarlet against his pale skin.

"If not treated soon, infection will set in. I'll need calendula and plantain and ..." Mother counted on her fingers.

Ephraim Carter stood. "I'll get Lucy. She'll know what he needs." He slipped out the back door.

"We need to get him to bed," Jenny said.

Without a word, Martin and Abel slid their muscular arms beneath Andrew and lifted him as if he weighed only a few pounds. "Show us the way."

When Andrew was settled in the guest bedroom, Jenny sat beside him. She winced as he grimaced in pain. "Sarie, please bring the elixir we used for Father."

"We'll be leaving then," Martin said.

Jenny stood, taking his hand. "I am indebted to you," she looked at Abel, "to both of you for saving Andrew's life. And for bringing him here."

Martin studied her. "We suspect he was keelhauled by Tories, which marks him a rebel. If so, all due respect, ma'am, you are as well. You're in a mountain of danger here in a city full of lobsterbacks."

Mother drew in her lips then nodded slightly. "We were making plans to leave New York tonight, but there are complications now."

He looked at Andrew, whose pale face matched the cotton pillow cover. "Ah, yes. Andrew can't be moved."

Jenny nodded. "Not only that, a British officer has asked for my hand. He wants an answer tomorrow or he will accuse us of being spies."

The brothers looked at each other.

"It would be best if you left the way you came. Get away from this house as quickly as you can, for we are being watched," Mother said.

"But we can help," Abel said.

Jenny smiled at them. "You are most kind, but you have already done so much. To add to the danger, our friend, Laurence Montclair, was murdered today. We were … helping him."

Martin stared at Andrew for a moment. "We'll take our leave then, Miss Sutton. Mrs. Sutton." He bowed to each woman and the brothers left.

"What are we to do, Mother?" She returned to sit on the bed beside Andrew.

"We are to nurse Andrew to good health. Until he is able to travel, we must stay here."

Sarie brought in the amber bottle containing a tincture of laudanum and poppy seed oil, and a pewter spoon. She handed the bottle to Jenny and stepped back. "Mathias, Isaac and me'll help when you're fixin' to leave. We be goin' with you, cause you ladies can't be travelin' alone."

"Thank you, Sarie. We could never leave you behind." Mother said, taking her hand.

"For now, though we must stay," Jenny said. "And tomorrow, Lieutenant Ashby will return for my answer to his proposal." What would she say? Ashby held their safety in his hands and was truly trying to offer protection, but surely the protection of a British officer was not what Father had in mind with the promise she'd made him.

What would Ashby's reaction be if she said no? She glanced at Andrew. How could she marry someone else when she loved this man so completely? But without Ashby's protection, she and Mother were closer to arrest every day. Marry Ashby and leave Andrew forever, or don't marry him and …

She held too many lives in her hands. Did she have the courage to save them all?

CHAPTER EIGHTEEN

(

J ENNY OPENED THE JAR CONTAINING the balm Lucy Carter had delivered the night before. Lifting the covers off Andrew's arms, she gently massaged the herbal remedy into his wounds. In his sleep, he protested at first, but as the mixture took effect, he quieted. He had awakened this morning long enough to eat a bit of porridge and drink some cider, but he had slept throughout the afternoon.

Every sound on the street below brought her to the window to see if Lieutenant Ashby had arrived for her answer. She rubbed her temples. How could she refuse him and keep Mother and herself safe? There was no way. She could not tease out a solution to this dilemma.

As Andrew settled into a deeper sleep, she paced the room.

"Jennifer, it will do no good to walk a rut into the floorboards." Mother sat at her embroidery, still stitching the same red poppy she had been on an hour ago.

"I am finding it difficult to sit still. Mother, what am I to do?"

They had stayed up into the early morning hours, keeping vigil over Andrew and discussing all possible options for dealing with Ashby. Jenny knew it was imperative to flee New York as soon as possible. Mother had refused to leave without her, though it was the perfect solution. Trying to escape with just Andrew would be far less conspicuous than with Mother and the entire household. Besides, Father's original plan had been to return to Boston in September, which was only a few days hence. Surely, their acquaintances would be aware of this, so it would appear they were simply following the original plan.

Mother bent her head over her sampler, though her fingers were idle. She, too, was teasing out solutions.

The knock on the door startled them both. Jenny clutched her waist. Listening to Mother's footsteps descend the staircase was like listening to a death knell. Andrew stirred at the noise. Sitting beside him, she took his hand. She caressed his forehead with her fingers.

"I love you, Andrew Wentworth."

Did one corner of his mouth lift? Just a bit? It was enough. It gave her strength to face this moment. She rose and headed toward the stairs.

Lieutenant Ashby was staring out onto the street when she entered the parlor. He stood, as always, as if at attention. Did he never relax? Hearing her enter, he turned. A crease etched between his brows melted away, and he smiled. "Good evening, Miss Sutton."

"Good evening, Lieutenant."

"Please, I've asked you to call me Nigel." His gaze held hers, his eyes warm, but did she detect uncertainty?

Was he unsure about her involvement with Montclair? Did he believe that she was at the church simply to pray for Father? The suspicion that colored his behavior when he escorted her home was lacking today. Perhaps she and Mother were safer than she'd thought. Her heart beat faster.

She sat in a chair. She wanted no opportunity for him to sit beside her.

He took the settee. "You appear weary. I hope the excitement of my proposal did not hinder your sleep last night."

"I appreciate your concern. I did have trouble sleeping last night." *But not due to excitement over your proposal.*

"I will not linger, for I would hate to disturb another evening's rest for you. I know ladies get engrossed in planning details of weddings." He smiled.

Sarie appeared with a tray of tea and cakes. She offered the refreshment to him, but he brushed her away like a fly. She turned to Jenny with the tray, blocking Ashby's view of her. Jenny bit her lip, her nostrils flaring. Sarie crossed her blue eyes. Jenny disguised her laugh with a cough.

"Are you well, Miss Sutton?" He rose.

"Yes," she choked out. She sipped her tea. "This tea will help the dryness in my throat." She smiled into the cup.

Until the seriousness at hand again struck her.

Ashby stood before her. She studied the floor since his proximity brought his body too close for her comfort. He dropped to one knee.

"I suppose I must do this properly. Miss Sutton, will you do me the honor of becoming my wife?"

For the last twenty-four hours, she had been dreading this moment. This was so wrong. It was Andrew, not Ashby, whom she'd dreamed of in this scene. It was love, not a threat, that caused a man to kneel before her asking for her hand. Her hands clutched the folds of her skirt so tightly that her knuckles were like white pebbles along the fabric. She could not feel her fingers to relax them.

If she only knew his true intentions. Did he truly care for her? Was this proposal based on the ardor he professed? Or was it a sort of blackmail? If so, she was cornered, like an animal in a trap. She had no choice. If she refused, she and Mother might hang.

"Miss Sutton?" He took her hands, squeezing them until she almost cried out.

She met his gaze. A soft smile played at his lips, his eyes searching. Perhaps he did care for her. But the harsh way he squeezed her hands sent a message.

He knew.

"Yes, Lieutenant Ashby, I will accept your proposal."

His eyes glittered at her, triumph shining through. "Jennifer."

Her name, from his lips, sounded discordant, nothing like the soft, loving endearment when Andrew whispered her name.

He swept her into his arms, his kiss harsh, his teeth bumping against hers. There was no tenderness, only conquest. He released her.

"We will post the banns together tomorrow."

She nodded, wanting to wipe her lips with her napkin.

He rose and bent over her hand. "I will call tomorrow morning to take you to St. Paul's."

His words brought gooseflesh to her arms. *How can I return to the place where Laurence Montclair was slain?*

Now, more than ever, she wanted to flee.

☾

Andrew's improvement overnight was remarkable. He had eaten more porridge at supper, drank a full mug of ale, and even nibbled some melon. A good night's sleep was the tonic he'd needed. When Jenny entered his room, he was propped against the pillows and Mathias was shaving him. At the sight of Jenny, he broke into a broad grin.

"Careful, Mr. Andrew. You smile like that again, and this razor gonna give you a big dimple along the side of yer face."

Jenny hurried to the bed and took his hand. "You look much stronger this morning."

Mathias wiped his face with the towel, gathered up the razor and bowl, and smiled at him. "Good ta see you lookin' so fine today." He nodded at Jenny and left.

She sat on the bed. This close, she could see the exhaustion in Andrew's pallid face, tiny lines etching worry in his brow. It would be some time before he could travel. She brushed his lips with hers. He lifted one hand to stroke her hair, but the exertion was too much, and he dropped his arm back to the blanket.

"Jenny."

How different her name sounded from his lips. Her belly tingled and warmth spread though her. She kissed his forehead, his cheek, his lips. "Beware, Andrew. When you are healed, I will have my way with you."

He smiled as a flash of passion gleamed in his eyes. Then he closed them and drifted off.

She laid her head on his chest. "Beware."

The knock on the door that she had dreaded all morning echoed through the house. She didn't move. She'd put this off as long as possible, but now she must put in writing her betrayal of him. She ran her finger along Andrew's arm beside the gash she had covered with ointment in the dawn hours. No sign of infection yet. At least something was going right. And he was stronger this morning. Soon he would be strong enough to travel.

"Jennifer." Mother stood in the doorway. "It's time."

Her body felt leaden as she tried to sit up. She held Andrew's hand for a moment. What she was about to do was not an act of infidelity to him; it was a duty to ensure their very survival. Yet, even to have her name connected to Ashby's seemed disloyal, to Andrew, to Father, to the Patriot cause. She shuddered.

"Jennifer."

"Coming, Mother." She rose, her attention lingering on Andrew's face. He no longer thrashed in his sleep. He no longer moaned in pain. But with what she was about to do, she might as well stab him in the heart.

☾

Lieutenant Ashby handed Jenny from the carriage, holding her elbow as they entered St. Paul's Chapel. She wanted to shake away from him. Before his proposal—and insinuation of his awareness about her Patriot sympathies—Ashby had been cordial and considerate. This morning, a coolness had crept into his demeanor, a severity into his attention.

Jenny's knees trembled as the two of them entered the

church. She averted her gaze from the spot where Montclair had been slain. But as they progressed down the aisle, Ashby stopped beside that very pew, turning to face it. She studied the floor.

"I find it interesting that I found you … ill in the church-yard around the time a man was murdered here yesterday. I know you are far too delicate to have committed the murder yourself." He let his words echo in the empty church. "But I suspect you might know something about the incident."

Her mind raced. He knew that she had seen Montclair, but he also knew she didn't kill him. Because he did. So, Ashby must have known that, rather than the Tory sympathizer he professed to be, Montclair had been working with the Sons of Liberty. To deny that she saw him would increase his suspicion that she was here to meet up with him, thus confirming her involvement in what he would consider treason.

"Please, Lieutenant …" She tried to move forward down the aisle.

He gripped her arm tighter. "You will call me Nigel."

"Please, Nigel." She swallowed against the building nausea. "I … I did see Mr. Montclair when I came into the church yesterday. As I told you, I came to pray for the repose of Father's soul. I was already distressed with grief." It wasn't difficult to feign this grief since she was already feeling lightheaded. "I only saw him from behind as I made my way to the front pew. As I was leaving I saw …" She clutched her lurching stomach. "I saw the blood, his staring eyes." She swayed. "I ran outside and got sick. When you appeared, I was afraid I would be accused of the murder."

Another lie. Her life was becoming one lie after another.

His grasp lessened.

She stared at him. His stern gaze softened for a moment. Perhaps he believed her. Was she becoming that good at being deceitful? "Once I had lied to you, I didn't know how to extract myself from that untruth." *I am going to burn in hell.* But she had to convince him that she was not a spy. Even though she was.

At that moment, Pastor Farr emerged from the vestry. "Oh, there you are. What a happy occasion during such difficult times." He glanced at the pew beside them. His cheery voice grated on her ears. "Come with me, and we shall prepare to announce your banns of marriage." Despite his portly size, his movements were quick and smooth as he strode to them. He took her arm, leading her away from the site of the murder toward the vestry. Candlelight reflected off his glasses as he smiled down at her. "Yes, a pleasant task in the midst of such sorrow."

Pastor Farr had them fill out the document that would officially announce their engagement.

The priest's gaze settled on her as she took the quill pen from him. Did he also know of her parents' allegiance? She stared at the document. Finally, she lifted the pen. It felt cold in her hand, and the cold traveled up her arm to her heart with a chilling self-loathing. When she finished signing, she met his gaze. Sorrow. Indeed, he knew of her parent's allegiance. But he must wonder at her reason for this marriage.

Ashby signed his name with a flourish, his signature sharp points and strident strokes, as rigid as he.

"I would like to meet with each of you—separately—to discuss, well, marital issues." Pastor Farr winked at Ashby.

Her stomach flipped.

Ashby bowed his compliance. "At your service."

"Miss Sutton, I would like to meet with you this afternoon."

So it begins. Instruction on how to be the wife of British Lieutenant Nigel Ashby. While Andrew lay deathly ill in her home.

€

Pastor Farr met Jenny at the door of the rectory. As she followed him into the parlor, she inhaled the comforting scent of beeswax candles and starched linen. Sunlight dappled the Oriental rug on the parlor floor, choreographing a dance between the reds and oranges. Dreading this meeting, she sat in the chair he indicated and steeled herself for an unpleasant lesson on Ephesians 5 and the requisite obedience of a wife.

He smiled at her as the housekeeper entered with a tea service. After pouring a cup for each of them, she quietly departed. Everything in this manse was quiet: the ticking of the long-case clock, its muted chiming on the half hour, the footfalls of the housekeeper as she retreated along the wood floor to the back of the house. Even the priest's smile was quiet in his somber face. Gone was the boisterous humor of the morning.

They sat in silence. Was he waiting for her to speak? Where did his sympathies lie? Would this marriage preparation trap her into revealing her alliance with the Patriot cause?

"Miss Sutton." His voice was quiet. "Are you well?"

A sudden urge to burst into tears swelled within her. Taking out her handkerchief, she wiped her brimming eyes and pressed the linen to her nose, stalling, trying to compose herself. Let him think it was due to Father's death. How she wanted to pour out her heart. What was it about Pastor Farr that homed in on her vulnerability? The air of serenity that surrounded him like a warm cape? His gentle gaze that, when searching hers, reached into her soul? His tenderness reminded her of Mr. Gates's ministering to her aboard the *Destiny*. But Mother's voice was clear in her head.

Trust no one.

Reining in her desire to reveal her distress, she took a deep breath. "I am well, thank you, Pastor Farr."

He nodded, allowing the silence to envelop them.

Damn. He will wear me down with this serenity. "Mother and I are still in mourning. It is a short time since Father died."

"I saw you yesterday."

She jumped. "Excuse me?"

"I saw you. Outside in the churchyard. Vomiting into my juniper bush."

Her face flamed.

"I saw Lieutenant Ashby join you. He came from the side door of the church. A short time later I discovered Laurence's body. You were the only people I saw about after my meeting with Laurence."

"I did not kill Mr. Montclair." She choked the words out. Was the decision to be whether she would be hanged as a murderer or hanged as a traitor? Is that what her life had come down to now?

"Of course you didn't."

So, he, too, knew it was Ashby. And both of them were powerless to prove it or call him to account for his action. They were at the mercy of the British army. She sighed. Was it relief or frustration? Perhaps both.

"Do you wish to marry Lieutenant Ashby?"

Her nostrils flared. "No."

His gentle smile returned. "I thought not." He stroked his chin. "I will post the marriage banns—indeed, I must. Meanwhile, you must devise a plan to escape this."

She must tread carefully, for he could be drawing her in to reveal information that would prove sedition.

"The British are watching our house. Lieutenant Ashby, in particular, has been skulking around at night."

"Miss Sutton, I, too, have received and passed on, shall we say, items other than herbal remedies from Laurence. I will miss my dear friend and mentor. Your mother will confirm her trust in me in matters of loyalty.

"Now, we have spent a sufficient amount of time to have allowed me to impress upon you St. Paul's directions on how a wife must act." He pressed his hands into the leather arms of his chair, lifting his bulk to standing. "I suggest you speak with your mother for assurance that, upon our next visit, you will be at ease during our 'marital' instruction. In the meantime, I will ponder this dilemma."

Her face flushed at his awareness that she didn't yet trust him. But hadn't a supposed minister betrayed—no, killed— Father?

"Fear not, for it is difficult to know whom to trust nowadays. What you need to decide is how far to take this. Will you, indeed, marry Lieutenant Ashby? How will that serve you and your mother?"

She shuddered. Living as a British officer's wife—what hell that would be. How ironic that the only way to protect Mother was to betray Father. But how could they flee now? The trip would kill Andrew, and she could not leave him behind again.

For now, she had to go through with the marriage to Ashby. Any other choice would cost them all their lives.

CHAPTER NINETEEN

A NDREW TRIED TO FEED HIMSELF, but the spoon wobbled as he navigated it toward his lips. After two attempts resulting in more broth down his shirt than in his mouth, he dropped the spoon in the bowl and his head back on the pillow. Was he more hungry or tired? He didn't know. Hearing someone enter, he cracked one eye expecting to see Sarie.

Instead, Jenny rushed to his bedside and kissed his forehead.

"Look at you. I leave for an hour and you perk up like a daffodil after a rain shower."

How could just the sound of her voice invigorate him so? He grinned and took her hand. "Good day, Jenny. Where were you off to this afternoon?"

Her smile didn't fade, but her eyes clouded over. What was distressing her?

"You were sleeping so soundly, I went to church to pray for your health." She bustled about, smoothing his covers, but a blush reddened her face.

The burst of strength she had inspired seeped away. Something was wrong.

"You need to eat more." She took the bowl he held.

"I'm weary."

Her hands were warm against his arms and chest as she inspected his wounds. He tried not to flinch as she lightly touched the ugly rope burns that blistered where his wrists had been bound. Though he couldn't see them all, his wounds—the long gashes etched along his torso, around his sides to his back where barnacles had gouged his skin— still burned like a well-stoked fire. When he'd arrived, he couldn't move his arms, so he was exhausted with the simple effort of feeding himself.

She took the bowl and spoon.

"I shall feed you." She bent toward him. "I need to bring you back to full health so we can fully enjoy each other's company." She gave a wicked wink.

He smiled, easing back against the pillows. He wanted to pull her back with him, feel her body against his. But even in her seductive wink, her eyes had lost their usual luster.

She offered a spoonful of broth, and he sipped it. He closed his eyes for a moment then looked at her.

"What are you hiding from me, Jen?"

She paused, the spoon halfway to his mouth. She moved it to his lips. "Why do you ask that?" She lifted one shoulder, cocking her head.

"Because you are an ineffectual liar. Your eyes widen, and you blush. See? There you are."

She narrowed her eyes, but she could do nothing to hide the blush.

"Tell me." He stopped her hand in mid-air. "Trust me."

He tried to hold her gaze, but she looked toward the window, biting her lip.

"You do that, too. You bite your lip."

"Damn." She dropped the spoon into the bowl.

Lucy Carter entered carrying a basket with assorted jars and bottles. "Good day, Miss Sutton, Mr. Wentworth. Time to tend to your wounds."

As Lucy busied herself, preparing an ointment, Jenny rose, taking the bowl and spoon.

Andrew held her wrist. "You need to be honest with me." His voice was low. "If we can't be honest with each other, all our professions of love have been false."

She recoiled.

He squeezed her hand. "And I don't believe they have been."

She glanced at Lucy, who was occupied with her task.

"We will talk later. I promise."

"I survived only because of your love, Jenny. It was your face, your voice that saved my life. Nothing you can say can destroy me now."

She turned away, and his heart sank.

☾

Lieutenant Ashby sat beside Jenny on the settee. He eased back comfortably, more relaxed than his usual rigid posture. He balanced his brandy snifter on the arm of the sofa, his other arm brushing against hers.

She clasped her hands in her lap, fingernails digging into her palms. She wanted to run out of the room. She wanted to scream at him to leave. Here Nigel Ashby sat, as if he was entitled to everything he saw, including her, when his fellow Tories had killed Father. They had torn the flesh from Andrew, who lay in the room above them, fighting back from near death. Oh, what she wouldn't give to see this bastard tossed into the water and sliced to ribbons on the bottom of a boat.

"I hope your meeting with Pastor Farr was agreeable this afternoon."

"Yes. Yes, it was. And yours?"

"Most agreeable." He reached for her hand, breaking it from her grip. "Now that we have set the wedding date for four weeks hence, we shall need to begin preparations." He looked around the room. "This house will be quite adequate, I think. There is no need for you to move out or for me to remain billeted in someone else's home. Perhaps you have a room where I can move my things?" He glanced at the ceiling.

Her heart pounded. Surely, he would not ask to see the rooms now? Putting Andrew at his mercy?

"We will prepare a room for you. It will take some time."

"Perhaps you could show me, even though it's not ready."

He smiled. "Perhaps my enthusiasm is premature, but I want you to know how happy you've made me. I would be most grateful to see what's upstairs."

Did he know about Andrew? Was he playing a game with her?

"I would be more comfortable if we readied the room first ... Nigel." His name stuck in her throat. But he smiled again when she said it.

Mother entered. "Good evening, Lieutenant."

He stood and bowed over her hand. "Good evening, Mrs. Sutton."

"Nigel was just discussing the idea of bringing some of his personal items over as the wedding nears. He wanted to see a room he might use for storage."

Mother's brows shot up. "Oh. Oh, my." She played with the amethyst pendant resting against her bodice. "Well, we would need to prepare a room for you."

Something banged on the floor above them. Then another crash.

She caught Mother's anxious frown.

Ashby jumped up and started for the stairs. Jenny grabbed his arm.

"It must be Sarie cleaning. I'll go check."

"It could be someone injured or an intruder. I insist on accompanying you."

Mother stood in his path. "I believe Sarie is up there. She will call if she requires help."

Another noise thumped above them.

"I have pledged to keep you safe. I will honor my duty." His eyes slid from Mother to her.

"There is no need ..."

But he brushed past Mother, who stood gaping, as he

strode toward the stairway.

Gathering her skirts, Jenny tried to keep up with Ashby's long strides up the steps. As they reached the hallway, Sarie was closing the door to Andrew's room, her eyes widened when she saw Ashby. Jenny's breath came in short gasps as she ran ahead to block the door.

"So sorry, Miss Jenny. I dropped the basin and it smashed in two. When I picked it up, it fell again and broke to pieces. I'll fetch a broom to clean it up."

"Thank you, Sarie." She turned to Ashby. "Well, we are safe in our home after all. No reason to investigate any further."

He stood close, towering over her. His breath tickled the curls that framed her face. "No, but since we are upstairs, why not look at the room you had in mind for me? Was it this one?" He stepped toward Andrew's room.

She stepped in front of him. "This is most inappropriate. You should not be above stairs with me at all."

He cracked open the door then peered down at her. "You are to be my wife. If your reputation is sullied, it is no matter, since you will not have to present yourself for marriage to anyone else." He pushed her aside and threw open the door.

If he hadn't been suspicious before, he was now. He would certainly arrest Andrew—and Andrew would hang.

Jenny reached toward the pistol at Ashby's hip. She could shoot him. If that's what it took to save Andrew, that's what she would have to do. From liar to spy to murderer. *What have I become?*

But the bed was empty. She could see it had been hastily made, but perhaps Ashby wouldn't notice. She drew back her hand.

Where was Andrew?

Ashby scanned the room, his brows drawn down in confusion. He turned to Jenny, searching her face.

She stared back at him, arching her right brow as if to say,

"What were you expecting?"

He examined the room again.

Sarie entered with a broom.

"Let us return to the parlor so Sarie can finish her task."

His lips were a taut, grim line. His flinty gaze bore into her.

She turned toward the stairs, praying he would follow. Andrew was in that room somewhere. Under the bed? In the armoire? That would be a tight fit with the clothes hanging in it. *Please let Ashby follow rather than search further.*

When she had descended a few steps, his footsteps stomped behind her. She let out a sigh, realizing she'd been holding her breath since he'd opened that door.

☾

Beneath the bed, Andrew lay still, holding his breath. He'd been a fool to try to get out of bed unassisted. When he'd heard that damned British officer's voice in the room below, he couldn't keep himself from trying to get to Jenny. Surely, he'd just added bruises from his fall to his other injuries. But none of those injuries would destroy him. Not like what he'd just heard.

She is to marry that British officer? He exhaled a hot, steaming breath. Could Jenny betray him like this? Could he have misunderstood that rotten lobsterback—what was his name—Ashby? Could he have misunderstood what Ashby had said? No, he was sure of what he'd heard.

None of his wounds hurt as deeply as Jenny's betrayal. All these days she'd spoken of love and devotion, and the whole time … Were they engaged when he saw her with him at the apothecary shop? The night they delivered the message to Montclair? Her greeting when she first saw him was passionate—had it all been a lie?

He clenched his fists as his gut squirmed with anger and despair. It would have been better if he'd died at the hands of the Tories. *Oh, Jenny.*

Sarie's face appeared as she knelt beside the bed, and she offered her hand to help Andrew slide out. The gashes on his back reopened, and he felt the blood seeping into his nightshirt. His weakened arms grew limp as he tried to scuttle along the floor without making any noise. The coppery taste of blood oozed in his mouth as he bit his lip against the pain.

Mathias entered and hurried over to lift him to standing.

The room spun out of control. Everything went black save for pinpricks of light swirling in a crazy dance. He reached out to find support, but only air filled his grasp, and his knees gave out.

"I've got you. Don't worry, son." Mathias's voice echoed as if they were in a cavern. It was the last thing he remembered until the acrid odor of ammonia shocked him to consciousness as Sarie waved smelling salts beneath his nose. He pushed her hand away.

Jenny sat beside him. "Andrew. Oh, my God. Andrew." Jenny lay her face against his. Sitting up, she wiped beads of sweat off his forehead.

He turned his head away and pulled his hand from hers. She picked up the tincture of laudanum from the bedside table and tried to spoon a dose of the remedy into his mouth.

"No." He tried turning away, but the effort was too great. She administered the medicine, and he sank into the pillows. His brows creased as he fought the pain. He studied her face. Her eyes didn't glow as they had, she did not smile, there was no dimple to entice him. He looked away. Had everything been a lie? He closed his eyes.

She gasped. "Oh, my God. You heard what Ashby said."

He kept his eyes closed.

"Andrew, let me explain—"

"You are to be his wife?" Overcome with exhaustion, he could barely form the words.

"No, Andrew, no."

He lost focus as he drifted off with the effects of the medicine.

"Andrew, please listen."

Her voice sounded like she floated away. Then blackness.

CHAPTER TWENTY

❧

"WE MUST MOVE HIM. ASHBY knows Andrew is here. Mother, I swear he knows." Jenny twisted the handkerchief in her hands as she looked out the window into the evening.

"I believe you're right, but where can we take him?"

Jenny studied the street. Was Ashby out there now? Watching and waiting for the opportunity to return for Andrew? Clouds darkened the sky, but it would be wiser to wait for nightfall before moving him.

"Mother, did you get a message out about the risk of approaching our home?"

"Yes, I did. What plan is hatching in that brain of yours?"

"After sunset, I'll fetch Ephraim. He and Mathias can put Andrew in the carriage and take him to the apothecary. With Mr. Montclair's death, if the British had been watching it before, they no longer have a reason. Lucy can tend him, probably better than I can here. Andrew would be safe there until he can return to Boston with us."

"Jennifer, it could be weeks. Ashby will keep a close watch on you now. Andrew might not be strong enough to travel before your ..."

"Wedding day." She breathed deeply. "I know." She pivoted to Mother. "But what choice do we have? Either we chance moving him or Ashby will have him hanged." She rubbed her throbbing temples as blood pulsed there. Her limbs prickled with the urge to move, to act, to do *something* to keep Andrew safe. Mother's reasoning was logical, but logic didn't work in the world in which they now lived. Risk, lies, menace were the words of the day. She struck her palm with her fist. It was time.

"I'm going to tell Mathias to ready the mare. As soon as it is dark, I will ride to the Carters'."

"It will be dangerous."

"I know, Mother. Everything in our lives has become dangerous."

❦

Dressed in the clothes she wore the night Andrew first came to her, Jenny mounted the mare. She had secured her hair tighter tonight to keep it from tumbling out from beneath the slouch hat. A light rain fell. Good. It would discourage people from being about.

"Let's go, Aggie." She clicked her tongue and the mare walked along the side of the house toward the dark street. Turning in the direction of the main street, she nudged the mare to a trot.

"Where do you think you're going?" A rider rode out from behind the trees across from her house, approached, and blocked her way.

Terrified, she reined Aggie in. Expecting to see the scarlet coat of a British soldier to her left, she was puzzled to face a tattered brown jacket. Her gaze traveled up the buttons of the coat to peer into its owner's face.

Martin Wirth. He rested a rifle on his shoulder, using only one hand to handle his horse. A large steed to accommodate a large man.

"Mr. Wirth." She looked around for his brother. Abel appeared from the shadows on another large mount. "And Mr. Wirth."

"Now, where in God's great earth are ya' going? And dressed like a lad?"

She looked from brother to brother. They had already saved Andrew's life once. Perhaps they could help again. She explained the situation.

Without any consultation, as one they turned their horses toward her house. Jenny scrutinized the shadows but saw no one watching them.

Tying up their horses, they followed her into the house. Mother's frightened face met them at the door. "I heard you in the yard, Jennifer. What is wrong—" She clutched her shawl at the sight of the two men. Then her face broke into a grin. "The Wirth brothers—how fortunate."

The men ducked their way into the door, removing their hats.

"Good evenin', Mrs. Sutton." Abel made a half bow.

"Mrs. Sutton." Martin did the same.

Jenny frowned at them, curious. "What brought you to our house at such a convenient time?"

The brothers glanced at each other, shifting uncomfortably.

"We decided to hang about a bit, seein' as how Andrew was in such a bad way," Martin said. "We didn't think …we didn't know …we knew if he died here, you ladies would need to leave and quick. And we kept seein' that lobsterback lurkin' about." He looked at Jenny. "Lucky for you miss, he must'a gotten hungry or bored, because he was there until about five minutes before you came out."

Jenny shuddered.

"Jennifer was on her way to the apothecary. We need to move Andrew immediately because 'that lobsterback,' as you call him, seems to know Andrew is here."

The men nodded.

"You have a cart?"

"Yes."

"We'll take him."

Jenny slumped against the wall. She remembered how heavy Andrew had been when they had tried to lift him back into bed. Even Mathias had struggled to heft his weight. For these two, it would be like carrying a large doll. Hadn't they brought him here all the way from Hart Island?

"Thank you both." Her voice broke.

Martin patted her shoulder. "Don't fret, Miss Sutton. We'll get him to the apothecary safely."

☙

Lucy Carter led them to the rooms above the apothecary where Laurence Montclair had lived. She hesitated on the landing, wiping her tears with the edge of her apron. "This way." She held the candle high.

The Wirth brothers propped Andrew between them, his toes not even reaching the floor. His head dropped forward, swaying with their movement. When they reached the bed, Martin took Andrew's weight while Abel swung his legs up onto the mattress. Jenny pulled the covers over his trembling body, then took his hand.

Lucy returned shortly with a small vial. Popping off the cork, she dribbled some on a spoon and slipped it into Andrew's mouth. He coughed, spitting some back at her, spattering her shawl. She chuckled. "He's still got fight left in him. Leave him to me, Miss Sutton. We'll get his strength back."

"Thank you, Mrs. Carter." She lifted her gaze to the two men. "Thank you both." Her shoulders dropped as exhaustion—and relief—seeped through every muscle and joint.

After Lucy escorted the men downstairs, Jenny scanned the bedroom. She had known Laurence Montclair so briefly. It seemed intrusive, almost voyeuristic, to be viewing his personal belongings like this. His brush and comb lay beside the ewer and basin on his dresser, each item carefully placed before he left the morning he was murdered. She shivered. All the furniture was walnut, the counterpane and curtains, crisp, the linen, ivory. The four-poster bed sat positioned near the window to catch the morning sun's rays from the east.

The window! She snapped the shutters closed. *Dear God, please let us have been unobserved tonight.* She breathed deeply to quell the panic rising within.

Andrew shifted, groaning in his sleep.

She returned to his side. "You must get well, my love." A tear escaped, a tiny rivulet down her cheek. "We must keep you safe."

Lucy appeared in the doorway. "I will stay with him tonight. It's best if you return home."

She nodded. But how could she leave him?

"Miss Sutton? The men are waiting to escort you home now."

She rose, still holding his hand. Finally, she released it and started for the door. Looking back one last time, she stopped. Even in sleep, a crease formed between his brows. Sadness or pain?

☾

True to his word, Lieutenant Ashby arrived in the morning, hoisting a trunk of his clothing. When Jenny saw the trunk, she folded her arms, drawing her blue shawl around her shoulders. She had never imagined this marriage would actually take place, but seeing his belongings in her house brought the truth of it. He started toward the stairs, his expression eager with expectation of what—or whom—he would discover up there.

Jenny blocked his way. "We are not married yet, Nigel. It would be inappropriate for you to be abovestairs before we are."

He looked at her as if noting her presence for the first time, scrutinized the top of the stairway, then snorted softly in frustration.

Mother appeared beside her. "Jennifer is correct. I am sure as an officer in King George's army, you would never want to appear crude or cause your fiancée to appear compromised."

He inhaled deeply, planting his feet in an unyielding stance. "My apology, although my presence there last night seems to have set a precedent."

"Your presence there last night was on your insistence because you thought we were in danger." Sarie appeared at the top of the stairs, holding a broom. Mother glanced up at her, then back at him. "You can clearly see the only danger we may be in is from too much dust."

He bowed, but upon rising, his face was stone. "However, I cannot leave this heavy trunk here for you ladies to grapple with, so I will make haste to deposit it upstairs, leaving your reputation unsullied."

He pushed past them and mounted the stairs. Sarie allowed him to pass into the room where Andrew had recently lain. His footsteps were heavy as he tromped over the wood floor. The door of the armoire slammed, the scrape of his boots signaled his search under the bed.

"*Damn.*"

Mother smothered a laugh, but Jenny's heart raced at the thought of what would have happened had Andrew still been there. She listened as he opened the doors to her bedroom and Mother's. She balled her fists in fury.

Once he'd descended the stairs, she rushed at him, thrusting her face toward his. "You take inappropriate liberties, sir. You have no right to search our house."

"I have every right under the order of King George." He took her hand and pulled her closer, his breath caressing her face. "My tender feelings toward you grow more fervent every day, Miss Sutton, but remember, I am an officer of the Crown and I must perform my duty. However, as my wife, you will be protected."

Mother stepped between them. "But she is not your wife yet, Lieutenant Ashby. It would be best if you leave now."

"And I offer my protection to you, madam. You would be wise to be grateful." He bowed, planted his hat on his head, and left.

Mother placed an arm around her. "Are you all right, darling?"

Jenny nodded, wiping on her skirt the hand he'd just held. "He's a bastard."

"Generally, I would punish you for that language, but instead, I'll praise you for your accuracy. Though I believe his fondness for you is sincere."

"Be that as it may, he knows our lives hinge on his good graces. He is playing cat and mouse with us. I believe he knew Andrew—or someone we were protecting—was here last night. Which will win the day? His fondness for me or his duty to King George? We must leave as soon as possible."

"Jennifer, perhaps we should leave Andrew in Carters' care. I believe he will be safe there and—"

"No. I left him once. I can never do that again. And I can no longer live with lies."

CHAPTER TWENTY-ONE

A NDREW STARED AT THE LEAVES dancing in the tree outside his window. Birdsong filled the air, but nature's beauty could not assuage the despair that held him. For a week, he had grappled with the knowledge that Jenny was engaged to a British officer. How could that be? Were her sympathies swayed in so short a time? Could her heart be stolen from him in the time it had taken him to reach Manhattan? But what of their brief times together since his arrival? His head ached with confusion.

"Jenny." Her name escaped his lips in a moan as he dropped his head back on the pillow, his eyelids heavy. He remembered the joy on her face the night they reunited on the road in front of her house. Had she already fallen in love with Ashby then? Were her kisses and declarations of love all lies?

But he could tell when she was lying. How she blushed— even in the darkness he had sensed her face redden. He thought it was passion, passion for him. Perhaps it was because she was caught unaware. And she bit her lip when she lied. He snorted. She'd had no time to bite her lip as he was covering them with kisses. Kisses she'd returned with equal passion.

And her mission was to Laurence Montclair's to deliver intelligence within the Patriot spy network. It didn't make sense. Why was she working with Montclair if she was in love with a British officer? Unless ... was she passing information on to Ashby?

His stomach twisted at the thought. Not his Jenny. She would never ... why, she had ridden beside him to save Jonathon's life. She risked her own life to draw British soldiers away from Brentwood Manor when they were about to kill him.

Not his Jenny.

He smiled, hopeful. Then he remembered Ashby's voice.

You are to be my wife. If your reputation is sullied, it is no matter, since you will not have to present yourself for marriage to anyone else.

He had ridden for weeks to arrive in New York and keep Jenny safe. He had dreamed of her every night, his mind filled with her every day. She was his love. His life. And now she belonged to another. He threw his arm over his eyes to block the thought of a life without her, a thought that drained his will to live.

If Jenny was this fickle, he never knew her at all. But without her, life made little sense. He shifted to his side. Wallowing like this would help nothing. He was surrounded by the belongings of a man who gave his life for liberty. Andrew would do the same.

Outside a troop of soldiers marched past the apothecary shop. The captain boomed commands. "Company, halt. Present arms."

Metal clattered as they shifted their guns.

Was Ashby there? Just below his window? A viable target? He had killed men before—could he kill again?

The troop moved on and the street returned to its usual bustle.

He tried to sit up, but the movement stretched the scabs forming on his wounds, his arms wobbled beneath him. *Damn!* He had to build his strength. His only goal now was to fight the British ... fight them to his death.

❧

With Ashby finding any excuse to stop by the house, Jenny had been unable to visit Andrew until today—almost two weeks since the Wirth brothers had moved him. Not being able to tend to him and know how he was feeling had been agonizing. So had worrying about his reaction to her engagement.

As she climbed the stairs, her heart quickened. What state would she find him in? Upon entering his room, she stopped, and her hand flew to her mouth. The last time she'd seen him he lay helplessly in bed, unable even to feed himself. Now, he was sitting in a chair, reading a book. His face brightened at the sight of her, then the light disappeared from his face.

"Andrew. You look so well." She wanted to jump up and down with the joy of seeing him so hale. She rushed to him, taking his hand in hers. She bent to kiss his lips, but he turned his head. "I need to explain something."

He stared out the window.

"Andrew, please look at me."

"When were you going to tell me of your engagement?" He glared at her.

"No, Andrew—"

"Apparently while I was riding as quickly as I could to find you, keep you safe in this God-forsaken city, you were cozying up to another. And a lobsterback at that." His voice rose in fury. "How could you do this? How could you throw away our love, our fight against the British? Everything we believe in?" He threw the book to the floor, his body quaking with rage. And did she see fear through his angry tears?

"Andrew, please let me—" She knelt beside his chair.

"Is everything all right? Andrew, are you in pain?" Lucy's high-pitched voice preceded her into the room. She skidded to a halt, panting, as she flew through the door. "Oh, excuse me." She nodded to them then backed out closing the door behind her.

How inappropriate for the two of us to be secluded away behind the closed door of a bedroom. Jenny shook her head at the sudden incongruent thought. If Ashby knew she was here ...

The pain in Andrew's face tore at her heart. He frowned and turned his head to stare out the window again.

A clang sounded from below.

Andrew looked down at her. "You should leave."

"Yes, she should." Nigel Ashby's voice was soft.

Jenny leapt to her feet.

Rising, Andrew searched for his pistol, but he staggered and reached for the back of the chair.

Ashby stood at the door, ramrod straight. His nostrils flared as he strode to her, wrenched her arm, and pulled her to his chest. Though his face was a thundercloud, his eyes were filled with sadness. "I've tried to warn you, but you seem hell-bent on throwing away your life." He glared at Andrew, then at her. "So, your heart has been spoken for. Never mind. Once he is gone, your heart will be free to love me."

"I will never love you." Jenny yanked her arm away.

Andrew's face was dark with rage, his jaw set like stone. He stumbled as he stepped toward him.

"Still weak? Well, I have just the place for you to gain your strength before you hang. Andrew Wentworth, you are under arrest for treason to King George III."

"No!" Her scream was primal, ripped from her gut. She blocked his path to Andrew.

He pushed past Jenny and stalked to the chair. Seizing Andrew's arm, he hauled him toward the door.

Andrew groaned, his teeth clenched against the pain.

"No," Jenny cried again. "I will marry you. I will do whatever you want. Just, please, let Andrew go."

Ashby scoffed into her face. "Don't whimper. It doesn't befit you. You will marry me and do whatever I want whether I arrest him or kill him on the spot."

He jerked Andrew around and half-carried him to the

door. He turned back to her.

"Our banns are posted, remember, my dear? You are already mine."

CHAPTER TWENTY-TWO

"THERE, THERE, MISS SUTTON. HE is a horrible one." Lucy sniffled and wiped her handkerchief across her eyes, then kneaded the tight muscles in Jenny's shoulders.

"Thank you, Lucy." All Jenny could think of was how to save Andrew. And Mother. The one thing that stood in her way was her fiancé.

Lucy wiped her tears again. "It's just too much. First Mr. Montclair, then Andrew, and now that evil man has trapped you." She crossed the room and picked up the brass mortar that lay against the floorboards. "I tried to warn you." She held up the brass bowl.

Jenny nodded, remembering the clang she'd heard just before Ashby entered. "Thank you, Mrs. Carter." Oh, that she had been more aware of the warning. But could Andrew have moved fast enough to hide? She thought not.

Lucy rubbed her shoulders again, then turned to the shelves, running her finger along the labeled drawers. "I suspect sleep might elude you. Aha. This will be perfect." She withdrew an amber bottle and poured sweet-smelling oil into a small vial. "Oil of lavender. Rub it on your wrists and temples to help you sleep."

"Thank you." Jenny went to the window and studied the street. "I hope you will not be bothered by Ashby. After all, you worked for Mr. Montclair and housed and cared for

Andrew."

Lucy glanced toward the back room where Ephraim and Zachariah were inventorying stock. "Oh, do not fret. Mr. Carter will look after us. He is a good man." She smiled weakly and blinked fear away when she met Jenny's gaze.

"Yes, he is a good man." Since the incident in front of Fraunces Tavern, Ephraim had jumped to do Jenny's bidding whenever she came into the shop. She looked up and down the street again. "Do you know where Mathias is? He was to wait for me with the carriage."

"I haven't seen him since that lobsterback arrived." Lucy joined her at the window. "No sign of him out there."

Jenny shifted with unease. "I'll walk home. If he returns, please tell him I've taken the usual route. Perhaps he will catch up with me."

"Of course." Again, a flicker of fear in her eyes. "Mr. Carter could drive you home."

Jenny weighed the awkwardness of a drive with Mr. Carter against the possibility of encountering Ashby. "Yes. That would be very kind."

"You take care, Miss Sutton," Lucy said, laying a hand on her arm.

She covered Lucy's hand with her own and felt her trembling. "You as well, Lucy."

She checked the street for Mathias again, fighting back an ominous shiver.

&

Ephraim Carter offered his hand to Jenny, helping her onto the wagon. He did not meet her gaze.

She kept as close to her edge of the seat as possible. The seat squeaked, tilting and bouncing back as he climbed up from the other side of the wagon and settled in beside her.

For a while, they rode in silence through the bustling street. Jenny twisted the corner of her shawl, twining it between her fingers.

"I would never hurt you, Miss Sutton." Ephraim's low voice carried the weight of remorse. "I would never hurt anyone. I don't usually drink that much. We was celebrating my friend's good fortune. He'd just bought a small farm. He kept buyin' and pourin', and I, well, I kept drinkin'." He scrubbed the stubble on his chin. "Bah. I didn't know my own name that night." He wiped his sleeve across his nose. "I'm so ashamed. I hope you'll find it in your heart to forgive me. Me and my friends. I ain't had a chance to ask you before."

His mention of that night resurrected the fear she'd felt, but it was fleeting. She felt no fear here, beside him, now. She wavered between sympathy and anger. His drawn face and downcast eyes were evidence of his sincerity, but she could not let him off so easily. "If it had not been me— some young girl, someone's sister, or mother, or daughter— you might have followed through. That girl's life would have been ruined."

He was silent for a while then made a choking sound. He cleared his voice. "Don't think I haven't considered that myself. I have. Ever night since. I don't know what I can do to atone for that sin—for sin it was no matter I never went through … well, you know."

Now Jenny was silent.

"I don't blame ya'. I don't deserve your forgiveness. But I do ask that ya' never tell my Lucy … or my boy." Now his voice did crack.

Jenny laid a hand on his arm. "I promise you, Mr. Carter. I will never tell Lucy or Zachariah. What purpose would it serve but to break their hearts?"

"Thank you, Miss Sutton." His voice rose. Then he took out a handkerchief and blew his nose heartily.

Jenny believed he would have hugged her in that moment, the relief in his voice was so palpable.

"And I forgive you, Mr. Carter. I believe you truly are repentant."

He wiped at his nose again. "Thank you." A whisper. He sent her a sideways glance. "And you know, I am here whenever you need me."

"Yes, I know that."

He gave her a half-smile, then nodded and flicked the reins.

They pulled up to her house. As Ephraim helped Jenny down, she noticed the door to the carriage house was ajar. Was that the wheel to the carriage? Why had Mathias abandoned her at the apothecary and returned home?

"That's strange," she murmured. She walked toward the structure and called out. "Mathias?" Pushing the door open, she stepped back and screamed.

Mathias was sprawled in the driver's seat, eyes bulging out, mouth agape, blood seeping into his white cotton shirt.

❦

Andrew lay on the filthy blanket that covered a pile of rancid straw. He kept his breath shallow, attempting not to gag at the stench in the gaol from unwashed bodies, human waste, and utter despair. A thin stream of daylight filtered through the bars in the window high in the wall, high enough that he had to stand on tiptoes to see outside, but not high enough to block the view of the gallows from which traitors were hanged.

Standing on tiptoe, he grasped the bars and craned his neck to watch any activity, other than building a new scaffold, in the area. Along the green, farmers sold corn, squash, and apples. Children interrupted a game of ninepins on the lawn to throw rotten produce at a man in the stocks. Women strolled under umbrellas shading them from the early September sun. Life went on as usual beyond these bars. But within, men and women awaited sentencing, or worse.

When his calves quivered from the effort, he took one last deep breath of fresh air from the window, then resumed standing. The odor in his cell was as repulsive as the gruel that made up his meals. Visitors were welcome to bring the imprisoned food at any time, and Lucy Carter had been providing meals for him, which he devoured, hell-bent on regaining his strength. But he had not seen Jenny in the week he'd been locked up.

Despite the dire circumstances and the putrid surroundings, he held on to hope. Hope that he could find revenge on Ashby, who took any opportunity to taunt him about the mere days until Jenny became the bastard's wife. His cruel jeers were a side of Ashby that Andrew was certain he'd never revealed to Jenny. Else she would never agree to marry him … would she?

He had to get out of here. A hundred escape plans had run through his head each day as he lay on the straw, watching the sun travel across his wall and descend into sunset. He refused to yield. Even if he were killed attempting to escape, what did it matter?

He grasped the bars of the window again and shook them. They didn't budge. He had to find a way.

Behind him, a bark of laughter.

"Do you really intend to rip those bars out of the wall, Wentworth?" Ashby peered through the small barred window in the cell door, eating an apple. *Crunch.* "Are you going to escape to save your fair maiden?" He studied his fingernails. "Which begs the question, is she still a fair maiden? No matter, I will discover that in a week's time when we are married. If she is not, she will be punished. Oh, don't worry—I will comfort her after that. She will—"

Andrew lunged at him. He thrust his face toward the bars. "Shut up, you bastard."

Ashby snorted. "How brave. And how strong. Much stronger than the day I came and snatched you from your woman's arms. You almost fainted like a girl. How are you going to rescue her, you weak-kneed, dandy prat?"

Andrew scowled at him. He straightened, determined not to let Ashby see his despair.

"Watch your back, Ashby. Your undoing will come from where you least expect it."

He was rewarded with a flicker of doubt that flashed over Ashby's face before he quickly concealed it.

"You'll be hanged the day after my wedding. I want your last night to be spent imagining the wonders I will be showing your lover." He tossed the apple core into the cell. "Enjoy your dinner."

Andrew slumped to the floor. He would find a way.

☾

Again, Jenny couldn't concentrate on Pastor Farr's words. She'd had trouble the previous week when he had prayed at Mathias's grave, beside the minister who served the black free and enslaved people. Since his death, Sarie and Isaac wandered around the house, balancing grief and fear because they were unsure why Mathias had been murdered.

But Jenny knew. Ashby. If she told them what she suspected, they would tremble every time he appeared—which occurred less often now that Andrew was in gaol. He had her in his control. The man she would marry. Instead of Andrew.

On this Sunday morning, she sat in the pew beside Mother, staring at her hands, hands that had caressed Andrew's face, traced the lines of his body. She tried to block the image of his hands gripping the iron bars that imprisoned him. Suddenly, Pastor Farr's voice broke through.

"Three weeks ago, I published the banns of marriage between Lieutenant Nigel Ashby of London, England, and Miss Jennifer Sutton of Boston in the Massachusetts Bay Colony. This is the third time of asking. If any of you know cause or just impediment why these two persons should not be joined together in holy matrimony, ye are to declare it." He looked around the congregation, giving sufficient time—perhaps even more time than necessary—for someone to object.

Was he hoping, as she was, that someone would come forward and testify to Ashby's cruelty? That he was not fit to be husband to her? That he was coercing her? That he was, she was certain, a murderer.

Please, God, let someone speak.

Silence.

How could this be happening? She glanced at Mother, who squeezed her hand. Regardless of her fear, it was happening. And if she rejected Ashby, she and Mother would hang. Just as Andrew would. She fought down the wave of despair that threatened to make her cry out, "No." Clenching her jaw, she sat erect, head high. She would not hang. Neither would Mother.

Neither would Andrew.

As they left St. Paul's Chapel, Jenny opened her umbrella against the drizzle and searched for their carriage. A hand grasped her elbow.

"Good day, my love." Ashby's voice was low and intimate. "Just think, next Sunday you will awaken beside me in our marriage bed."

Since arresting Andrew, he had become crueler. Where was the concern and protectiveness he'd shown? Had it ever been sincere? Yes, the pain in his eyes when he'd found her with Andrew had been real. And even of late, that flicker of tenderness shone through when he was off guard.

But he had killed Montclair and Mathias—in the name of loyalty to the King, he would argue. And a British sympathizer had killed Father. She shivered against the claustrophobic feeling of being surrounded by danger. She had to force herself to merely stand beside him.

She twisted her arm away from him. She scowled, pulling back, his face too close, his eyes too probing, but she noticed passersby casting quizzical looks their way.

"Best behave like a smitten fiancée," he said, glancing at Mother. "Your mother has a lovely neck, it would be a shame ..."

"I despise you," Jenny hissed. She smiled at the couple walking by who greeted them, then glared at him again. "I will never love you, no matter what you do or say."

"Did you think this is about love, sweet Jenny?"

"I did once, Nigel."

The muscle along his jaw flinched, and his eyes grew moist. His body relaxed as he studied her. "Yes, I do love you." He ran his finger along her jawline and she recoiled. He looked away. Straightening his shoulders, he turned back to her, his gaze cruel. "But you betrayed me. Nevertheless, you will be my wife … and your lover will no longer be a distraction. He will hang the morning after our wedding night." Bowing over her hand, his tongue flicked against her skin as he kissed it. "I will exact my payment for your safety."

Her stomach writhed. He had calculated Andrew's death intentionally. Her nostrils flared, hot breath coming in gasps. What could she do? How could she save Andrew? She tried to pull her hand back, but he held it and glanced at Mother.

"I hate you."

"Which will make our life together even more interesting."

What if she slapped him, right here in the churchyard? Would that dissolve their banns? What if she grabbed his pistol, just a foot away from her itching hand, and shot him dead?

"Come, Jennifer."

Mother's voice floated to her, and she forced the thoughts from her mind.

Taking her arm, he assisted her into the waiting carriage. Isaac held the reins, his face a somber mask as he sat where his father's body had grown cold. On the same cushion marked with a reddish-brown stain where Mathias had bled out. Ashby's work. It had been a warning.

Oh, if she could only turn her wrath into fists of iron and

pummel Ashby. She had never known hatred like this. Nigel Ashby's life was not worth saving.

CHAPTER TWENTY-THREE

(

MOTHER PACED THE FLOOR AS Jenny sat, hugging a needlepoint pillow, staring at the flames dancing in the hearth.

"You must not marry that man."

"Mother, I have no choice. He knows of our activities. If I refuse him, we will hang." *Does it matter? Andrew will hang the day after the wedding.* How different life was supposed to be. They had dreamed of the life they would share—lying beside each other every night, sharing their journey, a house full of children. Now, his journey would finish at the end of a rope. Why not hers? She glanced at Mother. That's why. Mother could not die.

"I will put the light on for a message to be picked up tonight ..."

"Mother, that will be risky. Ashby is watching our house."

"I don't think he's figured out the lantern system yet. We must call for a courier. Perhaps there is someone out there who can help us get away before the end of this week."

"We must free Andrew, too. He must escape with us." Jenny's voice constricted with panic.

She recognized the look in Mother's eyes. It was the same look she had when Jenny had demanded someone call a doctor for Kathryn while her twin lay lifeless in the street. Mother knew the futility of such a demand.

Jenny stood, throwing the pillow to the floor. "*No.* I will not believe that saving Andrew is hopeless."

"Jenny." Mother's voice was gentle.

"NO!" The word erupted from a visceral place within. *Think, think.* She tapped her index finger against her head. Lucy, her fellow Patriot, was skilled in the art of herbs and medicine. A plan started to form. She couldn't save Kathryn or Father, but she'd be damned if she wouldn't save the man she loved.

❦

The next night, Mother had just lifted the candle to lead them to bed when a light rapping sounded at the back door. Mother smiled. Heart fluttering, Jenny took her hand.

Couriers' visits had trickled to nothing since Montclair's death. Surely, this was a response to their signal for help. Or would Ashby come to the back door for some reason? No, he was too bold, too secure in his control over them. Even at this inappropriate time of night for visiting, he would march up to the front entrance.

Tap-tap. Tap-tap. Tap-tap-tap.

Together they hurried to the back door.

Mother eased the door open.

Daniel Gordon. The courier who had frequently picked up and delivered messages stood in the shadows.

He bowed slightly. "Mrs. Sutton."

Mother ushered him in, scanned the yard, then closed and latched the door.

"I've—" Seeing Jenny, he stopped.

Mother quickly explained their predicament, including the circumstances of Jenny's engagement.

"I am encouraged to hear this, Miss Sutton." He stood with his arms crossed. "We weren't certain where this household stood anymore."

Jenny thrust her face into his. "Have no doubt, Mr. Gordon. I despise Nigel Ashby as I do the Ranger who killed my father."

He nodded. "I'll pass that along. I've seen your lantern. How can I help?"

"We must escape to Boston. But we must also break Andrew Wentworth out of gaol," Mother said.

He looked from one to the other as if they were insane. "That's impossible."

She took Jenny's hand. "Then we must either flee without him, or try to free him on our own."

"I'm so sorry, Mrs. Sutton. I wish I could help, but I must leave immediately to prevent the British from raiding a magazine to the north. I must be on my way."

Mother unlatched the door, again scanning the yard.

Daniel tipped his hat and slipped out into the inky night.

Mother slumped against the closed door. "I, too, am sorry, Jennifer. I did the best I could."

She hugged her. "I know. I intend to go through with my plan."

"Jennifer—"

"You, Sarie, and Isaac must leave. Tonight."

"I can't leave you to do this on your own ..."

"Ephraim and Lucy will help me. If you are safely on your way, it will be less for me to worry about. Please, Mother."

"But ..."

"I know. But this is the only way to save three lives, for you know he will kill Sarie and Isaac as well. And who's to say he won't kill us all anyway? He has complete power over us, and we are helpless to prevent any of it. I would rather be dead than submit to that monster. But I can't make this work if I am worried about you."

Mother sighed, her shoulders drooping. "Oh, Jennifer. You will be in such peril."

"No more than on a wedding night with a murderer."

❦

To still her trembling, Jenny clutched the handle of the basket with both hands. The thought of entering the gaol sent a cold spike of dread through her. She stopped, unable to move any farther. She studied the path to the stairs, up to the dried-blood, brownish red door that loomed before her. If she had any sense, she would turn and flee.

But Andrew was inside.

She gathered her nerve, took a deep breath, and held the basket as if it were a lifeline. She stepped forward on the path, each step a decision that her feet had to agree to and move forward.

Inside the dingy office, a soldier lounged, his feet propped up on the desk. Spotting her, he sat up, interest lighting his face.

"Good evening, miss," he said, his voice smooth and oily.

"Good evening, officer." He was not an officer according to his uniform, but he puffed up as she'd expected.

"How may I help you?" He studied the basket then inhaled the aroma of warm bread and spicy stew that wafted from it, suffusing the stuffy room.

"I have brought supper for a prisoner," she said, nodding toward the door leading to the cell area. He was the only soldier present. At least, visible.

The soldier deflated, glancing toward the door.

"I will need to inspect the meal." He almost licked his lips.

"Of course, sir."

She handed him the basket, snatching back her hands and folding them to hide her quaking. He examined her slowly, scrutinizing her body, no doubt thinking she had wanted to avoid contact with him.

"You seem a shy lady." His smile stretched over yellowed, crooked teeth.

She twirled a stray tendril around her finger and smiled, knowing that the dimple that made Andrew weak would have the same effect on the soldier. A bulky key ring splayed out on the desk. If she reached out, she could touch it. But not yet.

He chuckled. "Come, miss, sit with me a bit. I get lonely locked up here with all these miscreants and traitors."

"No, thank you, sir. My mother strictly forbade me to linger. She said bring the victuals to our Andy, and be off to home."

He stood, frowning. "Andy, eh? Do you mean the traitor, Wentworth? He don't need no food. Soon, he will dangle in the rising sun."

Jenny's stomach lurched; her knees felt like rubber. She placed one hand on the desk to steady herself.

"Yes, sir. Will you not help with my mother's last request for him? She is sick in bed with despair, so we have been unable to travel here to visit him thus far." She leaned in; it was not difficult to call forth tears. "Please, sir?" She smiled again, her dimple a volley on this soldier.

He softened. Shifting on his feet, he picked up the key ring, jangling it in his hand. "I don't know ..."

She matched his stare, then lowered her lids, a tear inching its way along her cheek. She looked up at him.

"I would be ever so grateful."

"Eh? How grateful would you be, miss? How grateful for your brother's last meal?"

His leer made her skin crawl, and the thought of his hands touching her made her nauseous. But he was a lowly soldier who could be flattered into doing her bidding. While she hated this pretense, he was all that stood between her and Andrew's freedom. She pressed her handkerchief to her nose against his putrid breath and worse body odor.

"I ... I would be happy to show you my gratitude, officer." Her voice was small, soft, but it was as if she'd lit him on fire.

He rounded the desk toward her. She stepped back.

"I meant this meal."

"I want to taste more than this meal ..." He reached for her, but she sidestepped him.

"In that case, you would need to build your strength. I'm

sure the army doesn't provide enough food for a strapping man such as you." She stepped forward and lifted the cloth off the stew releasing more of the spicy aroma.

He closed his eyes, his face beatific.

"You'll need your strength." Her voice was husky as she started to replace the cloth.

He held out his hand to stop her, almost touching her arm. She remained where she was, watching the fire in his eyes.

He took the pewter spoon from the basket and lifted out the bowl of stew. Looking at her, he scooped a spoonful of stew, blew across the spoon, and slurped. Jenny's stomach cramped, preparing to retch.

"Mmmmm, better than my own mother's." He licked his lips. Was that all he would taste?

"Surely you don't think I've hidden a knife in that bowl of stew."

His face darkened. He swirled the spoon around the stew. The temptation was too much. He took another, healthy sample. His eyes widened, then narrowed, trying to focus.

"This is thu …thu …" He swayed then a puzzled look covered his face as he slid to the floor.

Jenny snatched the keys from his limp hand and hurried to the door. She glanced back at the soldier, afraid he would rise and accost her. He lay still. Hopefully, she hadn't laced the stew with enough laudanum to kill him. Hands shaking, she tried the first key—it didn't fit. She flipped to the next. The lock clicked.

She blinked, trying to adjust to the darkness along the dim corridor. Four cells lined the passage, each sealed with a heavy wooden door containing a square, barred window. She peered into the first. A shape huddled in the corner of the cell, lying on straw strewn on the stone floor. The stench made her swallow down the bile that rose in her throat.

"Andrew," she whispered hoarsely." A dark-haired woman rolled over and looked at her.

"Jenny?"

She turned at the sound of Andrew's voice. "Andrew!"

❧

He must be hearing things. Existing day after day in this darkened cell with little food or water was wearing Andrew down. But when he heard Jenny say his name, he knew she was real. At first, his heart leapt at the sound of her voice, but then it plummeted. Why was she here? He pressed his face against the bars to see if Ashby accompanied her. No, she was alone. Had Ashby sent her?

She rushed to his cell, clutching a ring of keys.

"Jenny, what are you about?" Was this a ruse? An opportunity for Ashby to kill him himself rather than allow that privilege to the hangman?

"Hush, we must hurry." She tried one key, then another, flipping through them, her fingers shaking. Finally, she found the key that slipped easily into the lock. The rusty hinges screeched in protest as she struggled to swing the iron door outward.

She rushed toward him, but he backed away.

"What do you want? You need to leave—now." His heart was torn as she stood before him. His love for her had not diminished; indeed, he still dreamed of her every night. Soothing dreams that lulled him back to their idyllic days at Brentwood Manor when his passion stirred at her voice, her touch. But harsh reality struck upon awakening, surrounded by filth, imprisonment, and her betrayal.

"Andrew ..."

He backed away from her. "You must leave here—now."

"You will not hang. Hurry, Andrew, we must run. Now."

He wavered. She seemed so sincere. How he wanted to wrap her in his arms, to flee with her and live the life they'd always planned together. He stepped toward her.

"What in the name of heaven—?" Ashby's voice rang out from the front room.

Andrew pushed her out of the cell and pulled the door shut. He glared. "So, this was all pretense. Pretense to allow me to be killed by Ashby while trying to escape. How could you, Jenny?" His voice broke. He gripped the bars in the door. "He won't have that satisfaction."

"No, Andrew, please ..."

Jenny looked around, but she was surrounded by locked cells. There was nowhere to hide. She slipped as far into the darkened corner of the passageway as she could.

Andrew held the door closed.

Ashby rushed into the corridor, then, catching sight of Andrew, relaxed. "Awake, Wentworth? Trying to avoid dreaming about your wench in my arms? Writhing under me? Begging for more?"

"You bastard." *Control yourself. Do not give in to his taunts.* Andrew locked his fingers around the iron bars and stared at him.

"No angry words for me, Wentworth? Are you enjoying the thought of my taking my pleasure with your lover?"

Andrew spat in his face.

Ashby lunged at the door, grabbing the bars. The door swayed toward him, and from his startled look, Andrew knew he had the advantage. He threw all his weight against the door to swing it fully open, crashing Ashby against the wall. His skull struck the stone, and he fell forward then stumbled into Jenny. He pawed at her, trying to gain his footing, then his eyes rolled back and he slithered to the floor.

She tried to reach the hilt of his sword, but his body twisted away, his pistol exposed. She clutched it, pulling it from his belt.

Her arms trembled as she aimed the gun at him.

Andrew took the pistol from her. He aimed it at Ashby's head. He would blast the man to hell.

CHAPTER TWENTY-FOUR

☾

ANDREW'S JAW TWITCHED AS HE stood over Ashby's unconscious body.

Jenny swallowed. Andrew had never looked so fierce. On the contrary, he had always been so sweet. Could he kill a man?

"Andrew." Her voice was soft.

He looked at her as if he'd just realized she was there.

She placed her hand on his arm, and he lowered the pistol. He nodded, then used his toe to turn Ashby on his back. The man still breathed but in shallow gasps. An angry gash spilled scarlet blood in a pool on the floor.

Andrew searched him, finding a pouch of powder and shot for the pistol.

"Quick. We must leave now." She took his hand.

They ran to the rear of the building where Ephraim waited with a wagon. Clambering up, they tumbled onto it as Ephraim whistled and slapped the reins against the horse's back.

The wagon careened along the road, pitching and bumping at every rut.

"Faster, Ephraim, faster," Jenny called.

"This is as fast as this horse can go, Miss Sutton." But he clucked and shook the reins, gaining a little more speed.

The evening was clear, a new moon with stars splashing the midnight blue sky. If they could make it to the main road, the going would be smoother. Finally, houses and shops flew by, most dark, the inhabitants sleeping. The only sound was the frantic wheels against the cobbles.

She was afraid to hope that they would clear the city and make it to the farm where Mr. Gates had dropped her. *Please, God, please keep us safe.*

Andrew sat across from her, not beside her, his face hidden in velvet shadow.

"Jenny, if we're caught, you will hang, too."

"Then we mustn't be caught." She wished her insides were as brave as she sounded. She searched the road behind them as much as the bumping would allow. The road was still empty. They were going to make it.

"Ephraim, Ephraim," she called to him, but he didn't answer. "Ephraim. You must slow down now so you can get off."

That had been the plan. As soon as they reached the countryside, he would get off so, if they were apprehended, he would not be involved.

"Not yet, Miss Sutton. I must get you safely away."

The wagon thundered along the dirt road, leaving the lantern glow of the city behind them. Jenny's teeth clicked against the bumps as they became more erratic. Suddenly, the wagon listed, there was a loud crack, and one corner of the wagon thumped to the ground, pitching Jenny and Andrew into the road.

"Oooof." Jenny felt the stab of a stone in her knee, and her wrist twisted beneath her as she tried to break her fall. Strong hands grasped her shoulder, helping her to rise.

Andrew brushed her hair back. "Are you all right?" His worried look made her heart sing.

"Yes, yes. We must keep moving."

"Not in this wagon," Ephraim said.

The broken wheel lay in the road, the wagon tilted like a genuflecting penitent. Ephraim tried to settle the horse that whinnied and shook its head, jangling the harness in the quiet night. Once the harness was off, one corner of the wagon stabbed into the ebony sky.

"Ephraim, you must take the horse and return home."

"But you should …"

"No. I don't want you or Lucy implicated in any way."

He nodded. "I wish't I'd brought a saddle."

Andrew scanned the countryside. "Not a farm in sight where we could borrow a saddle … or a horse. Not that we could take that chance. We'll have to walk." He frowned at her and scrubbed his hands through his hair. "Are you up to it?"

"Yes." She had intentionally worn her sturdiest boots. Turning to Ephraim, she took his hand. "Thank you. You risked your life for us. Now you must return home, for I don't know if we'll be followed."

Ephraim glanced at Andrew. He may as well have spoken the words aloud. *You'll be followed for certain.*

The two men dragged the wagon off the road and hid it in a copse of trees.

"Will you be all right traveling alone?" Andrew asked him.

He hoisted his rifle. "I'll be fine, but yer gonna need this." He handed the weapon to Andrew, who stepped back.

"No, we can't take your rifle."

Ephraim nodded toward Jenny. "She saved your life. You may need to save hers." He thrust the weapon into Andrew's hands.

"How can we ever thank you?" Jenny kissed his cheek, the stubble prickly and coarse.

"Let me and Lucy know yer all right." He turned and led the horse down the road toward the city.

☙

The shadowy night held the rustling of raccoons and skunks, the air filled with the songs of crickets. A cool, westerly breeze whipped Jenny's blue shawl around her shoulders as she walked beside Andrew. She couldn't help looking up at him. Was this a dream? Would they finally have the life together they had planned? Perhaps, but his silence alarmed her. Certainly, his strength waned, but he hadn't even taken her hand. This was not how she'd imagined their reunion.

They had been walking for more than an hour when their steps slowed and she stumbled. They paused in a nearby clearing. To conserve water until they could find a spring, they had been sipping sparingly from the canteen she'd brought. Now she took two biscuits and two pieces of dried beef from a pouch slung over her shoulder. Handing Andrew his share, she nibbled on her own. He tried not to gobble it down, but she could see his hunger. Too bad she had wasted that delicious stew on the soldier at the gaol.

He lay back on the grass, and when she tried to cradle in beside him, he rolled away.

"Andrew," she whispered.

"I'm tired." His voice, thick with exhaustion, barely reached her. Soon his steady breathing signaled his sleep.

She squeezed her eyes shut against the stinging tears. Within the fear and tension of her plans to help him escape had been the excitement of being beside him again. To be able to touch him, to hold him. She believed their love would withstand any danger. She hadn't been ready for his rejection. She opened her eyes and stared at his back, reaching out, then withdrawing her hand. He wanted nothing to do with her. How could he believe she'd betrayed him?

She tried to sleep, but the night sounds kept slumber at bay. Small animals scampered through the underbrush, and larger ones crept through the trees between them and the road. The one time she did drift off, a dream of Ashby crawling through the tall grass toward them shook her awake.

A thin pale line etched the eastern horizon, signaling the coming dawn.

She cocked her ear. Was that Ashby? Or a deer? A wolf?

She sat up. Chills ran through her. They had to move. Now.
"Andrew," she whispered. "Andrew, wake up."

"Umph." He rolled to his back.

Something was wrong. Someone was out there.

"Andrew. Wake up."

He sat up, instantly alert. He aimed the rifle at the road.

"We need to go," she whispered.

He looked around. "What is it?"

"I don't know. A feeling. I just don't want to stay here."

"Let's go." He rose and stretched.

The sky was growing lighter, not affording darkness to conceal them.

They skirted the road, making their way through the thinner trees along the edge. This slowed their progress, as brambles caught in Jenny's skirt. She finally pulled the back of it between her legs, tucking it into her belt.

Andrew frowned and looked away. Was he angry? "We'll have to find a place to hide during the day." He tossed the words over his shoulder.

"Yes, I think it will take another day of walking to reach the farm of Uncle Jonathon's friends. On horseback or wagon, we would have been there by now."

"We can—" He was interrupted by the sound of hoofbeats barreling along the road. "Quick, into the woods."

Crouching behind a large log, they saw two riders approaching. Neither wore the scarlet coats of British soldiers. As the riders neared, she and Andrew lay flat on the grass behind the fallen ancient oak. She chanced a peek at them once they'd passed. Her jaw dropped. There were only two men she'd ever met who were that size. The Wirth brothers.

She jumped up, sprinting toward the road, waving her arms. Her voice stabbed the air.

"Stop. Come back." She was seven years old again, chasing Kathryn, her twin's laughter trailing back to her. *Can't catch me, Jenny. Ha ha. I'll always beat you.* The sound of the horse neighing as it shied to avoid her sister. The piercing scream. Kathryn's sightless gray eyes.

Jenny's arms dropped to her side, she sank to the ground. "I didn't run to the road fast enough. I never run to the road fast enough."

❦

Andrew followed Jenny as she scrambled from behind the tree and raced toward the riders. By the time he reached her, she had crumpled in the road, weeping. An iron fist twisted his heart as he fought the urge to gather her into his arms. Instead, he knelt beside her, the rifle balanced across one knee.

"Shhh, Jenny, shhh. Everything will be fine." His fingers itched to brush the tangled hair from her face, and sweep away her tears. He wanted to kiss her forehead, draw her into his lap, and rock her as they sat on the dusty ground. Instead, he held the rifle.

"I couldn't … save Kathryn, and I … can't save … you." Her words caught between her sobs.

"We're going to be all right, Jenny. You have saved me. I would be dead by now if not for your daring."

When she had told him about Kathryn, she had simply said her twin sister had been killed accidentally. Her voice had been steady. Her face, her expression, had given no clue to this depth of emotion … and guilt. Now, her body trembled with unshed misery.

He stared in the direction where the brothers had ridden. Jenny was reliving her nightmare. He balanced the rifle against his shoulder and looked down at her. He couldn't take her into his arms and comfort her. She belonged to Ashby.

When he looked away, he noticed the sky growing brighter, and his gut signaled the need to hide.

"We must move."

She nodded.

He helped her stand. The tears that glistened on her cheeks sliced into his gut. How could he not comfort her? "It was not your fault, Jenny. You were a child. What could you have done?"

"I was chasing her."

"You were playing a game. You had no evil intent. She would have run anyway."

Raising her face to his, her eyes shone. "Yes, she would have run anyway." A weak smile revealed her dimple.

It stabbed his heart. She could save the world with that smile. But she was pale, and the dark circles spoke of a night of little sleep. He had to move away from her.

"Let's conceal ourselves as best we can. Perhaps we can find berries or nuts as we walk."

"I thought we would be at the farm by now. I brought the biscuits and meat for our escape, but only enough to see us through the night."

He was still weak from lack of food during his imprisonment, but he had to force himself to keep going. Jenny's face was ashen and drawn, but the determined set of her jaw convinced him they should move.

"Perhaps we will dine in comfort this evening. To do so, we must make good progress." Would they reach this farm and safety? *I should have killed Ashby when I had the chance, for he will certainly kill me if he finds us. Would he blame Jenny because their plan to murder me went awry? Would he harm her?*

He called up all his strength.

The burden of her safety weighed on him like the ropes that had carried him beneath the whaler in the sound.

C

The sun shot brilliant tones of orange and crimson into the clouds as it settled into the horizon. They had about an hour left of twilight. Andrew hoped they would reach the farm tonight. She'd said they should arrive in another day's walk. His legs trembled with fatigue, and the trees and road ahead shimmered in a blurry scene. *Just keep one foot in front of the other.* He continued solely by dint of will.

Hoofbeats pounded on the road behind them, from the sound of it, several riders.

He took her hand and dashed toward the trees.

Jenny's scarf caught on a bramble. Reversing her step, she tugged at it, which only twisted the fabric into a knot. She looked toward the road and tugged again. "Damn!" She tore the blue cloth away and followed him into the trees. Had she done that on purpose? Left a sign to indicate where they were? She must trust Ashby enough not to fear retribution for the failure of their plan. Knowing the man's cruelty, he believed otherwise.

He pulled her down to crouch behind a fallen maple.

Nearing them, the horses slowed to a trot.

He held his breath as he eased up, peering through the trees. He gulped. Seven British soldiers approached, led by Nigel Ashby. Even from here, Andrew could see the pallor in his face, his wince of pain as the horse moved. But his jaw was set, his eyes stony cold.

Some of the soldiers walked their horses into the underbrush and trees along the road. Their hiding place would soon be discovered, and to try to run from it now would be useless. He scanned the area. Just trees and shrub. No place that would provide adequate cover for them from a determined murderer. Perhaps they wouldn't hang after all. Perhaps Ashby would shoot them on the spot. His gaze slid to Jenny.

No, not until Ashby had tortured them both.

She met his gaze. She hadn't called out to reveal their position. *Have I misjudged her all this time?* He still wasn't sure. Her brows lifted in question but not in fear.

I can't help myself. I love this woman who stares down death— and worse—without so much as a blink. She hefted the pistol they had loaded that morning.

Shoot straight, my Jenny.

He pulled Ephraim's rifle along his side until he positioned it to fire. They waited.

Darkness was descending, but the snagged scrap of blue fabric waved in the breeze like a beacon. The troop was getting closer. Ashby looked like a buzzard, turning his head from side to side as he scanned the road, as if his beaked nose could detect their scent.

A soldier was the first to spot it. He ripped the fabric from the twig with a flourish.

"Lieutenant. Look here."

Ashby kicked his horse to a trot, halting where the soldier stood. A grin broke across his face. "Hah!" Sitting erect, he craned his neck peering in their direction. Did he see them? "Find them. Search in there." He pointed, his sense of their position uncanny.

Andrew sighted the rifle. Jenny cocked the pistol.

Two soldiers dismounted and tramped around just beyond them, thrusting their bayonets into the shrubbery.

"Don't kill them," Ashby shouted. "Save that for me. That and a bit more pleasure."

Andrew seethed at his sneering voice. The scene before him was tinged with red; his blood ran cold. He would see this man dead before he could harm Jenny.

The soldiers were closing in. At best, they could each get off one shot before they would be at the mercy of the soldiers. If he waited until one soldier was close enough, could he capture his musket, giving them another round? It was risky, but it was their only chance. Of course, once they were detected, the whole troop would dismount and surround them.

Sweat dripped into his eyes, stinging them, blurring his vision. He was aware of Jenny, still as a statue, beside him. No matter how brave she was, what Ashby had planned for her was horrendous. Andrew couldn't allow that to happen. He nudged her. Pressing his finger to his lips, he mouthed, "wait for me to fire." She nodded.

Andrew saw the recognition in the first soldier's gaze. The man raised his musket then remembered his commanding officer's orders. He didn't fire, but he didn't call out, either. Instead, he glanced to his left where his partner was just behind him.

Come closer. Come closer.

Andrew's gaze locked on the soldier's, willing him to approach.

Treading softly, a triumphant smile playing on his face, the soldier did just that.

That's right. Save the prize for yourself. Gain the admiration of your lieutenant. Just a few more steps.

Andrew smirked at him, drawing him in. A few more steps.

The rifle's recoil jolted Andrew's shoulder, and beside him Jenny jumped. The soldier's face exploded in a cloud of red. Jenny remained still. Horses shied and neighed at the blast.

The second soldier spotted them, stepped forward, and Jenny shot him in the throat. His face froze, his eyes wide with surprise, before he collapsed.

They bolted forward, each snatching a soldier's musket.

"Get them," Ashby shouted, raising his saber, his face contorted in pain.

Four soldiers dismounted and circled them. They could kill two more, but there would be no more opportunity to steal weapons. Andrew and Jenny stood back to back as the soldiers closed in.

The man on the left was bulkier than the other, and closer to Andrew. A shot to his limbs might just wound and Andrew needed to kill him. If need be, he'd run the soldier through with the bayonet. Then they would be at the mercy of Ashby, who would show no mercy. He aimed for the bulky man's face. "I'll take the man on the left," he whispered to Jenny.

They fired. Two more soldiers fell. The last two came at them with their muskets raised, their bayonets aimed at their hearts.

"Do not kill them," Ashby repeated, striding through the underbrush. He stood before them, triumphant. "They are mine." He caressed Jenny's face, then pulled one tendril straight, the back of his hand brushing the top of her breast.

Andrew lunged for him, but Jenny grabbed his arm, restraining him. A soldier lifted his gun, aiming it at Andrew until Ashby pushed it down.

"No. Before he dies, he is in for a spectacle."

How could he save Jenny from this monster?

CHAPTER TWENTY-FIVE

C

WITH HANDS BOUND AND TIED to the saddle horn, Jenny rode on one of the dead soldier's horses. Ahead, moonlight lit the shape of Andrew's back as they trotted along the road. Her mind raced with possible ways to escape—most involving Ashby's death—and even though none of the plans seemed plausible, she refused to give up hope.

Ashby raised his hand to halt the others when they reached a clearing. Dismounting, he ordered a fire and some food. The two remaining soldiers scrambled down from their mounts, tethered their horses, and began to set up camp. Ashby held her and Andrew's reins, ordering them to remain mounted, while the others worked. Once the fire burned, he handed the reins over to one of the soldiers and strode to the trees to relieve himself. Returning, he smirked up at Jenny.

"I suppose I needn't be so discrete since you will be enjoying *all* of me very soon." He turned to Andrew. "And you'll have the pleasure of watching."

She kicked a foot out toward him, but he caught it before it could land. Caressing her ankle, he kissed it, his gaze never leaving Andrew's.

She wrested it away. "You're a bastard."

"Oh ho. I see I bring out the saucy side of you. How delightful."

He sauntered off, chuckling.

"Jenny, I swear ..."

"Hush, Andrew." She nodded toward the soldier who seemed peevish about being left holding their reins. He kicked at the ground and shifted from foot to foot. His face brightened when Ashby brought a fresh canteen to him. "Good work today." His gaze shifted to her. "See? I can be kind." He laughed as he sauntered to deliver the second canteen to the soldier by the fire.

The aroma of porridge cooking over the flames tormented Jenny. All they had consumed since morning were a few berries and some water. One soldier chewed on some salted meat while he tended the fire. He then took a draught from the canteen, and she swallowed against her parched throat. Her stomach growled as she regarded the pot.

"Hungry, my love?" Ashby appeared beside her. He untied her hands. She began to dismount, but he stopped her. "Allow me, Miss Sutton." He held her waist as she slid from the saddle. His hands ran along her side.

Never did she feel so filthy as when his hands touched her, sullying any sense of goodness she held. Recoiling, she turned her head away, her mouth pulled down in a scowl. She wanted to be as far away from him as possible. Hunching her shoulders, she folded her arms.

Her stomach growled again.

"How neglectful I've been. Come by the fire. You must have sustenance before we share what *should* have been our wedding night." He took her elbow, but she pulled it away. "Oh yes. It will be a delightful nuptial celebration." He added over his shoulder, "Let Wentworth down. Keep a close watch on him."

Jenny tried to look back, but Ashby tugged her forward.

He offered her a bowl of steaming porridge and a drink from his flask. She took the bowl but waved off the drink. She gagged at the thought of putting her lips where his had been.

"Have it your way." He took a long pull of the liquid.

She watched the others. One soldier tied Andrew to a nearby oak, glanced at his comrade, then at Ashby. He made a face, and the other one snickered. So, they disliked Ashby, too. Was there any chance they would help her? Would Ashby's cruelty drive them to mutiny? The soldier looked back at Andrew and kicked him in the side.

"Filthy traitor." He spat on the ground next to Andrew's hand.

Andrew glared at him, but his limbs lay motionless as exhaustion took its toll. Black circles darkened his eyes, standing out against his pale skin. But his gaze was defiant—until it met hers. Then a mix of sorrow and love softened his face.

When she finished eating, Ashby allowed her to step into the trees to relieve herself. Would he follow? Was he observing her even now? Though the thought sickened her, she had to ease this urgency. When she returned to the fire, Ashby bound her hands.

"I think you might enjoy this sort of thing, my dear." He tugged on the rope.

She turned her head, refusing to look at him.

Clutching her jaw, he twisted her head back. "You will look at me when I speak to you."

Andrew thrashed against the ropes.

The soldiers froze, watching their officer's actions. They exchanged glances and one shook his head. They disliked their officer almost as much as she did. Her mouth would have twitched if Ashby's hold hadn't tightened on her face.

He followed her gaze. "Do you men have something to say?" He glared at them.

"No, sir," they said in unison. They concentrated on the ground.

When Ashby suddenly released his grasp, he whipped her head sideways.

"Ow." She bit her lip against saying anything else. She

did not want to give him the satisfaction of knowing he'd hurt her.

Andrew struggled again, his eyes dark with rage.

"In pain, my love? I will soothe your pain soon." He stroked her cheek. His voice softened. "Oh, Jenny, don't you see how I love you? I will have you, and then you will love me, too."

A shiver crept down her spine, but she sat rigid. Why was he delaying what she now knew was soon to happen? Just get it over with.

He glanced at the soldiers.

As they sat on a log near the fire, drinking from their canteens, their voices grew louder and their speech slurred. Why were they allowed to drink while on patrol?

Ashby sat off to the side watching them, keenly interested in their behavior. He smiled when one keeled over and snored. The other's head bobbed as he tried to drink again. His eyes rolled back and he slid off the log, crumpling onto the ground.

"Ah ha. At last. They were stouter than I thought." He turned to Jenny. "Now, my dear, we shall celebrate our wedding night." He untied her hands, leading her to stand before Andrew. "And you will watch. And then I shall kill you."

Jenny wriggled against his grip, but he pulled her in closer. "Don't be shy. I will be gentle. The first time."

Andrew kicked out, but Ashby sidestepped and laughed.

"I have waited for this moment far too long. But, no need to rush, I shall savor every minute." His voice was gentle with a cadence almost like a lullaby.

Ashby untied her shawl and let it fall to the ground. The cool breeze chilled her shoulders, but within, she burned with a desire to run him through with a bayonet. His fingers singed her skin through the fabric as he unbuttoned her waistcoat. His breath quickened.

He ran his fingers along her cheek. "You captured my

heart the first I ever saw you. It matters not to me what you believe in. I will change that. And I will change your heart until you are mine completely."

What would he do to her? Rape her for certain, but what other atrocities would he unleash on her? And then he would kill Andrew. Somehow, she had foolishly believed she would escape this fate. Once again, she had failed. Which would be worse: enduring his cruelty or Andrew having to witness it? She fought the trembling that started in her knees and worked its way up to possess her body.

"So, you begin to understand what is in store. You finally realize your destiny."

Andrew fought against the ropes that trapped him. "Stop, Ashby. Stop or I'll kill you."

Ashby threw his head back and laughed. "I fear for my life, Wentworth. How can I ever defend myself from your superior power? Watch this, Wentworth."

He loosened the ribbons securing her shift and opened it. She felt the cool night air against her skin. Her face flushed with humiliation, but she lifted her chin in defiance.

A sharp intake of breath. "As beautiful as I'd imagined." His breath was hot on her face.

Her skin crawled as if infested with fleas as he inspected her body.

Andrew's thrashing increased as his voice rose. "Let her go. I swear I'll kill you.'

Ashby's voice was ragged. "You will determine just how *gentle* I'll be with my fiancée, Wentworth. The more you protest, the more it will cost her." He pulled her shift down roughly, exposing her breasts. Pulling her to him, he crushed her against a tree. The rough bark gouged her back, carving into her skin. Warm blood trickled along her spine. His lips covered hers, his tongue darting in and out. He bit her lip and she cried out.

"Jenny," Andrew shouted.

She fought against him, pushing his chest with her arms.

"You'll pay for this," she hissed.

He caught her hands and held them over her head against the rigid tree trunk. "That's what I like. When you fight me." He pushed his hips into hers, forcing her to feel his erection.

"I won't just fight you. I'll kill you." She spat in his face.

☙

Andrew pulled against the restraints. Suddenly, they gave way and a knife was thrust into his hand. It took him a moment to react.

"Go, boy. Go." The slurred voice came from behind the tree.

He tried to stand but was so weak from lack of food that he stumbled. Pushing himself up, he staggered toward Ashby, who was pawing at Jenny as she fought to escape.

Ashby spotted his movement and turned. Andrew lunged, aiming for his heart. Ashby twisted, deflecting the wound to his arm. The two wrestled, and Andrew's hatred for this man propelled new strength through his body. Ashby wrested the knife from him, but Andrew knocked the knife from his hand.

"Andrew! Be careful!" Jenny's voice spurred him on. She loved him. She had always loved him, and he had been a fool. Had he trusted her, they might have escaped sooner. Now they both were in danger. If Ashby killed him, Jenny would be at that bastard's mercy for the rest of her life. He could not let that happened. A surge of determination shot through him. He fought with renewed strength, jarring the knife from Ashby's hand. When it fell at Jenny's feet, she seized it and plunged it into Ashby's back.

Ashby arched and twisted toward her. Reaching out, he grasped her shoulders, clutching her for support as he collapsed, sliding against her, trailing scarlet blood along her blue skirt.

She stepped back, dropped the knife, and vomited, splattering Ashby's black leather boots. She trembled as she studied him then reeled toward Andrew.

His arms were around her, and he buried his face in her hair.

"Oh my God." She could barely form the words.

They heard a moan. At the base of the tree, sprawled across the severed ropes was one of the soldiers. He raised his wobbling head and tried to focus on them. "He deserved it." His voice slurred before his head slapped down on the ropes.

Underbrush rustled as someone moved through the trees. Andrew held the knife, crouching in front of Jenny.

"Good evenin', Miss Sutton."

Andrew turned and looked up into the face of Martin Wirth.

"We had a devil of a time findin' ya."

His brother Abel joined him.

"Best ya' sit down for a minute, miss. And, uh, straighten yer, uh, clothes."

She looked down and realized she clutched her loose shift against her breasts. Turning away, she yanked the shift up, tied the strings and found her waistcoat. As she buttoned her jacket, she turned back to them. "How did you know about us?"

"We met Ephraim as he came into the city. He told us where you was headin' and we took a guess as to your progress." Abel handed her a flask of water.

She relished the cool liquid as it slid down her dry throat. As she handed it to Andrew, he smiled and held up the one Martin had shared with him.

"When we made it all the way to the farm and you weren't there, we doubled back, searching the woods along the road," Martin continued. "It was right nice of the Brits to light a fire to lead us here."

He surveyed the campsite. "Not bad for an evening's work. Two lobsterbacks unconscious and one..." He kicked Ashby's foot and he moaned. "Almost dead. Well done."

CHAPTER TWENTY-SIX

❦

THE FARMHOUSE WAS THE SWEETEST sight Jenny had seen in two days. Smoke curled from the chimney, a gray snake coiling into the dark sky. Beckoning lantern light glowed through the front window, and the crisp smell of a wood fire promised a warm hearth within.

Her weary arms and legs were leaden, her body burned with fatigue. The way Andrew listed in the saddle confirmed that he, too, was exhausted. When Abel helped her dismount, every muscle cried in protest, stiffness thwarting her effort to walk. She shambled to the steps, each a challenge as she climbed to the porch.

Martin scooped her up as if she were a rag doll and carried her to the door. In answer to his knock, the door swung open and her heart leapt with joy as Mother rushed to embrace her.

"Jennifer." Mother's voice broke as tears streamed down her face. "My sweet child. I've been so worried."

"Mother. You're safe. Andrew is here." She tried to peer over Martin's shoulder, but it was like trying to see around a mountain.

"Yes. You both are here. Now we are all safe."

Tears ran unchecked down Jenny's cheeks. Andrew stood beside her, smiling, but his lids were heavy, and he swayed a bit. Abel propped him up.

Then Sarie and Isaac appeared. "Miss Jenny!" Sarie made

no pretense; she bawled like a newborn. Isaac's grin beamed white teeth against his ebony skin. "We got food for you. Come in and set down."

Martin placed her on a chair at the kitchen table. Andrew plopped beside her. Mother set bowls of steaming soup before them. Isaac delivered two pewter tankards, cool with freshly pressed cider, and Andrew patted his shoulder in thanks. Sarie sliced a loaf of warm rye bread and slathered two pieces with creamy butter. Jenny inhaled the yeasty aroma, watching the steam rise.

Mother hugged Martin and Abel. "Thank you both from the bottom of my heart." She sniffed into her handkerchief.

The farmer's wife stepped forward, gesturing to the brothers. "Please, have some soup and ale. You must be starving."

"No, thank you, ma'am. We have three lobsterbacks to deliver to an encampment of Continentals just north of here. With the shape the lieutenant is in, we'd best hurry."

"Take our wagon to transport the wounded man, else he may die in your hands."

"Thank you kindly. That would be a help. We'll return it on our way back through." Martin patted Andrew's shoulder. "Never met a more courageous young man." He looked at Jenny. "Or young woman." He winked.

Jenny swayed when she tried to stand. He eased her back down. "You just git some victuals in ya', missy." She pulled his lapel and he leaned forward. She kissed his cheek. Abel hurried to her, leaning in. Laughing, she kissed him, too.

Martin cleared his throat. "Well then. We'll be on our way."

The farmer led them out, closing the door behind them.

Jenny sat back and sighed after finishing the soup, two slabs of bread, and a mug of ale. She caught Andrew's gaze, and, in the candlelight, desire reflected in his eyes. A warm tickle started in her belly and spread through her body. She smiled, and given the way he shifted in his chair, her dimple had not lost its effect.

Andrew lay in the stillness of the night. He had recovered remarkably after, what seemed to him, a feast. Though exhaustion drained every ounce of his energy, he could not sleep. Every time he closed his eyes, the idea of Ashby assaulting Jenny invaded his thoughts. She had defied Ashby and his threats, never showing fear. Even the risk she'd taken to help him flee from the gaol showed more bravery than most men had.

God, how he loved her. How he longed to wrap her in his arms, protect her, make love to her.

The candle flame fluttered as the door opened, and Jenny stood there, her gaze alight with passion. Her linen shift draped her figure, highlighting delicious swells over her breasts and hips. She pressed her finger to her lips. "Shhh." Then she smiled tantalizingly, and he thought he would perish in a swirl of pleasure and pain.

She padded over the wood floor, sauntering to his bed. Holding his gaze, she loosened the strings of her shift, bringing the neckline to her shoulders. Heat spread through him like a forest on fire. She smiled as movement beneath the blanket revealed his desire when she pulled one side of her shift from her shoulder, exposing the swell of her breast.

"Oh, Jenny," he breathed. They had spent many nights snuggled in front of the hearth at Brentwood Manor, but they had always been clothed. They had explored each other's bodies, but through layers of linen, cotton, or brocade. He had never seen Jenny completely naked.

With a graze of her finger, she brushed the fabric from her other shoulder, and her shift dropped to the floor. As did Andrew's heart. Candlelight flickered off her alabaster skin. Her rosy nipples were taut with her longing. He reached out, running his hand along her thigh.

She trembled.

Lifting the blanket, she nestled beside him. "You seem to be overdressed, sir." She tugged his shirt and pulled it up.

He scrambled out of it, tossing it on the floor. Wrapping her in his arms, he was amazed at how each of her curves fit neatly against his body. She raised her face to his, and he captured her lips, moving, exploring, delving into her sweetness. She moaned, deep in her throat. He thought he would explode.

Her silky skin urged his touch. She writhed as his hands explored her body. Every movement, every sound, proclaimed her delight in his exploration. His earlier exhaustion gave way to renewed energy, emboldened by her response, her touch.

She slid beneath him, pulling him atop her. Wrapping her arms and legs around him, she smiled, her dimple destroying any resistance he might have entertained. He joined their bodies, her breath hot on his neck as they soared to the explosion of pleasure and release.

℃

Jenny heard the rooster out in the yard. Andrew slept curled around her, their legs intertwined. How she wanted to remain, warm and sated, in his arms. But the family had probably already arisen to begin work on the farm. Her escape back to the room she was sharing with Mother would be precarious.

Slowly easing from Andrew's embrace, she tried to slip out of the bed. His arms encircled her, drawing her back in, scooping her beside him.

"Andrew, I must return to my room," she whispered.

"Stay, love." His sleep-filled voice was husky, breaking down her resistance.

"Mother will awaken soon. She'll see I'm gone."

"Mmm hmm." He traced lazy circles on her stomach.

"I must leave you now."

"Never leave me again, Jenny." His hand moved to her breast. Desire flamed, heat spread through her body. He moved against her.

"Andrew..."

She remained.

❧

Mother was already in the kitchen helping to prepare breakfast. She raised a brow at Jenny when she entered, but a half smile played at her lips.

"I'm pleased to see you slept in, Jennifer. You needed the extra *rest*." She exchanged glances with Sarie, who turned to busy herself at the hearth. But not before Jenny saw her grin. "Be of some use, daughter. Set the table."

Jenny busied herself with the task, snatching glances at the stairs. As she passed, Mother pulled her in, planting a kiss on her forehead. She held her close for a moment, kissed her again, then released her. "Get that table set. Breakfast is ready." She brushed away a tear.

Andrew appeared, shrugging into his coat. "Good day, Mrs. Sutton. Sarie." His voice softened. "Jenny."

Mother strode between them, hefting a pot of porridge onto the table. "Good morning, Andrew. You must be starving." She glanced at Jenny.

"I am indeed." He winked at Jenny and sat down.

"No wonder," Mother mumbled. She patted his shoulder. He winked again as he took his place beside Jenny.

A commotion broke out on the porch. She went weak with fear. Mother ran to her as Andrew knocked over the chair, lunging for the rifle propped beside the door. It was as if time stood still. Had the British found them? Would they face the gallows after all?

The door burst open, and Andrew aimed the gun at the head of the intruder.

"Is this any kind of welcome for your brother-in-law?" Jonathon Brentwood's voice boomed.

"Uncle Jonathon!" Jenny jumped up and ran into his arms.

Andrew set the gun down and clapped him on the back.

"Rumors abound about the two of you taking out a troop

of British soldiers." His eyes sparkled, his grin spread over his face.

"You've been talking to the Wirth brothers." Andrew handed him a mug of cider.

"Indeed, I have. They speak of the two of you in glowing terms. Something about taking out four soldiers with only two guns. They bandied about terms like 'courage' and 'bravery' and 'unstoppable.' Sounded like a bit of hyperbole to me." He laughed.

Mr. Gates entered with two other crewmen. Mother bustled about filling pewter mugs while Sarie dished up more porridge.

"Good day, everyone." Gates removed his wool cap. "So good to see you again safe and well, Miss Sutton."

Jenny rose and took his hand. "Welcome, Mr. Gates. I'm so pleased to see you again. But I thought you wished to avoid landing in New York, Uncle Jonathon."

He frowned. "So I did. But we encountered a British frigate that engaged us. Let's just say, she limped off with the worst of it." He sighed. "But the *Destiny* took some serious damage. She is in a nearby port for repairs."

"What will you do?"

"I've already purchased another ship that will safely return us home." He placed his hands on Constance and Sarie's shoulders. "We hope you will join us. I think you'll find Virginia winters more forgiving than New York's or Boston's."

"Perhaps the winters are more forgiving, but I fear some people are not. Sarie and Isaac will be safer in Boston."

"But, Mother—"

"We will be safe there now. The British no longer occupy Boston. And it is my home." Her eyes glistened. "But your home is in Virginia." She stroked Andrew's hair. "Thank you for saving my daughter's life."

"I believe it was mutual salvation." Andrew grinned at her.

Jenny laughed and squeezed Andrew's hand.

Lively talk and gentle teasing ensued while all ate their fill. Jenny and Andrew recounted their journey, and Mother filled in with hers. Jenny relished the laughter, the safety, the love that filled the room. Beneath the table, she sought out Andrew's hand.

Jonathon detailed the plan to get them out of New York and back to Williamsburg. He had seen Lieutenant Ashby while at the encampment where he'd met the Wirth brothers. Ashby was still alive, though barely, but enough to know that it was Jenny who had stabbed him. Should he recover, she and Andrew would have a formidable enemy out there.

As they finished their breakfast, Jonathon finalized the plans, urging them to be ready to leave at dusk. Traveling at night would be safer.

Jenny looked around the table at the people whom she had saved, and the people who had saved her. She took a deep breath and counted her blessings.

☾

Andrew ran along the wharf, dodging porters carrying barrels, jumping over crates stationed on the dock before being loaded onto ships, skirting sailors mending sails and rigging. He shouted, "Excuse me," and "Pardon me, sir," as he sprinted to the end of the wharf where the ship was ready to sail.

Jenny stood at the brass railing watching, laughter bubbling up at his exasperating progress. Her heart was full to bursting as he dashed up the plank then hastened along the deck to join her. Reaching her, he embraced her like a man holding a lifeline.

"Just in time, Andrew. How do the two of you like my new ship?" Jonathon asked as he approached.

"She's beautiful." Jenny scanned the trimmed sails, the neatly coiled ropes, the glistening brass fixtures, and the polished mahogany.

"I named her for you, you know." He smiled down at her. "She's called the *Courage*. She's a proud ship, an intrepid ship, and a salvation to me while the *Destiny* is being repaired."

"Captain, we are ready to depart," Mr. Gates called over.

"I will leave you two to entertain yourselves as I set sail." Jonathon bowed.

Jenny looked up at Andrew. "You ran fast enough."

"So did you." He kissed her.

"Yes, I finally did."

They stood at the rail, their arms encircling each other, and sailed out of port toward the life they'd dreamed of so long ago.

Read an excerpt from

LOVE'S DESTINY:
Book One in The Brentwood Saga

(

EMILY VIEWED HER REFLECTION IN the mirror. Thick dark lashes made a startling contrast to clear, blue-violet eyes. She wrinkled her delicate nose.

"I am too short," she thought. "And my hair...I must wear it up."

She pushed her long, thick, tawny-colored hair up from the nape of her neck. Golden highlights danced off it in the evening sun that streamed through the window.

A plan had formed in Emily's mind as the weeks had passed, bringing the inevitable meeting with Captain Brentwood closer. She needed no guardian—why she was seventeen years old. Andrew and she could continue to live here in London. Surely their inheritance would be an adequate income on which they could live comfortably. It was silly to even appoint a guardian for them.

Her heart lifted as she thought of her foolproof plan. That was why she must appear a mature and self-assured woman. But she wrinkled her nose once again at her reflection.

"Bah! I look like a child, and Captain Brentwood will be here any moment." She rang for Mary, her maid.

"Quickly, Mary, dress my hair high, and... well, sophisticated. I need to look mature... older. Oh, you know what I mean."

Mary hesitated. Etta was only the housekeeper, but she clucked over Emily and Andrew like a mother hen. If she did not approve, Mary would really get a dressing down. As gentle as Etta could be with the children, she could be equally stern with the servants.

"Come on, quickly, Mary," Emily insisted. It was time to start asserting her authority and look the part of woman of the house.

Mary did not want to tangle with Emily's temper either, so she quickly picked up the brushes and began to dress the girl's hair.

Emily surveyed the results. Her black, high-necked dress set off her creamy white skin. With her hair piled high on her head, she appeared taller, more dignified. She was sure her plan would work, and in spite of her sadness, her spirits lifted. There was a knock on the door.

"Come in," she called.

Andrew entered. "He should be here...Oh, Em, you look so different ..."Andrew stared at his sister. The transformation was remarkable.

"Do I look older, Drew? Do you think our plan will work?" Her eyes sparkled for the first time in weeks.

"I hope so, Emily. But please do not set your hopes too high. What do you think Captain Brentwood will be like?" Andrew asked.

"Well, he was Father's friend, so perhaps he will be a bit like Father. Perhaps not as robust, perhaps a bit older...I do not know. I just hope he agrees to our plan. I do not see why he would not. He probably does not want to be burdened with us any more than we want to be uprooted and moved to those savage colonies." Emily was not to be dissuaded; her plan would work. "We could continue to live here...what does it matter to him where we are? I have to convince him that I am capable of running this household and Father's estate."

CAPTAIN JONATHON BRENTWOOD STARED OUT the window of his coach. Lamplighters were making their way along, igniting the lamps that lined the streets of London. The *clop, clop, clop* of the horse's hooves beat a rhythm against the night as he pondered his new role as guardian of his dear friend's children. It was not a role he relished, being ignorant of the ways of children. And his dealings in Europe were becoming more tenuous as friction mounted between the colonies and England. Most of his time would be spent in the colonies now as trade and prosperity were growing there. And as the rebellion grew, he had other duties to attend...

The timing of this guardianship could not have been worse. But George Wentworth had been a mentor and had become one of his closest friends. Jonathon would honor the promise he had made to him. His experience with children had been limited, and when he was exposed to them, he was bewildered by their endless energy and their proclivity to mischief. He hoped George's children were not quite as lively and imaginative as some he had spent time with. George had told him many stories of Little Em and Andrew. From his stories they sounded well-behaved and mannerly. They certainly would tie him down more than he had been used to in his 28 years of bachelorhood. He had written his sister Joanna explaining the situation. Surely she would help him watch over the children so he could continue sailing. She and her husband lived in Brentwood Manor, the family home. David was a good manager, and the plantation was thriving under him. Jonathon would soon have to take over, but he wanted to sail for a few more years. Well, he would get this situation settled soon, and then he could set sail again.

The coach came to a stop in front of the handsome London townhouse. As he stepped down from the coach, Jonathon noticed an upstairs curtain fall back in place. He took a deep breath, straightened his cravat, and went up to the door.

"HE IS HERE, ANDREW. YOU go down first. I shall be right there, but let me talk to him alone. I am so nervous; I have eaten nothing all day!" She ran to the mirror as Andrew closed the door. "Oh, dear God, please let this work," she whispered. She lifted her chin peering sideways out of her eyes. Raising one eyebrow, she nodded her head regally. She had been practicing all week. "It must work!" she breathed.

As she descended the curving staircase she saw a tall figure with broad shoulders and dark hair studying the portrait of Jessica, Emily's mother. Jonathon Brentwood turned and looked up at a younger version of the portrait he had just viewed. Surprise flickered across his face, quickly replaced by a lazy, engaging smile.

"So you are Little Em," he drawled. Not quite, he thought to himself. He gazed at the beautiful tawny-haired girl whose blue eyes threatened to drown him.

Emily was stunned. This was her father's friend? Soft brown eyes gazed at her with amusement. They were set in a bronzed, handsome face. He was dressed in a blue longcoat and cream-colored breeches which enhanced his tall, lean figure. His broad shoulders and brown curly hair tied back at the nape of his neck completed the picture of a strikingly attractive man. Emily's cheeks felt flushed under his close scrutiny, and a strange tingle ran through her body. She reached the bottom of the stairs and looked up into his warm, brown eyes again as she extended her hand.

"Captain Brentwood? I am pleased to meet you." Emily was annoyed at the tremble in her voice. He bent and kissed her hand, his lips brushing softly against her skin. Their eyes met as he straightened. Emily tried to steady herself, unable to make her heart stop beating so hard. She was sure he could hear it. She reminded herself of her plan, and quickly regained her composure, straightening to her full height.

"You must be exhausted after your long, hurried voyage. May I offer you some tea," she paused noting his suppressed smile, "...or some brandy?" she added.

"Brandy would be fine. Thank you, ... uh... Miss Wentworth," he replied still fighting back the smile.

Emily led him into the parlor and rang for the maid; Etta appeared. Emily knew this would be difficult for Etta still thought of her as a child.

"Two brandies please, Etta." She raised her chin as she had practiced before the mirror. Etta started to protest, but something in Emily's eyes stopped her, and she hurried off to get the drinks.

"Please sit down, Captain Brentwood," Emily said coolly as she sat on the end of the settee. To her confusion, Jonathon sat beside her rather than in the chair she had indicated. A crooked smile played around his lips as though he attempted to hide a joke. He thought of the "Little Em" of George's stories and chuckled to himself. Nothing had prepared him for this beautiful girl who was trying so hard to be a woman.

"We have much to discuss, Miss Wentworth," he said as Etta returned with a tray carrying the decanter and two crystal glasses.

"Indeed we have, Captain," she replied.

Etta set the tray on the table in front of Emily. The housekeeper poured brandy into the glasses, and Emily was grateful for she had no idea what an appropriate amount would have been. She thought Etta rather stingy based on what was in each glass, but she took them and handed one glass to Jonathon. "Thank you, Etta; that will be all." She turned to Jonathon dismissing the housekeeper.

"Hmmmph!" Etta grumbled as she left the room.

Jonathon silently saluted Emily and then took a drink from his glass. Emily sipped hers and tried to choke down the spasms of coughing that threatened to overcome her. She had sampled wine before at social gatherings, but had never tasted brandy. Heat spread down her throat and she blinked the tears out of her eyes causing her to miss the fleeting smile that crossed Jonathon's face. It was a few minutes before she caught her breath enough to speak.

"Captain Brentwood, I loved my father very much and always obeyed him as he had my welfare as his concern above all else. However, with all due respect, sir, I think in this last instance he erred."

Jonathon raised an eyebrow encouraging her to continue.

"I realize you were his dearest friend, and I appreciate your generosity in this matter, but as you can see, sir, I am perfectly capable of taking care of myself and Andrew. I think Father often thought of us as much younger than we actually are and so made provisions which we obviously do not need. With the wealth Father accumulated on his voyages, Andrew and I can continue to live here quite comfortably. Eventually, I will marry, and Andrew will stay on in this house. So you see, Captain Brentwood, I appreciate your willingness to care for us, but it is unnecessary." She took a deep breath. Would it work? She wanted to squeeze her eyes shut and cross her fingers for good luck. Instead, she maintained her composure though it took all of her strength.

Jonathon continued to look at her with that amused expression. He took another drink of his brandy and, putting down his empty glass he eyed hers and looked at her inquiringly. Emily lifted her glass to her lips and sipped again. It seared her throat and brought tears to her eyes once more. She could not speak for a moment, and when she finally took a breath, the fire returned. She cleared her throat and felt a warmth infuse her. Her cheeks felt flushed and her breath came in short gasps. Finally, she spoke.

"Well, Captain Brentwood, do you not agree that this is a simple solution for all of us?" The room seemed very warm.

"Miss Wentworth, I can see that you are a very sensible, as well as capable, young woman…"

Emily's spirits soared.

"…and you are correct when you say that your father thought of you as younger. Why, he would call you 'Little Em' and tell me of how you sat in his lap and begged for stories. Or how you would tease the cook into an extra helping of dessert, and how, on a hot summer's day, you would totter across the lawn with just your…ah, well, suffice it to say I was expecting someone much younger."

Emily was blushing furiously at his last reference to her childhood. She avoided his gaze. She had to convince this man that she was mature and responsible enough to be on her own. Goodness, the room felt warm, and it seemed to be tilting a bit. Not thinking, Emily reached for the last of her brandy. Again her throat burned as the fiery liquid made its way down. Finally, she spoke.

"Well, as you can see, Captain, Father was mistaken. I am quite capable of looking after Andrew and myself."

"Yes, I can see that. In fact, you are quite a lovely young woman." Jonathon leaned back against the settee, casually resting one arm behind Emily. He saw through her charade and could not help teasing her for she was so serious. "I imagine you have captured the hearts of all the young men in London. How many suitors have lined up at the door asking for your hand and whispered their undying love in your delicate ear, promising ever to be true." He had leaned forward and his breath touched her hair, his eyes held hers. His voice was soft and silken as his arm encircled her shoulders. Emily sat gazing at his warm, brown eyes, captivated. The room was warm, and the firelight flickered on their faces.

Suddenly Emily caught herself and sprang from the settee, her head swimming, desperately needing some air.

"It is a beautiful evening, Captain Brentwood. Shall we step out onto the terrace?" she asked trying to steady her trembling. It did not help that the room seemed to be moving, too.

The half-moon perched on a treetop, and the stars sprinkled across the ebony sky. They walked silently out to the garden, the smoky smell of well-stoked fires filling the crisp air. Emily felt a little steadier. They sat on a bench beneath a tall oak.

"May I speak frankly, Captain?"

"By all means, Miss Wentworth," Jonathon smiled.

"I do not want to go to Virginia with you any more than you want to be burdened with me. I fully intend to stay here with my brother. Father's intentions were good, but he was wrong to do this to either of us, and I believe you see the sense in this, too." Emily folded her hands in her lap as if to end the discussion.

"Miss Wentworth, may I also speak frankly?"

"Of course," Emily nodded.

"In the carriage on the way over here, I would have given anything to be rid of this responsibility. But now, having met you, Miss Wentworth, I am not so sure I want to be relieved of my duty. I was expecting a young child. Instead, I find a beautiful young woman who has made it perfectly clear that she does not need me. Yet I find that this is just what I want—for her to need me." Jonathon could see Emily's embarrassed blush even in the moonlight. He could not help but continue to tease her; she was so serious. "No, I do not think I will be remiss in my duty. In fact, I am sworn to my promise even more having met you. How can I desert this fair damsel in distress? Why, it is my opportunity to be a knight in shining armor come to rescue a fair maiden." He leaned forward taking her hand. "Is it possible, my lady, that out of many I might claim your heart?" His voice was low, his eyes sparkled. "Oh, but one kiss from your sweet, gentle lips to carry with me forever would be so kind."

Emily felt a new rush of warmth course through her that

had nothing to do with the brandy. She knew he was teasing her, yet she tingled with excitement. Just the thought of his soft lips against hers, being held in his strong arms... what was she thinking? She stood quickly.

"I fear you mock me, sir, when all I desire is to settle our lives so we can each go our separate ways. Please just agree with me that this solution would be best and we shall be finished with it."

"I do not mock you, Emily," Jonathon spoke softly, "but even if I wanted to, which I do not, I could not agree to your plan."

"Why ever not?" she cried near tears.

"Because your father's will states that I hold everything in trust for you until you marry. Or, if you do not marry, until you reach age twenty-one. I am afraid you cannot be on your own until such time."

Emily's face went white. Tears welled in her eyes, and she turned quickly so he could not see them. It would not do to cry. Not here, not now. Her mind raced. She would be packed off to the colonies, and she was helpless to stop it. What could she do?

"Then I shall marry." She had not realized that she had spoken aloud. Michael Dennings had called quite frequently lately. She was sure he would propose soon. Of course, now he would have to wait until Emily was out of mourning. "That is what I shall do."

Jonathon cleared his throat. "There is one more thing. I must approve the marriage."

"You what?" she shouted. "Do you think, sir, to take my father's place? How dare you come here and tell me what I can and cannot do? Whom I may or may not marry? Who gives you the right?" She shook with rage. Her upswept hair was coming loose; tendrils tumbled and framed her face and shuddered with her anger.

"Your father, Emily."

Emily stared at him, her mouth half open.

"Father?"

"Yes, it is in his will also. Your father loved you very much, Emily. He made it very clear that I was to watch over you and Andrew. You both were so dear to him. I promised that I would take the best possible care of you. George was one of my closest friends; my promise to him means a great deal to me," he said gently.

The loneliness Emily had felt for the past month flooded over her again. Tears stung her eyes and a dull ache settled in the pit of her stomach.

"Excuse me, Captain Brentwood, I am not feeling well. Good night." She swept past him. Jonathon heard her choke back a sob as she ran back in through the terrace doors. He stood there for a moment staring after her, confused. What should he do with this woman-child?

EMILY PEERED THOUGHTFULLY OVER HER teacup at Michael Dennings as he spoke to her. Many of the matrons in the social circles had already paired them and awaited an impending engagement this season. Michael's sandy-colored hair matched his eyes. Emily had never noticed his eyes before, and if someone had asked her their color, she would have been at a loss to answer. She did remember, however, the soft brown eyes that had warmly perused her during Captain Brentwood's visit.

She must stop comparing them. But she knew that would be difficult, for that was all she had done since Michael had arrived for tea. Of average height, he was shorter than Captain Brentwood, and not nearly so broad in the shoulders. He wore a tan longcoat over a tan vest and matching breeches. So close were they to the color of his hair and eyes that Michael just seemed to run together, nothing distinctive, and a passing stranger would take no notice of him.

Emily had known Michael for years, and, though he was amiable enough, rack her brain as she would, she could not think of a single extraordinary thing he had ever said or done. That was Michael, ordinary and predictable, but a good, safe husband who could keep her in England. And that, thought Emily, is what I need to make him see.

"...do you not agree, Emily?" Michael repeated.

"What? I am sorry, Michael, what did you say?" Emily smiled prettily, and Michael was appeased.

"I said it is dreadful what is occurring in the colonies. Why, they are close to open rebellion!" he answered.

"And I am sailing right into it," Emily murmured

"I do not like the thought of your traveling over there, Emily. In fact, Mother and I were discussing it just last night. She said it is not proper for a girl of your delicacy and upbringing to be thrust into a savage land. She said it is scandalous for a genteel young lady to go off across the ocean, unescorted, with some sea captain. She said it is a shame you have not been betrothed by now, and if you were not so opinionated...uh, that is..."

Emily ignored the last remark. She had heard it whispered before. She was more educated than was usual for a young lady of her station; consequently, no man wanted a wife who might have ideas and opinions of her own—not to mention a wife who might be smarter than her husband. She attributed this gossip to jealous girls whose mothers would not allow their education to proceed any further than French knots and curtsies.

"Michael, Captain Brentwood is my guardian, so I am properly escorted. Andrew will be with me also. And the colonies are not a savage land anymore. Why, there are large towns such as Boston and Philadelphia, and ships arrive from England frequently. I will not be shut off from the world in some remote and distant land."

What was she saying? This was not at all what she had planned. Why did she suddenly feel defensive about a land she had no desire to see?

"Well, as far as Captain Brentwood is concerned, Mother

says he has a reputation with women. She says that having you on his ship is as good as..."

"Captain Brentwood has been a perfect gentleman in my presence," Emily snapped. Her cheeks flushed as she recalled his silken voice in the garden and the feel of his strong, firm arm around her shoulders. Michael misread her blush for anger, which was partly true.

"Do not be angry, Emily. I just do not want to see your reputation sullied."

"It is good of you to be so concerned," she retorted.

"Oh, this is not going right at all," Michael moaned.

Emily silently agreed. What was wrong with her? She was ruining her opportunity to stay in England. Yet, as she studied Michael, doubt slowly spread through her. She imagined passing the years as his wife. It would be safe and comfortable, but certainly not exciting. They would live in London and have children. And Mother Dennings would visit on Sundays and expound on her pet theories. Or worse, perhaps she would live *with* them and subject them to daily sermons. And the years would run together, much as Michael's appearance.

Michael had been speaking again, and his last sentence brought Emily back with a start.

"Emily, will you do me the honor of becoming my wife?" He was on one knee in front of her.

"Am I interrupting anything?" Jonathon's clear baritone rang through the room causing Michael to jump to his feet, and startling Emily as much as Michael's proposal had.

"Captain Brentwood," Emily breathed feeling strangely relieved, "do come in."

Michael shot Emily a bemused look. Jonathon strode in and seated himself on the settee beside her. His eyes sparkled at her and he took her hand in his own and patted it in a fatherly gesture. She slipped it away.

"Captain Brentwood, may I present Michael Dennings. Michael, this is Captain Jonathon Brentwood." Emily glanced at Michael noting his sour expression. Jonathon extended his hand which Michael reluctantly shook. The two men sized each other up.

"Well, Captain Brentwood, when do you plan to set sail for Virginia?" Michael finally asked.

"I have some legal matters to which I must attend, and some supplies to order and load. I imagine *we* shall set sail in a fortnight," he stressed the word "we" while looking at Emily. Unable to meet the gaze of either man, she looked down at her hands folded in her lap.

Michael shifted uncomfortably wondering why Emily had invited Captain Brentwood in at such an inopportune moment.

"I imagine you are anxious to get home to see your family and...uh...dear ones." Michael emphasized the latter cynically.

Jonathon leaned back casually stretching long, lean legs out in front of him.

"Yes, I am anxious to see my sister and her husband. As for the rest of my family, they will be with me on the ship."

Michael glowered at him.

"I think not, Captain Brentwood. I have just asked Emily for her hand in marriage. She will remain in England, where she belongs." He breathed the last decisively.

"No, Michael," Emily whispered. If she had shouted it, the impact could not have been greater. Michael's head whipped sharply back to her, his mouth gaped open. Jonathon searched her eyes. "You are a dear friend, Michael," she continued, "but it would be wrong for both of us if we were to marry."

Michael rose in bewilderment. He looked from one to the other.

"You are responsible for this," he shouted at Jonathon's composed face. He turned to her, "Emily, please reconsider."

"No, Michael. I am sorry," she spoke gently.

Michael shot a baleful glare at Jonathon, then turned on his heel and left. Jonathon looked down at Emily, but she could not meet his gaze. Her head was whirling with the events of the last few minutes. Michael had offered her exactly what she wanted, a chance to remain in England, but she knew it was not right for her. The idea of sailing into an unknown life with the man seated next to her was, somehow, appealing.

"It is just as well," Jonathon teased. "I would not have approved the engagement in any event."

"You arrogant cad," Emily seethed. "How dare you assume what you can and cannot do concerning any matters in my personal life?"

"But you forget, Emily, I am your guardian. Your safety, your health, your happiness are all a precious burden that I will happily carry."

"Who do you think you are that you can presume so much? My happiness will never be dependent on you! I think it is best that you leave at once!"

"Oh, I cannot leave, Em. I am staying for supper."

"You are what? How...?"

"Andrew invited me. He, at least, has some manners." He hid a smile.

"And I do not, I suppose?" Emily rose from the settee placing a hand on each hip. Her blue eyes had darkened to violet with her anger, and a blush heightened in her cheeks. Her jaw was set, and her full soft lips clamped into a firm line.

Jonathon replied easily, "Well, he did have the courtesy to ask a new member of the family to supper. After all, if we are to spend weeks together in the close quarters of a ship, I would deem it necessary to become better acquainted. I am sure that by the end of the voyage we shall know each other *very* well," he smiled wickedly. "But things will go much more smoothly en route if we develop a closer relationship now."

"I have no intention of developing anything with you, Captain Brentwood. And as for the family, I consider all of this to be a totally unnecessary, legalistic mix-up and nothing more. If I never get to know you better, it will be fine with me. Mrs. Dennings was right; you are a rake. Why, you probably have a woman in every harbor. I should have accepted Michael's proposal. He knows how to treat a lady with decency and respect."

"And now you are without the benefit of Mother Dennings' exhortations, too. You've told me of her strong opinions and disdain for anything not of England. Oh, I can picture all of you gathered 'round the cozy hearth listening to her prattle on about the immorality of the savage colonies and their provincialism," he laughed. "No, Em, no such life for you. You have too much spirit, too much drive for what Michael Dennings and his mother could offer."

Emily was startled at how his remarks mirrored her thoughts of just minutes earlier. Could he read her mind? She gathered her thoughts.

"And I suppose you could offer so much more? Tell me, sir, would traipsing off to some backward land with you be so much better? Will you then find me a suitable mate who will offer me all I deserve? Hah! You will probably deny me any suitable young gentleman who is courteous and kind. You will keep me a spinster. To what end, sir? What game do you play?" She had paced across the room during her tirade, unaware of admiring eyes that followed her graceful gait.

"Aye, Em, I could offer you more than your Mr. Dennings. I could show you places of such beauty and wonder as to take your breath away. Mountains that soar up and kiss the floor of heaven. Lush forests that stretch as far as the eye can see, full of trees so big that two men with arms outstretched would be hard pressed to span the diameter and touch their fingertips end to end. Our 'backward' land, as you call it, has cities with shops to rival London's. What is more, we judge a man, not by what his ancestors were, but by what he can wrest out of life and shape into his own. A man can build his worth from nothing; he can become wealthy, influential, anything he wants, on his own merit, not someone else's. It is a rich land, Em, full of promise for people with spirit. People like you and Andrew who draw strength from an inner reserve. Come with me because you *want* to, Em. See for yourself what Virginia is like. I believe one day you will love it as I do." Jonathon's eyes were shining as he spoke passionately of his land. Emily felt a sudden warmth for him. But he was asking so much.

"I cannot say that I *want* to go, Captain Brentwood, but I have no choice in any event," Emily sighed.

Jonathon saw the confusion in her eyes. She seemed to look deeply into the realm of possibilities before her, and complicating it all was the still-fresh grief for her father. He watched her internal struggle, and he began to realize his own growing hope that she would indeed *want* to go with him. He understood her pain and the enormity of her decision, for he knew it must be her decision. He tried to lighten her mood.

"Emily, must you be so formal? Please call me Jonathon."

Andrew burst into the room. "I have been down to the wharves, Jonathon. Everything is progressing smoothly. What a beautiful ship the *Destiny* is! Mr. Gates sends word that the mizzenmast is repaired and we should sail on schedule," his eyes danced with excitement.

Jonathon grimaced. They had run into a pirate ship far north of the Barbary Coast, and the *Destiny* had sustained considerable damage. But the pirate ship had suffered her wrath and limped off the worse for wear. Jonathon would have pursued her had he not been on his way to England at the behest of George Wentworth's will. He hoped their crossing to Virginia would be without incident.

"That is good news, Andrew," he replied.

Emily noticed his concern. "Did you encounter trouble,

Captain?"

"Nothing we could not handle," he grinned.

Supper was announced, and Jonathon offered his arm to Emily. She could think of no reason to refuse without appearing rude, so she tucked her hand through the crook of his arm. She felt the firm muscles of his forearm through the fabric of his sleeve. She glanced sideways at his strong profile with its aquiline nose and square jaw. He caught her glance and winked at her. She quickly looked away. Why did he disturb her so?

Discussion at the table was lively with Andrew firing a myriad of questions at Jonathon about Virginia. His excitement was apparent, and he was anxious to set sail. Jonathon answered his questions patiently, laughing at his enthusiasm.

"I wish your sister was as eager about this voyage as you are," he laughed gently, glancing at Emily. She had enjoyed listening to his tales of the colonies, but had remained silent for the most part. Now she raised her eyebrows at Jonathon.

"Captain Brentwood, I am leaving everything I know and love. Allow me my reluctance, sir."

"But, Emily, have you not been listening to Jonathon? It sounds like paradise over in Virginia. Can we set sail earlier?" Andrew's eyes shone.

"No, Andrew," Jonathon laughed, "I need time to ready my ship. And to convince your sister that she really *does* want to come."

"You have a difficult task ahead of you, Captain Brentwood," she replied. Andrew chuckled at her proper form of address.

EMILY WATCHED IN THE MIRROR as Mary brushed out her hair. She had to admit that the evening had passed pleasantly enough in Captain Brentwood's company. He had piqued her curiosity with the tales of his homeland. And he was even more handsome, if possible, when he was caught up in stories about Virginia as his eyes sparkled and his smile showed straight, white teeth against skin bronzed by the sun and the sea.

Emily climbed between the lavender-scented sheets and closed her eyes. It had been a trying day. Michael's proposal had been her goal on rising this morning, but the day had not gone at all as she had planned. None of her plans were working out lately. It was as if someone were interfering with her destiny...*Destiny*...she slipped off to sleep.

Jonathon had stopped off at the Golden Pheasant Inn and sat in the corner table of the common room drinking his ale. He needed time to think before returning to his ship. It had been an enjoyable evening. Andrew was an enthusiastic as well as knowledgeable boy. George Wentworth had hoped Andrew would follow in his footsteps when his education was completed. He was already well-versed in the ways of sailing, and seemed to have the natural talent of his father.

Emily was an enigma. She vocalized clearly her reluctance to sail to America, yet her eyes had glowed as she listened to his stories, leaning forward, chin resting in her hand, concentrating on every word, then catching herself, sitting up primly, feigning indifference. He caught her lost in thought once and wondered if she were reconsidering Michael Denning's proposal. He thought not. Searching her eyes today he had seen only firm resolution. No, Michael Dennings was not the man for Emily Wentworth.

"'Scuse me, Captain Brentwood, can I git ya' another ale?" A plump, pretty girl was smiling down at him. Millie leaned forward to take his empty tankard revealing much of her ample bosom. "Can I git ya' anything else, Love?" she asked invitingly. Jonathon had been at sea a long time, and normally this invitation might not have been unwelcome. But he had much to think about, and his mind was preoccupied with his new station in life – that of a guardian.

"Not tonight, Millie," he replied.

Disappointed, Millie turned and left the table, swaying her hips provocatively in hopes he would change his mind. Captain Brentwood was the most handsome figure of a man Millie had ever seen. So anxious was she to bed him, she would have willingly given him a toss for free. Most men just in from the sea were chomping at the bit to sample Millie's favors, but this one seemed preoccupied.

Jonathon rose and went out into the night. Settling George's estate and readying the ship for departure were enough to busy a man. But the problem of what to do with Emily taxed his mind the most.

ACKNOWLEDGEMENTS

AS ALWAYS, MY BELOVED HUSBAND Rich has been my main supporter, cheering me on when I despair, listening to my ideas even before his morning coffee, and celebrating success with drinks on the deck. I am eternally grateful to you, my beloved.

I am fortunate to be surrounded both locally and online by amazing authors who share the blood, sweat, and tears of our crazy profession. To my CR Sisters, my Crimson Romance family, and especially to my MMRWA Chapter mates, I thank you. A special shout-out to my critique partners, Maris Soule and Diana Stout, and my Monday write-in group, Kate Bode, Patty Seino-Gordon, Diane Flannery, Laurie Kuna, and Loralee Lillibridge, who traveled the journey of this book with me. Thanks to my Plotting Peeps, Anne Stone, Deb Moser, Linda Fletcher, and Sue Glover whose wisdom and wine-sharing offered new ideas—in *vino veritas* indeed.

A special thanks to H.J. Smith, Luana Russell, and Sara Yoder, who traveled with me during our journeys as teachers and continue to support and encourage me as beta readers, but more importantly, as dear friends.

Finally, my thanks to Julie Sturgeon who, with every stroke of the pen (or stroke of a character in Track Changes), helps me to become a better writer through her insight and expertise. And to all you readers who trust me enough to enter the story my characters and my Muse, Boris, have whispered to me.

ABOUT THE AUTHOR

C

AUTHOR, BLOGGER, POET, AND BELIEVER in dreams coming true, Elizabeth Meyette has journeyed through a career in education to a career in writing. To coin a friend's phrase, she's not retired, she's "refired" in her career as a writer. Her historical romances, *Love's Destiny, Love's Spirit,* and *Love's Courage* are set during the American Revolution. Her mysteries, *The Cavanaugh House* and *Buried Secrets,* are set in 1968 in the Finger Lakes region of upstate New York.

Elizabeth and her husband, Rich, enjoy living in west Michigan surrounded by the beauty of the Great Lakes. They made an agreement that she cannot cook on writing days after he endured burnt broccoli and overcooked chicken. Fortunately, Richard is an excellent cook.

She credits her muse, Boris, for keeping the stories coming. When Elizabeth is not working on a novel or poetry, she is busy keeping up with her blog, *Meyette's Musings.*

D EAR READERS,
Thanks for sharing my characters' journey. Want to know more? Visit my website and be the first to know about new books, freebies, and giveaways available only here. Be privy to deleted scenes and upcoming ideas from my books, so you can step into the world of my characters and know them better than any other readers. You may even help me name characters or decide on a plot direction - see your ideas in print!

Elizabeth

℀

VISIT ELIZABETH AT:

Amazon Author Page:
www.amazon.com/Elizabeth-Meyette/e/B0087F27JM/
ref=dp_byline_cont_ebooks_1

Website:
www.elizabethmeyette.com

Facebook page:
www.facebook.com/elizabethfmeyette/

Twitter:
@efmeyette

92604388R00155

Made in the USA
Columbia, SC
28 March 2018